MAY DAY

A GRAY WITCH NOVEL

R.R. BORN

To Stef
Thanks for pushing the wagon and letting me ride

CONTENTS

MAY DAY

CHAPTER 1

"he death card!" the young woman wailed after she looked at the 10-card tarot spread on the table. "My life is nothing. I am nothing."

Ari Mason shook her head at the Barbie wannabe. Brittania was very pink, very blonde, and very plastic. But Ari knew she had a good heart hidden beneath all that makeup. She'd read the young woman's aura the first time she sat at her tarot booth, more than a year ago.

Ari pulled the oversized, colorful tarot cards towards her into a neat stack. "Brittania, that's not what that means. That card's talking about change." Ari snagged a box of tissues from under the table and held it out. "Here."

Brittania snatched two tissues from the waiting box. "My life is perfect. I don't want change. I don't need change." She blew into the tissue. The honking noise she made was very unladylike. After she gave her nose a good wipe. "So, um, same time next week?"

The corner of Ari's mouth quirked up. "Of course, maybe, then we can sort out your love life."

She knew it was evil to torture the poor girl, but Brittania visited every week and cried every week. The young woman had a self-imposed dark cloud around her, and she never seemed to be happy about anything. Ari doubted if the girl had even taken a sip of the specially created, calm and jovial tea she had prepared for her last week.

"What? What did you see?" Brittania moved to sit back down.

Ari touched her forehead, closed her eyes and nodded in a very soothsayer-I-know-the-future fashion. "My next appointment will be here at any moment."

Brittania looked crestfallen with her pouty, pink glossed lips.

"But, I have this for you." Ari handed her a small brown paper bag and the young woman's face lit up. "It's a soothing lotion. Try it before you go to sleep. Tell me how it works."

The young woman walked away happy. That was a first.

Ari wrapped her cards in a white silk cloth, before placing them in a rowan oak box. Rowan oak had long been associated with protection from evil but also health and rejuvenation. By surrounding her cards with this particular wood, they reaped the same benefits.

"Heavens to Betsy, I think Hades has bought a home in Houston," Ari said as she popped open a fan.

The black silk hand fan moved back and forth quickly, the pictures on it became animated. The bats flapped their wings, and the full moon rose and set. Unfortunately, for Ari, the fan only moved the hot air around, not cooling her off at all.

Discovery Green is a huge greenspace in the middle of downtown Houston. This particular stretch of the park had a few trees, a long line of pop-up tents, soft green grass, and a concrete reflecting pond. Ari's 'Tea & Tarot' booth took up the last spot on the row. She had opened this booth shortly after leaving her coven. She wanted to use her abilities to help people. That was part of the reason for the fallout with her former coven.

A melodic, tinny sound came from the tent next to Ari's when a light breeze flowed through. When she stood to stretch, she'd spotted the owner hanging up a wind chime.

"Morning, Topaz," Ari said, before pulling off her kaleidoscopic head-scarf. Her shoulder-length braids fell into her face.

"Good morning, Ari," Topaz said.

The leggy Native American woman stood about five-ten, nearly as tall as Ari. Topaz flitted around her tent, graceful as a ballerina, setting up mobiles made of red and silver soda cans and other hand-made items. She created moveable art from aluminum cans.

"Lovely weather we're having," Topaz said with her rich Texas drawl. They laughed right after she said it because they both had to dab their brows of sweat.

According to the calendar, spring would start in a couple of weeks. Ari found that hard to believe as she fanned her peasant top from the collar, moving it back and forth to cool her sweaty skin. She wanted to hitch her ankle length maxi skirt way up, but she was sure that would've been frowned upon by others in the park. And getting arrested for indecent exposure was not on her list of things-to-do today.

The ladies paused as a cool breeze flowed over them. The zephyr ended way too quickly. Topaz continued to set up her booth, but Ari looked around with apprehension. She thought she'd felt a tingle of black magic carried on the wind. Houston was home to a variety of supernatural beings. At any given time, she would feel the darkness of black magic, the wildness of shifters transforming, but also the crispness of white magic being worked around town.

Not long after leaving the coven, she'd found an old copy of 'The Good Witch,' and it had taught her to work mostly with herbs, spices, and the power of positive thinking. Basically, teaching her the path of the white witch. It had been much more cathartic than working blood magic — her family's style of magic.

Ari feared she still had too much darkness inside of her to approach the white witches. No matter how much good she tried to do, she didn't feel worthy yet. It would be nice to be a part of a coven again but more than that she wanted a family. Sometimes the best families were the ones you picked for yourself.

A strong breeze rocked the wind-chimes, and they jingled a little louder, the mobiles spun a little faster. Then finally whipped Topaz's pink ruffled skirt up. Any other time, Ari would have laughed at the woman's Marilyn Monroe impression, but she knew trouble was on the way. A strong wind blew, picking up various canned art pieces and carrying them down the green. Topaz ran after them.

Goosebumps blossomed on Ari's arm, but she'd become accustomed to this particular ghost's otherworldly chill years ago. "You've got company," Remy whispered.

Ari had accidentally released Remy-Pierre from a cursed locket when she was eight. He always appeared as he died, a Private in the Civil War. A young man of twenty with black hair, two deep dimples, and haunting blue eyes. His Union uniform had light blue pants, black boots, and the dark blue jacket that hung unbuttoned and a bit too big. He told her his family didn't believe in slavery even though they lived deep in the South.

She'd placed her hand through Remy's ghostly one at her shoulder. When she was younger, he would only appear if she had the locket with her. But they didn't need it anymore, they're connected in a way where he just knew if she needed help. Magic was funny that way. She could also yell. He hated that, which was why she liked that option the most.

A tall man walked towards Ari's table with a slow swagger. His brown, shoulder-length wavy hair seemed to have its own wind machine as it flowed behind him. "Hello," the young man's low-pitched voice rumbled, "I was hoping you could help me."

"Please have a seat." Ari waved towards the chair. "How may I be of assistance?"

"I'm looking for my cousin. She's been missing for nearly seven years."

Ari nodded with her eyes closed, and both hands pinched at her temples while she frowned in deep consternation. "Your cousin, I see her. She's a beautiful girl. Tall, sexy, and curvy with long hair, hazel eyes and flawless, caramel colored skin." She opened her eyes.

He shook his head. "Naw, she's not sexy at all and I distinctly remember her having big feet and big hands."

Ari's eyes went wide. "What? I do not have big hands!" She jumped up and swung to hit his arm. He stood up at the same time dodging the hit, then came around the table, wrapping her up in a big hug.

"Hey cuz," he kissed her cheek. "How ya been?"

Ari pulled back and looked him over. "Good. I've been good. Oh, my goddess, Lucas, how have you been?"

She'd been born a day before Lucas and his twin sister, Luca Bea. Due to the similarites in their names Luca Bea was often called Rumble because of her earth magic. They had done most things together, school, swim, archery, go to camp...until he was taken away by his mother. Her Aunt Tatem had decided he would be best suited for the witch's guard when he turned thirteen. That's when Lucas' wind magic came into fruition. She only saw him on solstices and holidays after that. But he had remained her favorite cousin, no matter the distance and time.

"I've been good. Staying out of trouble." Lucas laughed a little too hard for that to be true.

"You know I don't believe that."

He laughed. "I know. Where the hell is Remy? Is he still with you?" Lucas looked around as if would actually see the ghost.

Remy moved from behind Ari and put a hand on Lucas' shoulder. Her cousin gave a deep, full body shiver. "Damn, you're as cold as ever. Good to know you are still around though." He laughed through the chill, rubbing his arms.

"What's really brought you all the way out here? I'm sure Erissa wouldn't approve."

When Ari walked away from her coven, they shunned her. Her mother made it absolutely clear that all communication with her was forbidden. If anyone contacted her, they would be punished or possibly kicked out themselves. What would make him risk coming to talk to her now?

"No, your mother doesn't know I'm here. But I'm here for a good reason. I'm sure you're not keeping up with news in the community."

Ari knew when he said, 'Community,' he meant the witch community.

"You're out here alone and unprotected."

Ari bristled at the fact that he thought she couldn't take care of herself. "I've been fine all this time."

"That was before someone decided to start killing witches."

"What?"

"Yeah, it started about two months ago."

"Did someone in the coven get killed? Anyone, I know?"

"Yeah, Candyce. You remember her. She had that weird power where she could touch you and locate your heart's desire."

"Wow, I remember her. She was a sweetheart. Why would anyone kill her?"

"Easy prey."

Ari frowned. "Lucas, you know better than to speak ill of the dead."

He nodded but didn't look a bit sorry. "Lately, it's been dismages as well." Dismages are what the witches liked to call humans without magical abilities. "It wouldn't be a big deal if it was just the humans, but when witches from other covens sent out word that some of them had gone missing. Then a few weeks later, the disfigured and mutilated bodies were found. So you see, you need to be careful. You have a habit of collecting dismages, and you can't protect them all."

"You know, witch on witch crime isn't new," she said.

"True. But a lot of the victims were young witches. They hadn't even figured out their powers yet. Then they just disappeared."

They both looked over as Topaz walked back towards her booth, arms full of her canned art. Lucas stood up and twirled his index finger and a dust devil whipped through the park. Topaz's skirt flew up, and she dropped the cans to hold it down.

Ari leaned in and hit him. "That's mean," she whispered.

He stared at the woman. "I know, but damn look at those legs."

Ari shook her head at him. He finally looked back at his cousin when the wind died down and grabbed her hands. "Aramais, you sure you don't want to come back to the coven? I'm sure auntie would take you back."

"I'm so sure she wouldn't, but I just can't. There's too much broken between us." She shook her head.

"I figured, but I thought I'd ask." He stood up, then pulled her in for a hug before he kissed her forehead. "Be careful and take care."

CHAPTER 2

*W*hen Ari's regular customer hadn't picked up her order, she'd decided to check on the older woman after closing the Tea and Tarot booth for the day. Mrs. Haversham lived in a 19th-century mansion in one of the oldest communities in town.

Remy stopped at the edge of the driveway as Ari walked up. When she realized he wasn't with her, she looked back and asked, "What's wrong?"

He looked at the house then to her. "You don't need me. You can handle this."

"Remy, what's going on?"

He hunched a shoulder. "Rien."

Ari studied him carefully. It made her worry anytime he used Cajun French. Rien meant nothing in Cajun, which meant whatever was going on was *something*.

"I'll see you back at the house." He didn't speak much of his old language anymore, but he still held a thick accent.

She opened her mouth to speak, but he faded away before she could say anything. *That was odd.*

Ari shivered as she walked through the threshold into the parlor of the old house. She got the distinct impression, someone or something not living was still on the premises.

"Thank you for coming," Mrs. Haversham said as she stepped into the room. The beige tweed dress hung a little loose on the petite, pearl-wearing woman.

Ari pulled a small paper bag from her khaki messenger bag.

The woman's wrinkled hands shook as she took the package. "This tea has helped me so much." She looked around the room like something would jump out and get her at any moment. "Things have been much better here."

"Just let me know if you need anything else. I'll be happy to come by," Ari said before leaning down to hug her client. At six-feet, she towered over most women and a good set of men as well.

When Ari reached the doors to leave, they slammed shut. A cold thrum of energy emanated from the doors like a slow moving fog. The tingle down her spine was something she'd always associated with ghosts. That's the feeling she had right now.

"No. No, not now." Mrs. Haversham looked around the room worriedly as she twisted her hands. "This is not real. This is not real." She repeated it like a solemn mantra.

Ari stepped away from the doors and looked around the room. The crystal chandelier swayed in a slow circle. "Mrs. Haversham, I'm pretty sure this is very real."

The older woman opened her eyes. "What? No. My daughter assured me this was all in my head."

"Well, if that's true, I can see what's in your head."

The woman groaned as the sheet from the baby grand piano slid to the floor, and it began to play the old-timey tune, The Entertainer. "I suppose you hear that as well?"

"Yes, ma'am."

Mrs. Haversham nodded. "Okay, what are we going to do? This can go on for hours."

Ari didn't have time for this, she had to go to work. From what she remembered an exorcism could be a time-consuming process. And the one time she'd seen it, the ritual had been performed by a person of faith. Upon birth, her soul had been tainted with darkness. She doubted that she had enough good in her to perform a rite to cast out demons because she still had one foot in rooted in black magic.

"Ghosts are a pain in the ass," Ari mumbled.

She could always see ghosts, that was rare for a witch, especially since she wasn't a necromancer. But after she released Remy, they seemed even more drawn to her.

She looked the older woman in the eyes. "Okay, I'mma need for you to trust me." On occasion, her Texas accent came out thick. The small woman clutched her pearls and nodded, only then did Ari continue. "I'm fixin' to try to get rid of this thing. Can you hide over there for me?" She pointed to a cream brocade and mahogany trimmed divan in the corner.

Mrs. Haversham gave a tight nod. "Be careful." Her thin fingers gently touched Ari's arm. "That thing is pure evil." After giving Ari a light squeeze, she moved towards the lounger.

Ari looked around the room. She hadn't come prepared to perform an exorcism. For there to be any chance of expelling this apparition, she needed to trap it. She looked around the room and spotted something that might work if she could reach it. She dragged a Louis XVI style chair to the marble fireplace. She kicked off her new leopard print stilettos to climb up and pull the ornate gild framed mirror down. The thing looked at least five feet wide and just as tall. She used muscles she hadn't known she'd had to keep from dropping the heavy antique.

She used the sheet from under the piano to cover the mirror. Mirrors could be used as doorways, and she didn't want any more unexpected visitors, nor did she want this one to get away. Who would have thought that when she'd decided to drop off some tea, that an evil spirit would hold her hostage. She was a witch, not a psychic, dammit.

The wind began to pick up around Ari as she dumped her messenger bag out on a small table to see if she had anything that could help in this situation. Some tarot cards fell out of the box, a sage stick, three orange plastic containers, a bag of trail mix, bottled water, and a graphic novel about a female vampire bounty hunter.

The wind sped up and whipped the tarot cards up into a tornado reaching the nearly thirty-foot ceiling.

Snick. The thin edge of a card cut her neck as it flew by. She grabbed the spot, and only a smear of blood covered her fingers. Just as fast, another card clipped on her cheek. *More blood.*

The intense blood scent filled Ari's nostrils and made her stumble backward. Her body reacted instinctually, skin tightening as her fingers prickled with energy. She didn't need to see her eyes, to know they had turned to a luminous honey brown. She closed them and took deep breaths to dispel the urge to use the dark magic raging inside her. Only death and destruction had ever followed when she used her powers. She rarely used them for this reason. When the *need* subsided, she opened her eyes to find she'd been enclosed by a swirling tarot card tornado.

At the far end of the room, the edges of the massive burgundy, gold, and blue Persian rug began to flutter. In a matter of minutes, a cylinder shape formed under the rug and moved towards her. It didn't take long for the rug wave to gain momentum and crest at about twelve feet. Ari had to really concentrate to focus her internal will. She thrust out her hand, and a swell of power flowed around her just in time to stop the thing from swallowing her whole.

Ari hadn't used her telekinesis in years. If she used her power with any type of regularity, she could've stopped the rug with a thought. Unfortunately, she hadn't been practicing this power or any other. Hopefully, Mrs. Haversham didn't see what she had just done. Witches weren't supposed to reveal their abilities to the non-magical community, but this fell into the realm of extenuating circumstances.

The rug toppled through the tornado as it crumpled into a large mass at her feet. The cards floated to the floor like snowflakes. The music stopped abruptly, and then an eerie silence rolled over the room. The only movement was when the older woman peeked over the back of the divan. When nothing happened, Mrs. Haversham walked out dusting dark gray particles from her dress and out of her white hair.

She looked around worriedly then asked, "Is it still here?"

Ari opened her mouth to say, I'm not sure. But before she could, the apparition appeared no more than a yard in front of her. A transparent, sepia-toned female watched Ari with empty eye sockets from a skeletal face. Not much creeped Ari out, but this did. Out of the corner of her eye, she could see Mrs. Haversham move back behind the divan. Smart woman.

Those eerie empty eye sockets stayed glued to hers and didn't notice the older woman moving around. If eyes were the windows to the soul, then this ghost had a depth of stillness in those dark orbs that screamed death, loneliness, and horrors not meant for the living to experience.

The spirit's tattered wedding dress barely clung to her bones and left a trail like a comet as she flew around the room. Judging by the few patches of hair, she might have had light brown or blonde hair when she was alive. The dress looked like it had been the height of fashion in the 1920s, with its high collar and lace trimmed long sleeves revealing only skeletal fingertips. Dead-Bride's mouth opened as she roared with rage through the room, then disappeared into the wall. The lights began to flicker.

Ari ducked when Dead-Bride made another pass through the room. Floor lamps went haywire, and a blue and cream vase that looked like an antique from the Ming era, shattered into a million pieces.

The wild-eyed Mrs. Haversham peeked out again and shrilled, "What does she want?"

"I'm not sure," Ari answered, never taking her eyes from the ghost's mouth as it opened and closed. The gaping maw didn't form words. Nothing coherent anyway.

Dead-Bride shot up like a rocket, then flew around Ari in furious circles.

"What do you want? I can help…if you let me." Ari had no clue how to help this ghost, but she had to try something to stop this.

The spirit took another spin around the room in desperate circles before she did what all ghosts attempted with her. "Oh, no, not that." Ari cringed when Dead-Bride surged forward.

The ghost bounced backward like it had hit an invisible brick wall, and Ari toppled back because she was that brick wall.

Ari rubbed her chest where the ghost had attempted to enter and pulled away a thin, clear string of slimy goop.

Ectoplasm.

Even if she didn't get possessed, this stuff ruined an outfit quicker than a red sock in a load of whites. Also, she didn't think transparent beings should be able to leave bruises. She found out at a young age that she couldn't be possessed. Her mother said it was a gift from her father. She had only a few short years with the man but remained ever grateful because she seemed to be a ghost magnet.

After the failed possession, Dead-Bride's attention turned towards Mrs. Haversham. The woman had been stoic the entire time, but when the divan lifted into the air and spun around, the old girl passed out. When the small sofa crashed down, Mrs. Haversham slid out onto the floor in a wide sprawl.

Ari took a deep breath as she ducked and dodged flying projectiles to reach the limp body of her client. She placed Mrs. Haversham back on the divan gently. The older woman didn't seem to be breathing. When she couldn't get a pulse at Mrs. Haversham's wrist, her own heart skipped a beat. She quickly pressed her fingers to her carotid artery at the woman's throat. *Still alive.* Ari sighed with relief, but she didn't rejoice too long over Mrs. Haversham's liveliness, because the ghost hadn't given up yet.

Dead-Bride stood near a collection of various sized vases, and two were at least five feet tall. The apparition thrust her hands forward with her mouth wide and released an ear-splitting scream. Each vessel seemed to waver from the paranormal energy heavy in the air before they flew in Ari's direction.

Ari crouched down as fragments of the vases shattered against the wall behind them. When the pieces finally stopped falling, she looked down at her arms, not a scratch. She pulled the unconscious woman to the floor and pulled the lounger on its side, using it as a shield to protect them.

Ari needed to get that ghost into the large mirror across the room. Her current situation had brought on the same anxiety that had crippled her during coven missions. Her heart pounded like it would burst through her chest at any moment, but she only had herself to get her and Mrs. Haversham out of this alive.

She looked around the room from the base of the divan. She spotted the three containers from her bag. They contained the only defense she had against ghosts... blessed rice and salt. It wouldn't banish spirits, but both items used in tandem was a good deterrent, much like mace. That may have been the only thing worth remembering that her mother taught her.

One orange bottle was in the corner to her right. She stayed on all fours as she made the dash. A wooden floor lamp crashed across her back. The heavyweight knocked the wind out of Ari, then she crumpled to the floor with a thud. Spasms blossomed from where the lamp landed, but she continued, just a bit slower.

Ari looked up to see another lamp coming her way. A burst of adrenaline roared through her, and her legs burned as she dug deep to get out of the line of fire. She couldn't waste any more time. For whatever reason, her presence made the ghost homicidal. It had only been torturing Mrs. Haversham. Now, the spirit's anger and hostility filled the room, thus, making her a full-on poltergeist. Ari did have a way of rousing a person's ire, and apparently, ghosts were no exception.

Her hands trembled as she popped the lid of the salt container and poured it around Mrs. Haversham. She didn't want the poltergeist to possess the old woman once the exorcism started. End tables began to wobble behind her. She had no interest in getting hit with those. They looked like they were made of real wood. She needed Dead-Bride's attention away from her client. Ari dashed across the room and slid under the piano just as the table crashed into pieces behind her. Definitely made of sturdy stuff.

A line of salt at the parlor doors would prevent the ghost's escape. Ari needed the other small container. It laid under the table in the middle of the room. It was now or never. She snatched the cover from the mirror before she ran. One end table missed her, hitting the fireplace, but a footstool slammed against her thigh. This parlor had too many projectiles, she thought as she crumpled down on one knee.

This ghost had deadly intentions. Ari was done with this, then pushed herself up, and limped the last few steps to the table. She grabbed the container and popped it open. Then used her teeth to pull the cork from the glass bauble around her neck. She flicked holy water in a large X in the ghost's general direction. Droplets hit the poltergeist on both passes. Dead-Bride's body flickered.

For the first time, the apparition showed fear. Her head shifted left and right while moving backward. Holy water affected spirits in many ways. Dead-Bride looked up and stretched her body with her arms extended like she would fly away. A bellow of annoyance filled the room, the ghost just realized she hadn't disappeared or flown away.

It was time, Ari recited a prayer she had learned as a child to repel ghosts. "Now, my eyes will be open," Ari threw a handful of rice from the small container, "and my ears attentive to the prayer that is made in this place."

The ghost made a gut-wrenching scream, backing away from the assault of grains.

"For now, I have chosen and consecrated this house that my name may be there forever." Another handful. "My eyes and my heart will be there for all time."

Dead-Bride stood at the rim of the mirror. Ari needed one more blast of rice to contain the evil spirit. She tapped the container, then tapped it again. Nothing.

Their eyes connected just when the apparition figured out Ari was out of ammo. The evil spirit's mouth opened wide in maniacal glee as she surged forward with arms extended. Ari screamed, unleashing all her pain, and all her anger at having to do this. A familiar heat surged through her entire body before two golden balls of flames blasted out of her hands, knocking Dead-Bride over the gilded edge, and into her prison.

CHAPTER 3

"*Y*ou're late!" Bull's deep voice boomed through the closet masquerading as an employee locker room.

In the mirror, Ari rolled her eyes at her boss. "Bull, don't start." She touched her braids, and a few had started to unravel. "I've had a hell of an evening already." She chipped at the dried mud and clear ectoplasm crud on her top. The dark blue blouse looked more like a homemade tie-dye job now. She frowned at her favorite shirt, it was destroyed.

The shirt wasn't salvageable after she'd dragged the antique mirror through the mud into Mrs. Haversham's back garden. It had to be destroyed to dispel the spirit. She pulled the top off and threw it into the trash. Luckily, she had worn underwear that could pass for outerwear. She lifted her arm and picked at the dried ectoplasm. It looked like globs of dried lotion on her dark skin. She washed her arms in the small sink. The only thing that had survived the ordeal intact were her gold hoop earrings, her jeans had splatters of the crud, but it looked like white flecks of paint or bleach. Not a big deal.

The path of the reforming dark witch was fraught with ruined clothes and hair appointments. She unraveled a few more braids to make her hair look halfway decent, then tied it into a ponytail. With all visible evidence of ghost nastiness washed away, she took a deep breath, put on a big smile and walked out into the insanity of a Friday night at the bar.

Bass thumped throughout the Cave. Most of the people inside the goth club were decked out in black or something leather. Some sported piercings in their noses, eyebrows, and lips, but even body modifications like horns or fangs weren't unusual.

People pushed in towards the bar with their fingers up. Bull kept the pitchers of beer flowing. The six-foot-seven tattooed behemoth moved with surprising grace within the tight space behind the bar. It was crammed with a full back bar of bottles of alcohol, beer taps, glasses, and small fridges for wine.

Ari poured a line of tequila into four shot glasses for the preppy guys in front of her. The two broad-chested guys that bookended them seemed to be bodyguards. They didn't let anyone near the out of place young men. One of the other young men waved a bill up and down in front of her. She snatched the fifty and placed it snugly between her all-too-prominent breasts, bound tightly in a deep purple brocade overbust corset.

A tall blond with hazel eyes reached towards her breasts. Ari popped his fingers.

"Hey, I just wanted to get my boy's change," Blondie said.

"Ain't no change in there for you." She spoke loud over the crowd and music. She pushed a saucer of limes towards them. "Now, drink up."

A group of young goth girls took up the spaces the boys had left. Ari raised her brows and nodded when they asked for Cosmopolitans and Appletinis. Back in her day, no self-respecting goth girl would have been caught dead with a fruity drink. These new millennial goth kids were a new breed, cheerful and smiling. It sent a chill down her back. She whipped out a silver shaker and quickly made their drinks.

Finally, she stood in front of a guy who hadn't raised his finger once, but she'd felt his eyes on her the entire night.

"What can I get you, handsome?" Ari asked.

If gods still walked the earth, this man would be one. A dark god. He looked about her age, twenty-five at the most. A few strands of gray escaped the tight ebony bun. She wondered if the color was natural. The intensity of his pale colored eyes unnerved her, but she couldn't tell if they were blue or not. Sometimes she wanted to turn a light on in this bar.

"That's some nice ink." Ari pointed towards his arm. Three, black, jagged ink tips peeked from under his collar and down his left arm. A tribal tattoo style, if she had to guess.

The guy looked down and nodded.

When he stayed quiet, Ari asked, "You need a minute?"

He shook his head and cleared his throat before his eyes met hers. When he spoke, she saw he possessed two things that made her knees jelly every time.

Two deep dimples.

"No," he stammered. "No. I'm ready."

Ari lifted both brows. "Scottish?" Make that three things.

"No," his brogue seemed to thicken, "I'm Irish," he said with a fair amount of pride.

You're sexy. "Nice." She leaned in like it was only the two of them in the bar and she didn't want to miss a word. "So, what can I get you?"

"Bushmill 21 with a drop of water," he answered. "If you please."

She pegged him as a vodka man, maybe even Jäger, but certainly not a BM-21. "Wow, you sure? People rarely ask for that here. If we have it, Bull might have to retrieve it from the vault. Why don't I make you a Bushmill Black on the rocks? It's pretty good."

He shook his head adamantly. "I'm celebrating. I recently found something I've been searching for," he nodded, "for what seems like centuries. Now, you see, only the 21 will do."

He smiled and her heart nearly melted. For a moment, she thought this guy possessed *panty-melting* magic. It usually took more than a pretty face and a smile to get her to this point. It had to be the dimples.

She turned around and yelled with unladylike manner, "Bull! Unlock the 21."

The big tattooed man frowned and held up two pitchers of beer at her demand. She turned back to her Irishman. "You want to open a tab?"

He shook his head. "No."

Ari nodded. "Okay, I'll be back." She turned around to throngs of outstretched hands. "Calm down! I'm coming." She knew it would be a while before the whiskey arrived. Bull didn't move fast on a regular day.

About ten minutes later, Bull appeared from the back. Ari retrieved the bottle of 21 from his outstretched hand and tucked it under her arm. She deposited two bottles of beer to waiting customers as she made her way back to her Irishman.

She grabbed one etched glass from under the back bar and placed it in front of him. Then cracked the seal on the bottle and attached a steel speed pourer. She poured two fingers worth into the glass, opened a bottled water, and topped it off with a splash.

"Enjoy." She turned to leave.

"Wait, I'm celebrating, and I can't toast alone."

She lifted her brows because she didn't really understand what he wanted.

"Pour another glass and have a drink with me."

"No, I can't." She waved him off.

"Please." He reached out and touched Ari's hand, then snatched it away, just as fast. "What was that?" He rubbed his fingers, blinking wildly.

A jolt of electricity had pulsed through where they'd touched. "Whoa." If she didn't know better, she'd say this Irishman had magic.

He didn't seem to know what had happened. He tentatively touched her hand again. Nothing. Just static electricity, she supposed.

Never taking his eyes from hers, he slid the glass in front of her. She began to shake her head before the word, no, came out of her mouth.

"I couldn't possibly," she finally said.

He pushed the glass until it brushed her fingers. "No one should celebrate alone."

Those eyes broke Ari's heart. Something in him seemed sad… maybe even broken. Of course, she shouldn't do it, but Bull was always harping about her customer service skills or her lack thereof. "Fine." She grabbed another glass and poured.

He waggled his glass once she finished, smiling a smile that had lured many women into trouble, she was sure. She picked up the freshly poured glass of whiskey and clinked it against his. "Cheers."

"Slainté," he said at the same time.

Ari closed her eyes as the explosion of spiciness and hints of raisin and vanilla flowed over her tongue. She couldn't help the smile that spread across her face. The whiskey went down warm and smooth. After she swallowed, she opened her eyes to meet his. "That has to be the most spectacular thing to touch my lips in a really long time."

He coughed, barely catching his breath. Ari quickly grabbed a towel. "Sorry. Sometimes I just say things," she said wiping the bar.

"No," he gasped. "I just wasn't expecting to hear that." The corner of his mouth quirked up before he spoke again. "Happy to be of service…" He paused.

"Oh." She dried her hands on the towel, then extended one towards him. "Ari. Nice to meet you."

"Heath. A pleasure."

Heath's warm hand enveloped Ari's without the shock of electricity this time. She couldn't read minds, but everything he wanted to do to her blazed in his eyes. She wanted to look at his aura, but the lights and the music made it difficult to see anything. There was something about him that called to her. She wasn't sure what it was, but she wanted…no, she needed to find out more about him.

The crowd stayed thirsty until last call. Between serving pitchers of beer and shots of tequila, she managed to talk to Heath and even take a selfie with him. She promised to send it to him before the week was out. She knew she would call him sooner than that. She could feel it in her soul. This guy was something special.

CHAPTER 4

"Mother, no!" Ari woke on a scream. She looked over at the clock, the red LED lights held steady on four. It was still morning. She'd only been asleep for an hour. And in that time, over and over, her last mission with her old coven replayed: a little girl with bouncing blonde curls in a white dress with cherries smiled at her, then her beautiful brown eyes, so full of life widened, just before all the color faded out into a dishwater gray. Her mouth contorted into a macabre slash as her body convulsed on the ground.

Ari's mouth opened to scream, but no sound came out. In frustration, she ran towards the thrashing body. As Ari held the small, and broken body of the young girl, the convulsions ceased and their eyes met. The little girl blinked and Ari knew what she'd wanted without her saying a word.

Help me.

That was a memory she'd thought had long since been buried. There was no going back to sleep now. She wiped her eyes as she walked to the kitchen to get a glass of water. As great as it had been to see her cousin, his visit also brought back so many memories of her time in the coven. Time she had worked hard to forget. As a child, she'd been ecstatic at any chance to perform spells, even sneaking around to do it, but she had no way of knowing that the magical books or grimoires, as they are called, had been steeped in the darkest of magic.

Ari's condo was a mixture of new items, and garage sale finds. A long weathered country table, that she used as a prep area for her spells, filled the entire dining room. She saw it on the side of the road, on her way to a small country bee farm one day. The table could easily seat ten, not that she would ever have that many people in her place at one time. Instead of all those chairs, she'd distressed a wooden bench to match the aged look of the table and placed potted plants all around.

The kitchen contained various hanging baskets of sage, basil, chives, and oregano. Various herbs hung by twine to dry. She even grew garlic in a large container near the balcony. That always made her place smell like an Italian restaurant.

She used the dining sideboard to store all the finished potions and containers of various items she used. Ari gathered a few herbs to start her wards. Wards are magical shields anchored to a physical place. Mostly used to keep out malevolent visitors. She had learned a new style of making wards from a grimoire she had acquired from a small metaphysical store called the White Cauldron. What Lucas had said scared her a little, more for her friends than herself. Her place had been warded since she left the coven and she reinforced them once a month.

It took a little time to learn new wards that her coven wouldn't be familiar with. Each coven had their own set of spells and symbols they used with wardings. She didn't want to come home and find her mother in her condo one day.

When Ari burned the rowan wood on the stove, the smoke filled the place. You could have sworn she was trying to burn the building down. A sure sign the wood was perfect. She chipped the ashes into a red marble mortar. The mortar is a traditional bowl made of a material like wood, marble or metal to crush and ground ingredients with a club like item, often called a pestle. This was one of the few things she'd snagged when she left the coven. It had been her grandmother's on her father's side. Her mother would have only thrown it out. She had hidden it in her room after her father had left or disappeared. She'd been too young to fully understand what had happened between her parents. One day he was there, the next her mother said his name was never to be uttered again.

After Ari had worked the ashes into a fine powder, she'd mixed it with oil, and poured it into three small glass bottles and corked them. Just as she had gathered straw to begin twisting protection crosses, her cell phone rang.

"Who would be calling me at this hour?"

She found her cell under a heap of rosemary. It was her best-friend Leise. She swiped the picture of a sprite looking girl with sky blue eyes and sprouts of short black hair. "Hey Leise, what's up?"

"Did I wake you? I'm sorry," Leise rambled softly. "You know what. I should let you sleep. You should go back to sleep. I just didn't know what to do? Who to call…"

"Leise, slow down and tell me what's wrong." Ari chimed in before Leise hung up the phone.

She hadn't heard Leise like this in a long time. Her friend's personality was often laid back and quiet or go, go, go. The latter meant she was scared or nervous about something. The phone line had been quiet for such a long time, Ari thought she'd hung up. Then she heard a loud sigh. Her heart raced. "Leise, please, talk to me."

"I'm really tired."

"Then go to bed and call me later." Ari wanted to believe her friend only needed sleep. But her instincts kicked up a notch, and she knew it was something more.

"That's just it, I can't sleep. I can't remember the last time I did. In all honesty, I don't think I've slept more than six hours this entire week. There's something seriously wrong."

There was a hiccup in her voice. Could've been from tears or from frustration. Either way, she had to check on her friend. "Okay. I'll be right there."

Ari had already started to get her purse and keys when the conversation had first started. She walked along the sideboard to find a sleeping potion. She also grabbed the protection crosses she had just made and placed one into her bag.

"Hey, Ari."

"Yes."

"Could you bring your cards?"

CHAPTER 5

ring your cards? Those were words Ari never thought to
hear from Leise. The last time they did anything witch-
related, or 'woogie' as Leise liked to call it, they were thirteen, and it
hadn't gone as planned. She brought an old tarot deck she liked to
use for special occasions.

It didn't take long for Ari to reach Leise's place. There wasn't
any traffic as she whipped through town in her twenty-year-old,
light blue Beemer, she affectionately called Tiffany. When she
knocked on the door, it just opened. No 'Who is it?' or a peep
through the curtains. Leise just held the door open, her face
shrouded by disheveled midnight black hair.

"I could have been anybody. You have to be more careful," Ari
said. Her friend gave a nearly imperceptible shrug. "Leise? What's
wrong?" Ari touched her shoulder. When Leise looked up, her
sunken eyes swallowed her pale face. Ari held back a gasp; her
friend looked like a native from The Walking Dead.

"Is this about your mom?" Leise's mother passed away a few
months back. They hadn't talked in a while, but when they did,
Leise always said she was fine. Now she could see that wasn't quite
the truth. Ari wanted to be able to say the right thing to make it all

better. But she didn't have a great relationship with her own mother, so she had no idea what to say.

Leise waved her in, then waited. "Remy?"

"He's not with me," Ari said as she stepped inside.

"He's always with you," Leise said softly.

Ari mumbled, "Not lately."

Leise had closed the door and walked past her. Ari stopped in her tracks to cast her eyes around the living room. Her finger slid under her nose as the stench of old pizza and stale beer hit her hard. "Oh, honey," she said.

She moved cautiously through the minefield of discarded takeout containers. Then hopped over a plastic water bottle, only to step into a soiled Chinese food container. Ari closed her eyes with a soft prayer to the shoe gods, in hopes that her new shoes weren't ruined.

"Girl, what the hell?" Pieces of lo mein slid off the front of her leopard print stilettos when she shook it. She exhaled slowly and remembered how much she loved this girl.

Leise picked up the bottle and takeout containers. "Sorry."

No, no, no. Before Leise could run away, Ari held up her hand to stop her. Most days Leise was soft-spoken, but Ari hadn't heard her friend go monosyllabic since middle school. Back then, Leise used to answer everything with a yes, no, or a shoulder hunch. "I can help you…if you let me."

"Tea can't fix this," Leise whispered.

Leise had no way of knowing how much more powerful she had become in the last ten years. "Okay." Ari threw up both hands in surrender, but to also let her friend pass. It might take some time for her to open up.

Ari cautiously walked towards a huge pile of clothes in the center of the room. Once upon a time, a futon had taken up space somewhere near that spot. "Annaleise," her voice sounded skeptical, "have you been sleeping down here?"

Ari lifted a blanket and pillow with two fingers from the far end of the clothes pile. Tongs and a hazmat suit would have been better suited for this job.

Leise seemed very interested in cleaning all of a sudden. She averted her eyes as she picked up a pizza box and a few hard cider bottles, then walked to the kitchen without answering.

Ari watched her friend move slow as molasses to throw away the items. Without ever looking up, Leise threw clothes on the floor to clear a spot on the futon to sit down.

Ari sat on the arm of the futon behind Leise. To see her friend in this kind of shape, disturbed her deeply. She wanted to rage and yell, "Why didn't you come to me sooner?" But didn't, she took a deep breath to still her nerves then simply asked, "Why?"

Leise pulled her knees to her chest and took a deep breath. "After mom's funeral, I guess…maybe about a week or so, her lawyer called me to his office."

"Aww, sweetie. You should have told me. I would have gone with you." Ari patted her best friend's shoulder.

Leise nodded. "I know. But I felt like it was something I had to do on my own. You know?"

Ari understood her friend's need for independence and stayed quiet, as she rubbed Leise's back in circles. A silent show of support.

Leise took a deep breath and started again. "Mom left me everything, of course, but also a key to a safe deposit box. It contained a family heirloom." She rolled her eyes. "I didn't even know we had things like that in our family. Long story short, I haven't had a good night's sleep since I brought that thing in the house."

"How long?" Ari asked.

"I don't know — six weeks," Leise said with a sigh.

More than a month without sleep. Well, no wonder her friend and this place looked like hell. "What can I do to help?"

"I don't know. A spell. An exorcism…something. All I know is, I got a box with some bad juju."

MAGIC HAD NEVER SCARED LEISE, but there was something weird about the gift she'd received from her late mother. She stood in the door of her bedroom, and a chill went down her back as Ari handled the box. *How could she touch it like that?*

"What do I need to do?" Leise finally said.

Ari patted the bed across from the box. "Come. Sit."

Leise rolled her eyes. Why couldn't Ari do this without her participation? But she didn't want to string this out any longer than necessary. The queen-sized bed seemed hella small now. She sat as far away from the box as she could, even to the point of putting a pillow between her and it. If she moved any closer to the head-board, she would've become a part of the design.

Ari laid the tarot cards in front of her in a circular pattern. "Anything else I should know? I see you never opened the box."

Leise leaned her head back on the headboard and closed her eyes. "No."

How could she tell her friend that she had fought with her mom before she'd died, and she couldn't forgive herself? That she was slowly losing her mind? Every time she closed her eyes, she dreamt that someone was watching her. Stalking her.

Leise opened her eyes to the overwhelming silence. Ari had crossed her legs and sat quietly, waiting. Leise licked her lips with every intention of speaking, but the words wouldn't come. She picked at a thread on the comforter until it loosened. A warm hand covered hers, probably saving the quilt from a messy demise.

"Tell me," Ari encouraged.

Leise closed her eyes and kept them closed as she spoke in a barely audible voice. "I feel like it's watching me."

"The box?" Ari responded.

Leise nodded. "Yeah, or whatever's in the box. And when I do fall asleep, it's the same dream over and over: A dark forest, no stars in the sky, no wind, and no sound. The place is so ominous, then I see a dark shadow. I suspect it's a man, but he's always hidden in the trees." Leise shook her head. "A good night's sleep has been an impossible dream."

Ari picked up her tarot cards and put them in a purple silk pouch. "Okay. We're going to do something else." She jumped off the bed and grabbed a white pillar candle from the windowsill and something out of her bag.

"Before we start, could you please wear this?" Ari handed her a weird looking homemade necklace attached to a leather strip.

Leise looked at it from all sides. "What's this?"

"It's a protection cross. It helps if someone tries to use magic on you. I know it's not the prettiest, but it will save you if attacked."

Leise shook her head. "This might clash with my style." In other words, it was ugly.

"Leise, please wear it. I'll be right back. I need few things from the kitchen, if you have 'em." She laid the candle on the bed.

Leise opened a drawer and threw the necklace in before Ari came back. She could only deal with one problem at a time. No one was going to attack her. She didn't have anything. All she wanted to do was sleep in her own damned bed. When Ari returned, she had a ceramic bowl filled with small plastic containers of spices and tea bags.

"From what you just told me, we need to do a house cleaning spell." She placed the bowl on the bed and moved the box back to the nightstand. "It should remove all the negative energy in this room. Oh," she pointed to the opposite nightstand. "Hand me those matches."

Leise rolled onto her shoulder to reach them.

Ari lit the white candle, then handed it to Leise. She poured a nice heap of garlic powder and ground cloves into the palm of her hand, before throwing it into the bowl.

Leise's brow furrowed in curiosity. "What's with the tea bags?"

"I needed mint leaves for the spell. You, my dear, only had these old tea bags." She tore the bags open and poured the tea leaves into the bowl.

"Yeah, I kept them for when mom visited," Leise added. "You know I'm not big on tea."

"Yeah, I know, but it's good for you." Ari looked around the bowl, then under it. "Damn it."

"What's wrong?"

"I need one more thing." Ari looked around. "Oh, wait." She

jumped off the bed, then pulled her messenger bag from the floor. She rummaged through it intently. A big smile crossed her face as she pulled out a dried stick of leaves tied by a string.

"What's that?"

"Sage," Ari said, as she hopped back on the bed.

"Do I even want to know why you have that in your purse?" Ari shook her head with a smirk. "Okay." Leise laughed it off.

Ari crushed some of the dried sage into the bowl. "Ready?"

"No, not really." Leise looked around at the candle, bowl, box, and her friend. "But this will work, right?"

"This? Yeah, think of it like," Ari tapped her chin, "feng shui." Her radiant smile screamed confidence.

Leise nodded like she understood, but didn't. As long as it worked, that's all that mattered.

Ari took the candle from Leise and lit the contents of the bowl, then placed the candle on the nightstand. Once the spices began to smolder, the bitter smell of the smoke prickled Leise's nose. Ari carried the bowl around the room, and the smoke lifted in slow-moving whitish-gray wisps from the bowl in a trail behind her.

"In the name of the goddess I bid thee part. I sanctify and cleanse this room. Let nothing but jubilation linger here." Ari placed the bowl on the bed, then grabbed the candle and box from the nightstand. She lowered the box into the smoldering smoke and repeated the spell. Once completed, she blew out the candle.

Ari closed her eyes as she took Leise's hands and held them over the box on the bed. A moment later she opened them and said in a squeaky voice, like from the lady in the Poltergeist movie, "This house is clean."

Leise snatched her hands away laughing. "Shut up."

"For real. No more bad juju in the room." Ari patted the box, "Or in this bad boy...good boy."

Leise went wide-eyed, "Really? You don't feel anything weird or evil?" She wanted to believe it was that simple.

"Nothing weird," Ari winked. "But, I do come from a long line of witches. Some of them are less Glenda and more Wicked Witch of the West." Ari smiled wide.

Leise knew she wasn't kidding. "I'll be sure not to invite any of your relatives over then."

Leise inched back as Ari pushed the box closer to her. Unlike the first day, the box felt different. She waited for the cloak of dread to insulate her. So captivated by the box, she didn't even notice when Ari touched her hand. Warmth, love, and much-needed support surrounded her, as Ari's hand held hers on the lid of the box.

Ari moved her hand away, leaving only Leise's. "Open it."

Leise rubbed the box. "I feel like I should say something."

"Then say it," Ari said softly.

Tears welled up. Leise wiped them away with her free hand. Now that she could touch her mother's gift, she didn't want to lose contact. "Mom, I'm sorry it took so long to open your gift." In that moment, everything became very real, although she knew it had been real for a long time. "I love you." She picked up the box and pulled the top off.

The steady beat of her heart strummed loud in her ears. She pulled out a rough cut, deep purple amethyst on a long silver chain from a black velvet bag.

"That is so beautiful," Ari gasped through her hands. "The amethyst is the crystal of spirituality. Some believe that it calms the spirit and mind. It also helps with insomnia and recalling dreams and prevents intoxication."

"Wow," Leise whispered. The necklace swung between them. The light seemed to get absorbed by the crystal, which was truly breathtaking and unique.

"Breathe Ari," Leise whispered as she took a deep breath of her own.

She heard Ari exhale across from her. They both stared at the brilliance of the deep purple. Many thoughts ran through her mind, but foremost, that she wasn't worthy.

Ari picked up the box and pulled out a small, yellow folded piece of paper. "I knew it," she said with soft excitement. "Most antiques come with some sort of certificate, or history, or something."

Leise didn't care. This was a present from her mom.

Ari read it to herself.

Leise laid the necklace on the bed, "What does it say?" She asked absently as she ran a finger over the grooves of the amethyst.

"Apparently, this necklace has been in your family for centuries," Ari laid the paper down. "Did you know your family's from Ireland?"

Leise's brows pulled together. "That's weird because mom said our relatives were from Eastern Europe, but they moved around a lot."

"Your people were gypsies." Ari said with a smile.

"I don't think they go by that anymore, but maybe. Mom never said exactly where, but it doesn't matter now anyway, I don't have any family left."

Ari frowned. "You have me."

Leise grabbed Ari's hand. "You're right. You're my sister in every way that counts." She gave Ari a big smile, and they both laughed.

Ari laid the paper back in the box and jumped off the bed. "My work here is done." She grabbed her bag from the floor and beams of sunlight came through the window. "I'm kinda sleepy now. I'm happy I don't have to go to the senior facility until tomorrow."

"You still volunteer there?"

"Sure, I can't abandon my seniors. They're so funny and they tell the best stories. I love them. Speaking of which, don't forget next Saturday we are working the Children's festival."

Leise clicked her heels and gave a stout salute. "Aye, aye cap'n."

Ari grabbed her tarot cards from the dresser. "Next time, I'll give you a proper reading."

"Oh, joy," Leise said dryly, with her arms held wide. But she couldn't hold in the smirk forming at the corner of her mouth.

Ari eyed her suspiciously. "You are such a smart ass." She leaned in to wrap her arms around Leise's shoulders, before whispering in her ear, "Happy I could help. Sweet dreams." She pulled back and said, "Now, can you please dream about a hot guy."

CHAPTER 6

*L*eise wiped the sleep from her eyes as she looked up at the dark, star-filled sky. When she reached out, instead of cool sheets, her fingers found dampness. She snatched her hand back like she'd been burned. She looked around nervously before turning her head, wetness greeted her cheek, and her eyes were filled with green. She stretched her fingers out again into the short, dew ladened blades of grass.

She stood up, and her toes curled in the damp, chilly lawn. As she walked in no particular direction, she inhaled the scent of jasmine and salt water on the wind. Also, a hint of ozone permeated the air, letting her know rain wasn't too far off. Out of nowhere, a large oak tree appeared. She looked around, not a soul for miles in any direction. Everything seemed so real, but she was sure she was dreaming. She placed her palm hesitantly on the rough bark of the tree. The sky began to lighten from pitch black to various shades of purple, orange, and pink. It was as if an artist had waved a wand, and color with white puffy clouds appeared.

When Leise looked behind her, the field of grass had disappeared into an abyss of darkness. Her nightmares began like this, every time. For a moment, her heart had overflowed with happiness.

She'd thought Ari's spell had worked. When she looked forward, a forest of redwood sized trees lay ahead of her with a gravel path up the middle. A few trees in, she saw the silhouette of a man.

Him.

Apprehension overwhelmed her as she stepped onto the path. Sure she was afraid, but the logical part of her brain pointed out that this was a dream. And if she confronted the monster in her nightmares she would be able to sleep peacefully. Or was she remembering the rules from a movie and she would die here? Instead of thinking on that, she concentrated on his face.

Unlike in the nightmares, every step she took this time revealed a piece of the man. Whoever he was, he'd driven her from her comfy bed and had robbed her of her piece of mind. She was getting more pissed off with every step.

When she made it to the house-sized tree, it had to be at least ten feet around. He still hadn't moved. She squinted, but his face was still shrouded in shadow. As she walked around the tree to get a better look, he moved slowly in the other direction. He wasn't exactly running, more like avoiding.

"Quit it!" Leise exclaimed. The shuffling of the grass stopped. "Just come out."

She heard the crunch of the grass as his hand came from the darkness to lay against the rough bark of the tree. The long strands of greasy looking hair fell sideways, effectively hiding his face from view.

"I'm not going to hurt you," she said then let out an exasperated sigh.

He lifted his head and stepped from behind the tree completely. Beyond the dirt on his face, full lips, or even his filthy, shoulder-length dreadlocks, his eyes made her suck in a breath.

How could that even be natural? His eyes reminded her of the amethyst she fell asleep with. She heard herself gasp before closing her gaping mouth quickly. Her eyes roamed from his dirty bare feet to his brown worn suede pants, and dirty peasant style shirt.

Ari would call him, 'A fine specimen of a man,' albeit a bit shabby. His clothes looked like they came from the medieval era.

Before this moment, Leise always thought the ominous feeling she felt would be a hideous, demon looking thing hanging around so he could possess her. Red eyes, claws, huffs, green puss oozing from open sores all over his body. A straight out of hell demon. She couldn't have been more wrong.

His lavender eyes followed her every move. It was like he hadn't seen another living soul in years. She knew she should be afraid of him but there was something about him that settled her.

Then a flicker of something crossed his face as he looked down at his clothes. He ran his fingers through the torn material of his filthy shirt. He even picked at the mud on his pants. His hand automatically went to his hair. He pulled one of the thick dreadlocks in front of his face.

She thought the matted locks were a deep, dull brown but upon closer inspection, the tips weren't brown at all but a reddish color and those clothes really needed to be burned.

She wanted to touch his hand and stop him from worrying about it. "It's okay. I don't mind." She reached out, then pulled her hand back, when he took a step back. "I'm sorry." She held her palms out.

His head quirked to the side like a bird. Then shook his head. When he spoke, the garbled words came out gravelly and unintelligible to her ears. His language has no basis in English.

She realized he didn't understand her nor did he speak English. She waved her hands for him to stop. "Okay. Stop. This would be much easier if you spoke English."

His somewhat calm changed abruptly. His eyes went wide just before he crumbled to his knees.

"Oh, my God. What's wrong?" Leise rushed to his side.

He shivered with a groan before he spoke. "Did you just use magic on me?"

"No." She answered him before she realized she understood him. His voice still carried an accent, British, or maybe Scottish. She was horrible with accents, but she understood him just fine.

"Then what did you do to me? I understand you, now," the young man said.

"Dude, it's a dream. Stuff like that happens."

He squinted his eyes again giving that weird look of confusion. "What is a dude?"

She smiled and pondered how the man in her dreams didn't know slang. "It's what we call friends or people when we don't know their name."

He nodded sagely like he was locking the term away. "Please forgive me," he bent in a courtly bow with a closed fist over his heart. "Let me introduce myself. I am Brennan of the clan *Dubhghall.*"

She couldn't pronounce the name, the first part — 'dove' came out breathy and the second part, 'hall' sounded a bit guttural. The interpretation in her head was probably wrong, but she had no intention of ever repeating it. "Brennan. That's nice. My name is Annaleise Morgan, but my friends call me Leise."

"Annaleise. That is a very beautiful name."

"Can you explain whatever this is?" She waved her hands around. "I'm dreaming right?" She could hear the pleading in her voice because she didn't want any of this to be real.

"In a way," he replied.

Her eyes squinted as she carefully scrutinized him. "You can't be real." She took on a dreamy smile. "Maybe, I saw a guy I thought was cute and now, poof, I'm dreaming about him…you." She was rambling and just needed to shut up.

A minute passed, then another. His silence made her heart speed up. For the first time in his presence she felt nervous. What was it about this place? Her dreams even before that necklace appeared were odd - just not this odd.

His eyes lowered. "I am very much a real person. Just not from your world."

From her world? "I don't understand."

"Are ye a witch?"

"What? No?" Did he say, 'ye'? Who speaks like that? Where did this guy come from?

"It tis just…" He paced away from her.

Leise got the feeling he didn't know how to break the bad news to her.

"You are here," he looked around, waving, "and now, I speak your language. You must be a witch."

She began to walk backwards. "I just told you. I am not a witch." Her ire rose. "I didn't do anything. All I did was go to sleep and then I was here." She turned towards the darkness. "This place. Oh, my God. I really need to wake up now." Then she half walked — half jogged away from him. She'd been wrong. Ari's spell worked a little too well. She started towards the darkness on the path between the trees.

His bare feet crunched loudly on the gravel behind her. "Please. Don't leave."

She turned with her hand out to him. "Don't follow me. Just go away." When she turned back around the scene had changed entirely. The darkness - gone. The forest - gone. Only a white abyss in place of it all.

"I really, really need out of here!"

Leise woke up on a scream. Her eyes popped open when she reached out and felt cool fabric under her hands. The morning sun warmed her feet. She reached up to touch the crystal. It laid heavy between her breasts. That dream might have been stranger than the nightmares. She waited her entire life to say she'd met the man of her dreams. Be careful what you wish for.

CHAPTER 7

The oversized couch in Ari's living room was more comfortable than her bed most days. And today was one of those days. The sun was going down; she'd slept well into the evening.

"Remy! Where are you?" Ari yelled from her campsite on the couch. "Where is that boy?" She mumbled.

Remy had been acting very strange lately. He hadn't been hanging out with her at the booth, or at the bar. He loved hanging at the bar. Bull was his favorite target. She barely saw him at home anymore. Sometime soon they were going to sit down and talk about it. But for now, she was embracing a little quiet time. She ordered her favorite meal when she woke up.

When the kettle whistled, she poured herself a cup of lavender-chamomile tea. This weekend had been a little busier than usual with the exorcism, her bartending gig, and Leise's house cleaning. Not to mention her impromptu family reunion with Lucas. She inhaled the fragrant bouquet before taking a sip.

She closed her eyes as she lay swaddled under a patchwork blanket she had snagged at an estate sale. The previous owners had had no idea the Celtic symbols sewn into the material actually created a protection spell. A shunned black witch needed all the help she could get.

The doorbell rang, and she flung the covers back. "I'll be right there."

She looked down at her red plaid flannel sleep shirt and white boxers, she looked decent. Then she ran her hands through her hair and cringed. The tornado winds had done a number on her braids. She grabbed a ball cap to hide the bird's nest on her head. "Coming," she yelled. She dashed into her bedroom to grab an orange cap. A few minutes later, she opened the door to one of her favorite people. "Spencer, I'm so happy to see you."

"You too, Ms. Mason. That'll be $12.82, and I threw in some extra chili garlic sauce, you know, the kind you like," he said as he handed her a plastic bag, with a brown paper bag stapled inside.

She handed him a twenty. "Keep the change."

"See ya next week, Ms. Mason."

"Later, Spencer." She closed the door and put the bag down. The steam from the nectar of the gods cleared her sinuses. "Pho has to be the most perfect food."

"No, Cher. That would be gumbo," Remy said.

She nodded as she cracked oped the lid on her soup. "True, but my skills are not in the kitchen." She blew on the plastic spoonful of soup, before taking a sip. She closed her eyes and smiled. Perfection. Grandma Pham knew her stuff.

"Aramais," Remy whispered.

Ari thought she'd imagined it, but when she looked up, Remy was looking at the floor. He'd rarely called her by her first name. She'd been 'Cher' for as long as she could remember and now he couldn't even look at her. "Yes?"

"I've been thinking that maybe it's time for me to move on," Remy said, still not making eye contact.

Everything in her went still, except her heart. It began to beat a mile a minute. "Why? Why would you want to walk into the light? Why would you want to *leave* me?" Her heart tightened as she remembered every time she was rejected and laughed at by her mother and others in the coven. "Don't you love me anymore?"

He reappeared in front of Ari in the blink of an eye. "Of course I do, but what I want…ce ne fait rien." He shook his head.

"Of course it matters." She threw up her hands. "Is this why you didn't come with me to Mrs. Haversham's? Distancing yourself? Are you searching for something? Is that why you're disappearing so much? I can help you." No point in having powers if you couldn't use them to help the people you loved.

"I can't remember the last time I saw you smile as you did with that guy from the bar the other night."

"What? This is about Heath? I just met him. He could be a total psycho for all I know. You can't throw us away because of him." That was the last thing she expected to hear.

"No, it's not that, but it made me think. You will have a family soon and where does that leave me?"

He thought she didn't need him. For most of her life, he had been the only person she could count on. "There has to be a solution. What do you want? To find a girlfriend? As much as I hate to admit it, I'm a freaking ghost magnet. Maybe I can start a Ghost Tinder and find you someone." She would not give him up.

"Cher."

"Remy-Pierre Arceneaux, I need you. And if you didn't know it, I love you." If she could've touched him, she would've wrapped him in a hold so tight he would never doubt how she felt. Instead, she wrapped herself in a tight embrace as the tears streamed down her face. A moment later, she felt his otherworldly chill surround her. He held her, and that made her cry even harder.

"Come on, Cher. Don't cry. You know I can't take your tears."

"Then no more talk of leaving." She held his chill inside her, close to her heart. She knew if he wanted to leave, he could. But she would do whatever she needed to do, to make him stay.

)O(

AFTER HER LITTLE 'Come to goddess meeting' with Remy, she couldn't get back to sleep, and her pho had a greasy overlay she wasn't too keen on diving in to. She still had items on the big table to make protection charms. After a few hours of twisting, knotting, and weaving the long pieces of straw her fingers began to tingle. She wished there was an easier way to do protection magic, but she had to pour positive energy into each strand she wove into a tightly bound square. As a special layer of protection against evil, she hid a tiger's eye stone within each cross.

About two hours later, the sideboard was full of small boxes tied with string. Ari had filled all her specialty tea orders and something extra for the seniors at Ravenswood Arms where she volunteered.

Over the past year, she'd noticed the rise in Alzheimer's at the senior home. Ari wanted to see if she could create something that would ease some of their suffering. There was a memory potion in her white magic spell book, but as it was written it would help a person remember where they put their keys or a forgotten phone number. She wanted to help recover years of lost memories, not just a few hours. Unfortunately, the only mnemonic spell she knew consisted of a lot of blood and losing up to a week's worth of memories. She would not want to perform that ritual on anyone.

She carried a small wicker basket and shears to the wrap around balcony that looked eerily similar to an L-shaped mini jungle. The herbs loved the warm weather and were growing out of their pots, but she used the sage, valerian, and mandrake the most. The small waterfall took up a corner. It helped with humidity, not that she needed a lot of assistance with that in Texas, but it kept the tropical plants happy year around.

The mint potted farm, as she called it, had the traditional peppermint, catmint, and spearmint, but her favorite right now was chocolate mint. She whipped up a mean chocolate tea with something special for couples. It was a big hit for Valentine's.

She clipped handfuls of lavender, rosemary, and chamomile. She even picked a few petals from the white rose bush and white periwinkles. She used her grandmother's pestle and mortar to ground all of the ingredients of the memory potion. But after an hour of rubbing herbs into a fine powder she was convinced her herb tool was once used as a medieval torture device.

"Why don't you use the blender?" Remy hovered crosslegged above the long wooden farmhouse table.

Ari stood and stretched her arms over her head. "Because that's not how it's done." She had to imbue her power and intention into the herbs, and that couldn't be done in a blender. If she didn't project positivity into the spell, darkness and disquiet would overrun it, and ruin all her hard work, and good intentions.

After their argument, she wasn't sure what to say or where they stood. She couldn't remember if they'd ever fought before. She didn't think so. With that, the silence stretched uncomfortably between them.

Finally, Remy spoke. "Are we okay?"

Ari flicked the powder into a mason jar with 'Memory' written in cursive on the lid. "I don't know. You still thinking about leaving?" Her hands stilled on the container after she'd closed it. Waiting.

"No, Cher. I will stay as long as you want me."

The weight on her chest lightened. She moved to place the jar on the sideboard. "Good."

She closed her eyes as a chill encompassed her entire body from behind. When she felt an extra cold spot on her temple, she opened her eyes and tears streamed down.

Her phone chirped, breaking the moment. She reached up to wipe away the tears and pulled away two perfectly frozen teardrops. The multifaceted pieces of ice melted almost instantly. Remy had faded away by the time she'd looked up, but nothing more needed to be said. They were okay.

She wiped the dirt and mint oil from her hands on a rag from the table before checked her phone.

A text message.

When she swiped the screen to open the message box, a smile spread across her face. *Speak of the devil.*

Heath: Are you up?

She smiled as she typed: It's the witching hour, what do you think?

Heath: Smiley face emoji. Nice.

Ari: What are you doing up so late?

Heath: Thinking about you.

"He is so full of it," she said aloud but typed: Nice to be thought of.

Heath: How 'bout lunch this week?

Ari: Hmm, kinda bizzy this week. Volunteer stuff.

Heath: E'ryday?

Ari: No.

Heath: Maybe after.

Ari: OK. Cool. But I'm really jonesing for some homemade pastries.

Heath: Done. I know a great place.

Ari: Interesting. I can't wait.

Heath: Night.

Ari: Nite.

She fell back on the couch kicking her feet back and forth in the air with a squeal. She hadn't waited a week to send Heath their picture. She didn't even make it a day. She'd been feeling pretty cocky when she put her number in his phone. She'd told him she didn't want him to think it was a telemarketer and not pick up when she called. Her smooth flirting skills may need to be documented for posterity's sake.

CHAPTER 8

*L*ate the next morning, Ari shook out the red petticoat from under her 50's inspired, red pinstriped dress. Of course, she could wear jeans and a tee, but where would the fun be in that? Besides the seniors always got a kick out of it when she dressed up. She admired the completed protection charm in the mirror. It looked a lot like a St. Brigid's cross and went nicely with her outfit.

She'd made a few items for people at Ravenswood. As she put their items in her bag, she threw a couple of protection charms in a paper bag as well. It never hurt to have some protection around, and if anyone asked she would tell them the necklaces were for good luck. And in a way, they were.

Before she reached Ravenswood Arms, she could see red and blue lights flashing at the end of the street. The facility was a four-story sprawling estate with gardens that took up more than fifteen acres. When she got closer, an officer with a bright yellow and blue safety vest directed traffic away from the entrance and main parking lot. Ari slowed and rolled down her window. "What's going on?"

The officer never stopped waving traffic through. "Ma'am, you need to keep moving."

"I work here." A white lie, but he didn't need to know that.

He actually looked at her then and stopped motioning traffic. He leaned in but his eyes didn't immediately look on her. Ari thought it was more like he was checking out the interior of her car for weapons.

Finally, he made eye contact. "Okay, you need to park in the back parking lot. Turn left at the next street, and go behind the property."

Ari nodded, and said, "Thank you," before driving away.

He had given her directions like she didn't know anything. Granted she'd never had to park in the back but he could have asked if she knew, instead of assuming she didn't. It poked a nerve when men treated women like they didn't have a brain in their heads.

Once Ari parked, she walked around to the entrance. The yellow police tape partitioned off the grass area from the main parking lot all the way to the covered walkway, leaving only one door available to enter. At once, she knew someone had been seriously hurt or possibly killed. Her cheery retro dress seemed out of place now. When the wind changed, she went stock-still as a familiar hot tingle ran through her body. The coppery smell of blood mixed with the sulfurous stench of black magic lingered all around but it was different, not like her coven's magic. She couldn't put her finger on it, but knew she'd recognize this magic if she felt it again.

As much as she wanted to run away, she couldn't. She had friends in this building. In her heart, these were the people she'd sworn to protect. Lucas was right, she did collect a lot of dismages. She exhaled, and a coolness passed over her shoulder.

"Are you okay?" Remy moved in front of her.

She looked up at him, feeling anger then determination roll through her. No one came to her town and messed with her people. "I'm fine." She moved around him.

"Your eyes."

She stopped abruptly, closed her eyes, then took a few deep breaths. She needed to clear her head and heart, in order to calm the darkness building inside her. When she felt centered, she opened her eyes. "Better?" she whispered.

Remy's cold arms wrapped around her. "Yes."

"Thank you," she whispered before she began walking again.

"Do you absolutely need to do this, Cher?"

She gave a half nod to a person passing by her before she answered him. "You know I do," she said barely moving her lips. It wouldn't do to have people think she was crazy.

"Be careful." He shook his head with a frown before he disappeared.

Under the covered walkway, the pungent smell of blood assaulted her senses. No matter what they used to clean the blood, the deep burgundy deformed circle could not be missed on the concrete. She stepped through the available door, only to have a hand whip up into her face.

"Whoa, Miss, how can I help you?" A tall, broad-shouldered man in an ill-fitting, dark blue suit blocked her path.

Taken aback, Ari looked the man up and down before speaking. Buzzcut, jet black hair with almond shaped brown eyes. The wrinkles at the corners made her think he squinted at everyone and everything. "Um, yes. I work here."

"And your name is?" He looked down at his iPad.

Ari watched him curiously. "Mason. Ari Mason."

His finger touched the screen and whipped back and forth, but she couldn't see what he was doing. "I don't see you on staff here, Mrs. Mason."

"That's Miss," she said tartly, "and I'm a volunteer. I visit every week."

He snapped the cover over his iPad. "Ah, well you won't be able to volunteer today. Only necessary personnel and family."

"Why?" The words slipped out before she had a moment to think. "From the scene out here, it looks like they need a distraction more than ever."

His mouth became a tight, straight line. His eyes assessed Ari in a most distressing manner. He scrutinized her at length, as if looking for a chink in her armor.

Ari was more than positive this man wasn't letting her in. "Mister, can you—"

"Detective."

"What?"

"I'm a detective. Detective Westin."

"Okay. Detective Westin, could I at least drop off the items I brought for my friends." She held up her messenger bag.

The detective lifted his eyebrows and put his iPad to the side. "What do you have in there?"

She took a deep breath as she rummaged through her large khaki bag, unfolded one of the paper bags, and held out a small bottle of lotion.

The detective pointed inside. "What's that?"

The tea.

Ari rolled her eyes. Sure, it looked like marijuana. She could already tell where this was going.

"Are you dealing to these old people?" He snapped loudly. Heads turned towards them.

"What? No!" Ari responded, but a scowl crossed his face and he wasn't hearing anything she had to said.

"Turn around."

"What? I will not. If you—" her words were cut off when he threw her into the wall. Unbelievable. Her messenger bag fell to the floor as cold, steel bracelets snapped around her wrists. "What is wrong with you?"

"I don't think he likes you very much," Remy chimed in.

Ari cut her eyes to him but didn't say anything.

"What are you doing?" A female voice came across the lobby. "She works here."

After the cuffs were in place, Ari turned to look at Lane Exley, Ravenswood Arms facilities manager, walking fast towards them, heels clicking hard on the tile floor.

"She's doing more than that." He lifted one of the plastic baggies that had spilled out on the floor. "See." He read the label. "Raspberry-mint Lane." When he loosed the twist tie, the fresh scent of mint filled the air.

"It's tea. My tea," Lane held her hand out. "For my cramps, if you need to know. Now, can you please release her?"

He didn't even have the good grace to look embarrassed as he handed the tea to Lane and removed the handcuffs from Ari. "She can't stay. This is an ongoing investigation."

"I'll handle my job. Please come with me, Ari." Lane turned her back on the detective.

Ari quickly placed everything back in her bag, and slung her bag over her shoulder, then walked quickly to catch up with the feisty admin. She knew now she never wanted to get her riled up. "Thank you for that."

The entire interaction had taken Ari by surprise. Mostly, she feared what words might come out of her mouth. Namely a spell that would have left him writhing on the floor.

"No, problem. He's been a douche all morning. We've had someone nearly die today, and he's not even pretending to understand our pain." Lane lifted an index finger to try and stop the tears. It hadn't worked. She snatched two tissues from the box on the front desk to dab the corners of her eyes. "I'll be right back."

Ari waited at the front desk. Detective 'Douchebag' Westin had walked back outside after their little misunderstanding. He talked to other uniformed officers before they shook his hand and walked away.

"I leave you for a minute, and you get into trouble," Remy chided.

There were only a few people in the lobby, but Ari made a point of not talking to or arguing with non-corporeal beings in public. The hairs on Ari's arm stood on end when a white-haired man walked past her. A staff member walked ahead of him rolling two suitcases. Heck of a day to move in.

The older man was a little overweight and walked with a cane, but his aura is what drew him to her attention. It had dark spots and broken points throughout an otherwise blue glow. He had gone through a terrible tragedy and hadn't yet found a way to live with it. She would have to do something to help him.

She leaned against the tallest portion of the desk, and placed her hand over her mouth and spoke softly. "I didn't see you helping me."

Remy gasped in mock horror. "Me? Accost the police? I would never. You, my young rebel, do not respect authority."

"Me? I—" Ari stood up straight.

"Thank you for waiting," Lane said from behind Ari.

Ari turned quickly. "No problem." The young woman looked like she would cry again. "You want to tell me what happened?"

Lane looked around, then took Ari's hand and pulled her into the small room behind the front desk. She closed the door once they were safely inside. Lane waved towards a chair, indicating Ari should sit. Ari thought it looked like Lane needed it more, but if this would help the woman tell the story…she pulled out the chair and sat.

Almost immediately, Lane began to sniffle. All remnants of the strong woman from just a few minutes ago was gone. "Nurse Francesca was attacked this morning. It was early, before dawn. I saw her coming up the walkway, and then I went to get a cup of coffee." Lane's trembling hand flew to her mouth. "I should have waited for her." Her words were garbled, but Ari understood well enough.

Ari reached out and patted the woman's hand "It's not your fault. You have to believe that."

Lane nodded as she wiped her tears. Ari didn't have the heart to tell her she had just smeared mascara to her hairline.

The young woman started again. "It's not much more to tell. When I came back, she was on the ground. Her mouth. Her hands…" She looked at her hands and clenched them. "They looked like the ragged roots of a tree. Contorted and bloody. There was so much blood. I thought she was dead, but then she wheezed. She was still alive. So, I called 9-1-1."

"And you didn't see anybody out there?"

She shook her head. "No, nobody."

Ari hated to ask because clearly the woman was still rattled, but she needed to know. "Anything weird?"

Lane eyed her suspiciously. "Like what?"

"I just meant, it's quiet here. Maybe you heard a car backfire or smelled smoke. Something different from a normal morning."

Lane seemed to understand, and her suspicion seemed to be assuaged. "Nothing like that, but I heard thunder, then it got foggy. And now that you said that, that fog was weird, it didn't move like any fog I'd ever seen. It crept along the ground, kind of like dry ice, then it was gone. I thought it strange for a moment, but then I heard the sirens and didn't give it a second thought. You think that meant something?"

"No, no I'm sure it was just fog. You know how Texas weather is." Ari was more than sure that wasn't just an atmospheric event. "I have some things for a few people, can I go in?"

"The detective was right. The police are still inside. It would best if you came back another day."

"I understand, but I made some cream for Ms. Myrtle's arthritis, and I have something special for Aracely and the gang. Please." Ari clasped her hands together and blinked her eyes like a cartoon character. "With cherries on top. Just for a minute. I promise, I won't take long."

Lane watched her with a stern face, and for a minute she didn't think the woman would do it. "Fine, fine. Come on. I think they're in the library."

Ari was idly wondering if there was a way to actually ward a building this size. She knew she couldn't do it. Small apartments and personal protection, sure, but this place. She looked around. Nope, she wasn't capable of magic on that scale.

"Hey, did I see someone new moving in today?" She followed Lane past the elevators.

"Yes, Mr. Pauppen Miller. He lost his entire family not long ago. Ah, here we are. I'll be right back." Lane straightened her jacket and skirt before she walked in.

A tangible relief rushed out of her when she saw the gray-haired woman roll through of the french doors of the library.

"Aracely," Ari whispered, then leaned down to hug the petite Hispanic woman.

"Not here, ladies." Lane walked quickly to an unmarked door

and peeked in. "Use this room. Don't take too long. I told the detective she had a phone call." She held the door.

Ari pushed Aracely's wheelchair, even though she knew the older woman liked to do it herself. "Until these old arms quit working, let me do it myself."

Aracely's thick accented voice had scolded Ari on more than one occasion. The room looked like a meeting room no one had used in a while. It had stacks of chairs and two eight-feet tables across the front near a drop-down screen.

Lane had said, "Five minutes," before she'd closed the door.

"Are you okay?" Ari pulled up a chair.

"I'm fine. I wasn't anywhere near the entrance," Aracely patted Ari's hand.

"Then why are you in for questioning?"

"I was in the library. I saw Nurse Francesca walking from the parking lot." Aracely looked at her hands then.

"What it is?"

She looked around. "I don't want them thinking I'm losing my mind. But I know what I saw."

A feeling of dread crept up Ari's spine. "Tell me, you know I'll believe you."

Aracely looked into Ari's eyes and watched her carefully. It felt like the old woman's stare could decree the truth. After a few moments, the woman nodded. "I went back to reading, so I didn't see the attack, that was too far away, you know. A few minutes later, I saw someone in a long coat calmly walking by. He threw up his hand, then a tornado appeared. It sucked him up, and then he was gone." Aracely's hands shook. Ari took the woman's cold, thin fingers into her own, and held them tightly.

As much as she wanted to panic, Ari took two deep breaths before speaking. "Did he…she…it see you?"

"I don't think so." Aracely browed creased in consternation. "No. I'm sure. I only saw the side of the long cloak."

Ari rummaged through her messenger bag and pulled out a small brown paper bag. She opened it and pulled out the protection charm and held it up. "I made this for you. You should wear it."

Aracely reached out. "Ohhh, I haven't seen one of these since I was a child. Mi abuela had something similar to this along with other crystals and candles around the house."

"Santeria?"

This explained why Aracely embraced her the moment she'd walked in and seemed to be accepting of all the homeopathic things she brought to help the seniors. Aracely smiled with glistening eyes and tapped her nose. Just like how Ari hadn't been overly forthcoming with her craft, Aracely still kept her grandmother's secret.

"I made a few more, so give them to the boys. Just tell them it will make them vigorous with the ladies. They'll wear it." She handed another paper bag to the older woman.

Aracely covered her mouth when she giggled and Ari could see the beautiful, young woman she once was and the beauty she was now.

"You know them so well. Michael and Luscious get a kick out of you calling them boys." Aracely tucked the bags between the chair and her leg.

"Ms. Aracely, when they interview you. I think you shouldn't tell them about the tornado. They won't believe you."

"I know."

The door opened behind them. "Ms. Hernandez have you completed your call?"

"Yes, Ms. Exley, I believe I have," Aracely said with a conspiratorial smile. When Ari moved to push her wheelchair, she swatted at Ari's fingers. "What have I told you?"

Ari lifted her hands in surrender. "That you can do it."

"Gracias, mija." Aracely rolled way.

"Doesn't she have a motorized wheelchair?" Ari continued to watch the older woman work her small arms to roll the chair.

Lane laughed. "Yes, but she won't use it."

"Oh," Ari finally looked at Lane. "This is for Ms. Myrtle. Tell her to use it once a day in the morning. It should give her some relief in her joints." She handed Lane a small round bottle filled with a beige cream. She'd heard the older woman's arthritis had nearly completely paralyzed her fingers, and she had been in terrible pain. The crisp, tingling sensation from the mint should reinvigorate her hands, and the rose oil along with the spell should leave a youthful glow.

Lane took the lotion. "Thank you. I'm sure anything would help her."

"I hope so. She'd been asking for a manicure. Since I can't do that today, maybe this will help."

"I'm sure it will."

"Take care."

))((

ARI HAD misgivings about leaving the people in the facility. She hadn't thought anything would actually happen to someone she knew when her cousin came to her the other day. When she stepped outside, the faint aroma of blood still lingered in the air, but not enough to trigger her powers.

A gentle breeze flowed over her and she stopped abruptly at the end of the covered walkway. It carried the scent of something not quite right. She lifted her head like a lioness scenting prey and the stench of rotting eggs made her recoil. She quickly covered her nose, but it didn't stop the assault on her senses. As she walked along the pathway towards the garden, the rotten smell got stronger. Every supernatural being's magic had its own feel and smell. The magic surrounding her felt malevolent and unfamiliar.

Could her presence have brought this pain to a place she loved? Maybe attacking nurse Francesca was a lure. The older woman wouldn't hurt a fly and had to be tapping seventy, but she was spry as a spring chicken. Bringing up retirement were fighting words. There was no reason to hurt her. She looked around. The path led to a seated area near a fountain, then through a grove of trees. Perfect place for an ambush, she thought. He or she could be watching her now? And for how long? Did they know about Leise?

Ari needed to see Leise for her own piece of mind. She turned around abruptly as she rummaged through her bag for her phone, only to run into the broad chest of Detective Westin.

"Ms. Mason, you're still here," he stated. "What are you doing out here?" Looking up the path, then back to her.

"Making a call," she waggled her phone. "It's illegal to drive and talk, you know. What are you doing, stalking me?" She realized with overwhelming vehemence, she disliked this man. There was an arrogance that clung to him like stink on a skunk.

"Not at all. I just don't like interlopers on my crime scene."

"You know what? I'm leaving right now." She went around him. How dare he? This was her place. These were her people. He had no clue what was going on, and he thought she was the interloper. The nerve!

"Have a nice day Ms. Mason," Detective Westin said.

She couldn't see him but she could hear the smile in his voice. She wasn't sure if flipping off a cop was against the law, but she wanted to. He was being an ass for no reason at all. She had no clue what she had done to bring out this much hostility in him.

He was lucky she had turned over a new leaf, because she knew a curse that could cause explosive diarrhea. Was it childish? Possibly. But would it be satisfying? Definitely.

CHAPTER 9

Technology was great until you actually needed to speak to a real person. Ari pressed the pound key on her cell over and over, not listening to the 'I can help you' recorded prompts. When a male's voice finally said, "Thank you for calling the Paper Trail, how may I help you?" She nearly pressed the pound key again.

"Oh, hi. Can I please speak to Annaleise Morgan?" Ari used her best, official sounding voice.

The male's monotone voice groaned. Ari was fairly sure this associate missed phone etiquette training. He didn't sound happy to help. The inflections in his voice sounded a lot like Eeyore. "Umm, yeah. She can't come to the phone right now."

That response made Ari sit up a little straighter in the car. "Is she okay?"

"Umm, yeah. Well, not really," he said.

Her heart was working double time now. "What happened to her?"

"Not sure I'm allowed to say."

Ari didn't know all of Leise's coworkers, but she was pretty sure this was Sylvester Telepsen. He frequented her bar a few times a month. "Sylvester? Is this you?"

The phone was quiet, then a long, hesitant, "Yeah," came through.

"It's Ari, Leise's friend." She heard him exhale.

"Ari, I told you to call me Telly."

"I know, I know, but I forget. Anyway, tell me the truth. Is Leise okay?"

"Sure, sure. She was late again."

This time, Ari exhaled loudly. "Can you do me a favor?" She continued when he groaned. She took that to mean, yes and continued. "If you guys get off work before I get there, could you please walk her to her car. She hadn't been getting much sleep. Could be her blood sugar, I don't know. I'm just worried she might fall in the parking lot." No need to scare them with the truth. For all she knew she was just overreacting.

"Sure. Whatever."

If Ari was sure of anything, that would be that Telly had a crush on Leise. He sounded like he didn't care about most things, but when he was deep in his cups at the bar, Telly talked exclusively about Leise's eyes and hands. Hey, everyone had their thing. A fraction of peace rolled over her knowing Leise would be safe surrounded by people at work for a few hours.

About fifteen minutes later, Ari pulled up in front of a nondescript, brown brick building. To dismages, the White Cauldron looked like a crystal and metaphysical store. But for practitioners, it was one of the best places to acquire real magical supplies.

Ari had been in this store many times before, but she would buy what she needed and leave. On occasion, her skin would tingle from the remnants of magic in this building. The white magic always reminded her being wrapped in a clean, hot towel from the dryer. She would inhale and hold that goodness inside her before leaving the store every time. She felt it was only right to protect them as well. She turned the brass doorknob in the middle of the weathered door. After fifty years of Texas heat and humidity, the door held only a hint of the original color.

The wards protecting the store were strong. It felt like she was pushing through sturdy cling wrap every time she walked in. But if a person tried to enter the store with ill intentions in their heart, the wards would repel them, but if they persisted, it would rip a large chunk of their power-base away. Lucky for her, it only made her ears pop.

A bell jingled as Ari entered. The store's medieval, round, iron chandelier whooshed to life. There wasn't any electricity because it messed with some people's powers. Despite not having any electricity, the tapers on the chandelier and the pillar candles around the store cast an almost ethereal, buttery glow. All the place needed was a fireplace and a couple of wingback chairs to give it that homey feeling.

Behind the vintage push button cash register, an apothecary cabinet encompassed the entire wall. It looked well worn, with yellowing pieces of paper on each drawer's tarnished card holder. The cards looked as if they would disintegrate if someone sneezed in their general direction.

"Merry meet, Ms. Mason." The petite woman gave a slight bow with the traditional Wiccan greeting. Her accented voice had a melodic quality, but it was more Scarlet O'Hara than Elizabeth Bennet.

Ari returned the bow with one of her own. "Merry meet, Ms. James."

"No, please call me, Elizabeth."

"Elizabeth. Okay."

"How may I be of service?"

"Um, I'm actually here to talk to you. It's kind of important." Ari looked around the room, then whispered, "Magically speaking."

Elizabeth gave a nod, then walked towards the front door and locked it. She passed Ari as she walked through the library in the back of the store. "Please follow me. I'll put on the kettle."

Instead of taking a seat on the long bench in the shelved book area called the library, Elizabeth opened the back door and held it for Ari. When Ari looked inside, it was a narrow stairwell that led upstairs.

Once on the next floor, Elizabeth unlocked an ornate wooden door. Ari examined the intricate patterns and noted the straight lines of the runes carved into the frame. The magic that emanated from this level wasn't just white; it was a little of everything. Ari held her hand out to feel the power crackling at the door.

"You are welcomed here. Please come in." Elizabeth stood at the door patiently. When Ari stepped through, she said, "Please have a seat." Elizabeth waved towards the round table in the middle of the room. "I'll be right back."

Ari looked around the spacious room. She lifted the black sheet from something hanging on the wall. She lowered it quickly, "Oh." Underneath was a silver framed mirror with rune symbols etched along the edges. This mirror could be used for scrying or summonings, and the runes kept any number of evil baddies from coming through from the other side.

As she walked around the room, she spotted remnants of chalk circles drawn on the hardwood floors. She stood in the center of one and could see faint squiggles and lines around the edges. She couldn't be sure what the circle had contained, but she didn't feel any maliciousness lingering.

"Welcome to my humble abode." Elizabeth carried a silver tray with a cast iron teapot and two small iron cups without handles. They looked like little bowls. Next to the cups was a small saucer of golden brown silver dollar sized cookies, and a small carafe of water.

When Elizabeth sat it on the table, Ari admired the kanji characters raised around the pot. She wanted to touch the characters. It called to her. Had to be a spell of some sort.

"What does it say?" Ari held her hands clasped tight in her lap.

"Truth spoken here." Elizabeth poured a faint green tea into both cups. Bits of colorful flower pieces and leaves floated in the hot liquid. The symbols along the cup flashed green. "Drink deep and speak true."

The tea ceremony was a test. Ari knew it instinctually, and part of her wanted to rebel against it. The spell would compel her to tell the truth. She had secrets. Everyone had secrets. But she didn't want to reveal any of them.

"You do not have to drink," Elizabeth said as she lifted the cup with two hands, pressed it to her lips, and sipped.

Ari watched the woman, then Lucas' words flashed in her mind, and she realized she came here for a reason. Her hands moved around the bowl-like cup in the same fashion as Elizabeth, and lifted the cup and inhaled the soft floral scent. It wasn't jasmine, but rose, and something she couldn't quite place. She closed her eyes as she blew over the hot liquid, then sipped.

When Ari lowered her cup, Elizabeth smiled. "How did you like it?"

"Oh my goodness, that's so good. I could smell the rose, what else is that made of?"

"Coneflowers and sunflowers. My own recipe."

"I have both of those in my garden, but never once have I used them together. It has a light, pleasant taste. I like it."

"I'm glad you approved. It's nice to have another tea connoisseur here. The others do not appreciate tea as much. May I?" Elizabeth indicated her cup. Ari nodded, and the woman looked at the remaining contents on the bottom. She turned the cup one way, then another.

For the first time in a while, Ari was nervous. When she entered the building her hands were freezing, now they were damp with anticipation.

"You are not what you seem." She set the cup down. "You are waiting for something before you can become."

"Become? Become what?" Ari lifted the cup, turning it side to side. Was that a scythe in there?

"Only you can answer that." Elizabeth poured Ari another cup of tea.

"Thank you."

"Ms. Mason—"

"Please," Ari cut in. "Call me Ari."

"Very well then, Ari. What is it that you needed to speak to me about?"

Ari took one more sip of her tea, before placing the cup on the table. "I don't know if you had heard about a string of murders…"

and Ari preceded to tell her about the witches who were murdered, and the attempt at the senior facility. "This power was like nothing I'd ever felt before. It was greasy and malevolent. And when I walked near the crime scene, I had never felt so much anger. Even hours later, evil clung to the area in a way that seemed nearly tangible."

"Would you mind telling the others what you just told me?"

Ari worried her lip as she looked at her watch. "I don't think that's a good idea."

"Ari, only you can fully explain what has happened."

"It's your group, and I just wanted to relay the info so they wouldn't be caught off guard. It's a dangerous time for witches."

Elizabeth nodded. "That's very true indeed." She stood, and Ari followed. "We don't like to call ourselves a coven. We like to think of ourselves as a family. We'll meet again two nights from now…if you would like to come by."

"I'll think about it," Ari said before she walked away.

"Merry meet, merry part, and merry meet again, Ari Mason," Elizabeth said with a nod.

$$) O ($$

WHEN ARI STEPPED OUTSIDE of the White Cauldron, it was dark. How long had she been in there? She looked at her watch and frowned.

Hours, that was the answer.

The shop owner had been so easy to talk to and the time flew by. She felt like it had been about forty minutes, one hour tops, but in truth, it was more like six. Something kept her in that building. She wasn't sure if it was the building or Elizabeth herself, but there was a cacophony of strong magic within the White Cauldron.

Tiffany had a cracked windshield and dents to which she called, 'Character curves.' Going by that logic, the BMW had loads of character. But she had a good motor with no major damage; even if Ari pushed it, the car should be able to reach Leise's job before it closed. With no time to lose, she stepped on it.

When Ari pulled up in front of the office supply store, the lights were out. "Dammit." She looked at the time on her dashboard. She couldn't have missed Leise and Telly by more than five or ten minutes. She drove around to the back parking lot. Leise had told her once that her boss blew a gasket when she parked in front of the store once.

Nothing could have prepared her for what she saw. She hit the brakes and stared at a hooded figure approaching Telly. Her heart raced when she didn't see Leise, but when Telly stepped forward with his hands extended, presumably to stop the approaching figure, she saw Leise on the ground slumped over.

Ari opened the door, but it slammed shut before she could get out. When she looked up, the hooded figure had turned its attention towards her. She couldn't see a face, only endless darkness within the cowl. She pulled the handle again, but the door wouldn't budge. The figure pointed a gnarly piece of wood in her direction. The six-foot wooden staff wasn't smooth, and pristine like most witches used today. The old stick looked like it had been carved from a tree in Sherwood Forest when Robin Hood still stole from the rich. When the stream of white, jagged light shot out of it, the strands moved like lightning on a jerky, horizontal path. Ari braced for an explosion as she cringed behind the steering wheel. She watched the white light envelope the car.

Then nothing.

She opened her eyes. The vehicle was still intact, but when she touched the door handle she heard the distinct sound of crunching metal. When she snatched her hand away, the crunching stopped. The spell would crush her inside her own car. This creature wanted her to watch as he killed her friends. A level of malice and hate bubbled up inside of her that she was terribly uncomfortable with.

For a moment, she entertained the thoughts of what she wanted to do to the creature before her. The golden light from around her hands illuminated the interior of the car like a small sun. She took a few deep breaths to calm her nerves and clear her mind. That level of anger could make her a mindless beast and her friends needed her right now.

The figure turned back towards Telly who leaned protectively over Leise's body. This was her fault. If she hadn't told Telly to watch out for her best friend, he wouldn't be in this. But then Leise would probably be dead already.

Get yourself together and think. She was a powerful witch, but in this moment she felt utterly helpless. Her emotions tried to drown her, but she wouldn't let them. She wiped away the tears that tried to consume her and looked around the car for something…anything that would help her get out of this car.

The spell seemed to be keeping her from getting out, maybe someone could get in. "Remy!" Her ears rang from the sheer volume and force she put into the call.

"I'm a ghost. I'm not deaf," Remy said, as he wagged a finger in his ear.

She had never been so happy to hear his snarky comments. "Remy, we don't have time for this," she pointed out the windshield. "Go help them."

His brows lifted then he looked back at her. "And do what exactly?"

"Help. I don't know, possess the guy if you have to." *Just don't let that creature kill them.* The words rolled through her mind unbidden. She couldn't stop the tears this time. "Please, Remy." With those words, Remy disappeared.

Ari spotted her cell phone on the passenger side floor amidst the scattered items from her overturned bag. She grabbed it and quickly swiped the screen and called 9-1-1.

"9-1-1, what's your emergency?"

"Gunshots at the Paper Trail on Main. A girl looks dead." The hooded figure loped with slow measure towards Leise. It moved a lot like a vulture - up and down with its hand outstretched. "Please get the police here. I think he's going to kill them. Oh my goddess, no." She dropped the phone as she let out a gut-wrenching scream.

The figure extended its staff, and parts of it glowed an orangey-yellow. From where Ari sat, she couldn't see what the small slits and curves were, but she knew with everything in her that those were runes and dark magic poured from them like water through a sieve.

Sylvester threw himself over Leise's body the same time Remy stood in front of the staff. The luminescence dimmed, but the staff didn't waver from Sylvester.

Remy was juggling cans in the air. To them, it must have looked like the cans were floating in the air. It paused the attack, but Ari knew it was only a momentary reprieve. "Good Remy." She touched the passenger side door, and the crunching metal echoed through Tiffany.

Ari looked up to see that Remy had disappeared into the dark cloak. Then just as fast fell through the back of the cloak coughing, then he collapsed and faded away.

"Remy. Remy!" She had no clue that was even possible because Remy couldn't breathe. Her hands burst in golden balls of flames, and launched them forward. The windshield creaked, then small spiderweb-like cracks formed around the frame before it exploded outward. The glass stayed intact as it slid off the hood to the ground. She didn't have time to think about what she'd just done to Tiffany.

"Hey!" Ari crawled over the hood and jogged across the parking lot.

The hooded figure didn't react to her yell, but continued to hold the illuminated staff high above its head. It seemed to be tethered to Telly's limp body and keeping it suspended in mid-air, at least ten feet up. Ari stopped short as she looked at Leise's co-worker. A rippling effect moved from Telly's hand up his arm to his face. It wasn't just his arms; something was happening to his entire body. His pants hung loosely only seeming to stay in place because of his belt. His mouth hung open in a macabre and half twisted gape. A bright silver-blue light moved in a slow undulating motion into the dark cowl. If this went on any longer, everything that made Telly, well, Telly would be drained away.

Ari lifted her hands and wound up like a Major League pitcher and let two baseball sized balls of fire fly. The first hit its target with gleaming accuracy, knocking the hooded figure aside. Telly's body dropped and hit the ground hard. Ari wanted to help him and let out a sigh of relief when she heard the sirens in the distance. But her relief was short-lived, the hooded figure had turned the glowing staff in her direction. A crack of thunder resounded as a bolt of light came forth, streaking towards her in a jerky, jagged pattern. She didn't get a chance to murmur a spell or anything before the lightning reached her.

Ari could faintly hear voices in the distance. When she opened her eyes, she didn't see anyone. As a matter of fact, she didn't see anything at all. She blinked, instead of darkness, a stark, bright whiteness was all she could see. The lightning must have blinded her, but luckily it didn't kill her.

Ari went to move her arm.

Nothing.

She concentrated on the slightest of motion, but it didn't budge at all. Both arms felt like fifty-pound weights and for one brief moment she was scared she wouldn't be able to use her hands again. Her fingertips tingled like sharp needles prickled just under her nails. It hurt like the dickens, but she was glad to have some feeling. When she made an effort to move this time her arm jerked.

Gravel moved under her hands when she had gained enough strength to sit up. She realized she was still outside in the parking lot. She opened and closed her eyes a few more times, and the brightness began to dim as darkness with flashes of red and blue started to fill her sight.

"Over here," a young man's voice called out.

A blurry yellow vest came towards her. "My name is Jeff. I'm an emergency medical tech." His warm hand touched her shoulder. "Are you okay, miss?" She stared at the young man for a minute before his handsome, but youthful features came into focus. She smiled at the light freckles across his nose and tortoise-shell round glasses. She was happy to see anything at all.

"Yeah, I think I'm okay." Gravel dug into her hands as she tried to push herself up and failed. "Could you please help me up?"

"Not yet, Miss. Let me check you out first." A bright light flashed in her eyes. Nothing like the blindness she had previously experienced, just a flicker this time.

"No, I need to check on my friend." She pushed him away and

stood on her own, but when she took her first step, the ground came rushing up.

For a scrawny guy, he had a firm grip. "Whoa, steady," Jeff said, as he helped support her. "Over here, I need some help," he called out, over her head.

"Wow, okay." Ari didn't let go of his hand until she was back on the ground. "Just tell me, is Leise okay?"

He paused before he spoke as he looked through his kit. "The others are on their way to the hospital, and I think you should go as well."

A female EMT arrived with a gurney.

"I just need to sit," Ari said faintly.

"Right here." He helped her off the ground. When Ari stood without swaying, Jeff guided her to the gurney and helped her up. When he touched her shoulder and urged her to lie back, she didn't fight it.

"Gunshot?" The female EMT touched Ari's shirt. "I don't see any blood, but she has a severe burn."

Ari reached up. Her protection charm was gone.

Just as they reached the ambulance, Ari heard a familiar, and yet unwelcome voice. "Ms. Mason." Ari closed her eyes and tried to play dead.

She felt him hovering next to her. When she cracked open one eye, yep, he was still there. "Detective Dou...Westin." She'd corrected herself quickly.

He lifted both brows but continued. "The others were unconscious when we arrived."

"I believe I was as well."

"But you are awake now. Can you tell me what happened?"

She closed her eyes as Jeff and the other EMT loaded her into the ambulance. "Detective, we have to go."

Thank goodness for Jeff. Ari turned her head towards the wall, but before the door closed completely, she heard the detective say, "We'll talk soon, Ms. Mason."

Ari was going to have to think up a good story because the truth was not an option.

CHAPTER 10

*H*ospitals always smelled of bleach, disinfectant, and death. The whiteness of the halls and rooms were misleading because the black stain of death clung to the entire building. Ari tried not to visit, if at all possible. Not because of the blood or even the stench, it was the damned ghosts. Thank goodness they didn't ask for anything. She had no plans of becoming a ghost whisperer.

When she woke up this morning only one ghost lingered in the room, it faded into the walls when the doctor appeared though. The ghost looked like a Native American shaman. A petite woman with long, white hair in a light-colored, fringed animal skin dress with a necklace of teeth and bones. Even as a ghost she had the most compelling light eyes. They seemed to look in her and through her simultaneously.

The doctor had discharged Ari the next morning. She had just gotten dressed when Detective Westin walked in. It was too early in the morning for him.

"Ms. Mason, how are you doing? Better I hope." His voice suggested he didn't care.

"Detective Westin, shouldn't you be out *detecting*?" Ari knew she shouldn't poke at him, but again, too early in the morning.

He gave a her wolfish smile. All teeth — white, sharp and far too many. "I kind of thought that's what I was doing. Now, tell me what happened last night."

He hadn't asked, it was more like a command. When men came at her like that, it set her teeth on edge. She looked at the detective, really looked at him right now. Something she failed to do up to this point because he just rubbed her the wrong way. She sat down on the bed and contemplated the muted colors swirling around this man. She couldn't remember the last time she saw an aura with so much negativity. The dark grays and reds let her know he didn't trust anyone or anything. And anger, whew. She did not want to be around when that powder keg blew. She took a deep breath and put out the fire burning inside of her.

"I don't know what happened," Ari pulled at a loose thread on the sheet. "When I arrived the store was closed."

"And were you there to shop?" He interrupted. He had a pen and pad in his hand, but not writing.

"No. I went to see my friend."

"The victims - Annaleise Morgan and Sylvester Telepsen?"

She looked at him then. *Victims.* Did he have to be so cold about it? "I know them both, but I was there to see Leise." When he didn't comment again, she continued. "I figured I couldn't have missed her by a minute or two. So, I drove to the back parking lot. They were being attacked and when I got out of my car something hit me."

He nodded as he scribbled on his notepad. "Hmmm, and that blue car at the scene was yours?"

Poor Tiffany. She closed her eyes at what she'd done to the old BMW. "Yes, sir."

"And what happened to the car? The windshield was melted and they couldn't open the doors."

Ari affected an innocent smile with a shoulder shrug. "I couldn't say."

"And did you see who attacked your friends?"

If for one minute she thought the detective could handle what she saw out there, she would have told it all. But she knew this wasn't something the Houston police could handle. "It was dark. I couldn't see much of anything. A person in dark clothes was looming over Telly and Leise. I called 9-1-1, and then I was knocked out."

He studied her for a long minute. "You can't remember anything else?"

"I'm sorry. That's everything."

He nodded again and wrote something in his notepad before flipping it closed. Then he reached into his jacket pocket and handed her his card. "If anything else comes to mind, please give me a call."

Ari took the card and gave a salute with it. "First person. I promise."

The detective walked out with a frown. Ari had never been a great liar, but she stuck to the basics and told mostly the truth.

"Remy? Remy, are you here?"

Nothing.

"What did he do to you?" Ari spoke aloud in the empty room.

"He tried to effing kill me, is what."

Ari turned around to see a Remy stretched out on the hospital bed. He had always been pale and transparent, but now he looked as if a fluorescent light illuminated him. A bit green around the gills. She rushed to his bedside. She wanted to touch him, feel his forehead, make sure he was okay. But she couldn't. "Are you okay?"

"Of course I'm not okay. What part of, 'he tried to kill me' did you not understand?"

Ari laid her hand over his. She shivered from the cold spot where their hands met, but she didn't care. "What happened? I was so worried."

"If I never possess another person it would be too soon. He was pure evil. Just rotten on the inside. I felt like I was being sucked into a black hole. If I had stayed any longer, I would have been a permanent guest."

"I'm so sorry. I would have never asked, if I'd known."

Remy nodded. "I know, Cher. But I did find out one thing. He wants someone called, Nyah desperately and he will kill every witch in this city until has her."

"I wonder why he thinks she's here in Houston," Ari said, more to herself. Then it clicked, that's why he killed poor Candyce. To help him find his heart's desire.

"I don't know. But what I do know is…you can't go against this guy alone. He's very powerful. Completely insane, and full of old magic. But he also has some new magic. I want to say it's not his own."

"How could you tell?"

"I was only in there for a moment ya-see, but there were small globes of bright, pure white light, that hadn't been taken over by his taint. It's kind of hard to explain, but I could tell that they didn't belong there."

"Stolen magic?"

"Je ne sais pas." Remy hunched one shoulder. "I suppose it could have been."

"Gods and goddesses, this is bad."

Her mother had said there was a way to steal a witch's power. Everyone thought it was an old witch's tale. Stories told to scare bad little witches. She stood and paced down the side of the bed and back, before she spoke again. "Remy, you should get home. You look a lot like Slimer from Ghostbusters right now. I need to check on Leise and Telly, then talk to some witches."

"Cher, I'm already…"

She held up her hand. "Remy-Pierre, I know perfectly well what you are. But that doesn't stop me from worrying about you. Doesn't stop me from loving you. What happened last night," she took a deep breath and wiped at a tear that hadn't fallen yet.

"Okay," Remy wrapped his arms around her and kissed her forehead. He whispered, "Prendre garde," before he faded away.

Be careful.

)O(

AFTER VISITING THE NURSES' station she found out that Leise was only down the hall from her.

"Hey," Ari said with a light knock on the door. The curtain was drawn around Leise's bed. "Leise?"

"I'm here," Leise said as she pulled the curtain back.

There were thin black and blue bruises around her neck and some bruising on her face. "Why aren't you in bed?"

Leise buttoned up her khakis. "I've been released. I had a concussion, but I'm okay now," she groaned as she slid her arm into the hoodie sleeve. Ari grabbed the hoodie and held it open as she slid her other arm in and zipped it up. "Thanks. Have you heard anything about how Telly's doing?"

"No. I was going to check on him after you. Are you up to it? Or…"

"I want to see him. I need to see him." Leise sounded desperate.

"Do you remember anything about last night?"

"Not really. I walked out and a man reached for me, Telly stopped him. I guess he hit Telly, then came at me again and slammed me against the car. I don't remember anything after that."

"Did the attacker say anything?"

Leise brows furrowed before she shook her head. "I think he might have said, 'finally,' but nothing else that I can remember."

"Were you wearing the protection cross?" Ari didn't see it.

Leise looked away. "I felt bad after I hid it in a drawer, but I wasn't going to wear that thing."

"What did you do?"

"I made it into a keychain. I had it in my hand, because I was at my car, then I got attacked."

Ari sighed in relief. That's what probably saved her life. "It's okay."

"Oh," Leise's brows went up. "Oh, wait, it was that kind of attack?"

"Yeah." Ari nodded. "Have you talked to the police yet?"

"No, she hasn't, Ms. Mason," a rich baritone boomed through the room, "and I'd appreciate it if you didn't interrogate people in my investigation."

Ari's closed her eyes at his voice. "Goddess, deliver me from insufferable men," she whispered, then held her lips tight to keep from saying anymore before she reached out and grabbed Leise's hand and squeezed it. "I'll be outside. Then we can go check on Sylvester."

Leise held Ari's hand and pulled her back, blocking the detectives's view. "I don't know if I want to be alone with him," she whispered.

Ari turned to look at the detective. He stood with his arms crossed and a scowl on his face. Nothing about him screamed friendly or helpful. She turned back to Leise. "I know he looks mean, but he's honest. Just answer his questions. I'll come rescue you in ten minutes. Besides, I have a spell I've been saving just for him." She winked.

"Promise?"

Ari held up her pinky. "Promise." Leise smiled and hooked her pinky around Ari's with a firm shake.

"Ms. Mason…"

"I'm going, I'm going," she said aloud, but whispered, "It'll be okay." Then hugged her friend. "If he gets overbearing, imagine him in his underwear. Personally, I think he wears a thong that's why he's so uptight."

)〇(

Leise had been in the room a little more than ten minutes when Ari had opened the door. Leise waved her out by saying she was okay. About ten minutes later, Leise walked out the room with a sad smile on her face.

"Thank you, Detective Westin."

He gave her a huge smile. "I told you to call me Adam."

"Adam. I know you'll find whoever did this," Leise shook his hand.

"A pleasure, Annaleise." The detective gave her a slight nod with a tight smile before he walked away.

When his eyes fell on Ari, his usual scowl appeared. She had started to think of this as his resting bastard face. Ari lifted her brows. *Was that a smile along with niceties?* Leise must have the gift to soothe the savage beast.

"Did you call him Adam?"

"Yeah, I thought it would be worse, but he was nice." Leise gave a shy smile.

"Wow. That's not the word I'd use for him."

"I kind of got that feeling." Leise touched Ari's arm. "No more talk of him. I want to go check on Telly. Do you know where he is?"

"Somewhere in ICU."

)O(

A NURSE DIRECTED them to Telly's room. Leise pushed the door open. Whirs and beeps echoed through the mostly quiet room. Leise gave a visible shake when she saw all the machines around Telly. Ari thought Leise was going to fall and grabbed her arm to hold her steady.

"Thank you," Leise whispered, as they walked closer.

When they reached Telly's bedside, Ari squeezed Leise's hand before letting go. Leise extended her hand, her fingers hovered, but didn't come into contact with the covers. Leise stood over Telly and finally moved the hair that masked his eyes. He didn't look much like himself.

His eyes were closed, but his cheekbones were sharp against the sunken in cheeks. His thin arms laid atop the sheet in a nice, folded, the mortuary isn't that far off style, Ari thought morbidly. She wanted him to move his arms, open his eyes, and talk. He looked like he was laying on the border between life and death. She had never seen magic that could suck the life out of a person. *What did he do to you?*

Ari looked around him, hoping to see his aura. The burnt orange light was broken in places, and it flickered. His soul and his life were in jeopardy. The doctors couldn't fix what had been done to him. She needed to ask a healer if his soul could be restored. It might be a more humane thing to let him die. Ari wanted to slap herself for even thinking it. She didn't kill people. That's something her mother would do without blinking an eye.

The machines sounds seemed to get louder in their silence. When Leise's shoulders shook, Ari placed a chair behind her and touched her shoulder. "Leise, sit down."

Her friend nodded as she sat, but didn't look back. Ari placed a hand on Leise's shoulder. "He'll be alright."

Leise turned around finally and looked at her, tears in her eyes. "He saved my life." Saying the words must have opened a dam. The tears rolled down her face in a steady stream as she talked. "I'm so grateful, and I wish I could do something to help him. He's like this because of me."

Ari wanted to assuage her friend's guilt. She wanted to scream that it was all her fault. Telly wouldn't have been there if she hadn't asked him to be. She felt the anger and sorrow fill her like a volcano about to erupt. Her free hand glowed, but there wasn't any fire. She snatched her other hand from Leise's shoulder just in case she went five-alarm.

"I'm going to wait outside."

Ari paced outside the door, but it only seemed to fan her fury. She sat down and tried some breathing techniques. One long breath in, one long exhale. She repeated the pattern a few more times. She opened her eyes when her temper had lowered to a manageable state.

She had to stop this monster before he hurt someone else, but she couldn't do it alone.

CHAPTER 11

*A*ri and Leise waited in front of the hospital for an Uber. "Maybe we should have asked your new best friend for a ride to the impound lot?"

"He's not my friend, I just said he was nice, that's all," Leise smirked. "Maybe it's you who likes him."

"Annaleise Morgan." Ari's hand whipped up over her heart as she stared in mock horror. "If I didn't love you, I'd curse you where you stand."

Leise laughed, then said, "I'm happy you love me, then."

The car stopped in front of them and the passenger side window rolled down. "You called for a car?"

Ari's eyes followed Leise's hand as it touched her necklace. "You wear it outside the house now?"

"Huh?" Leise looked surprised. Ari gave a nod with lifted brows towards the amethyst in her hand. "Oh, yeah. I've kinda gotten used to it." She opened the back door, and they both got inside.

"HPD impound lot on Navigation, please," Ari said to the driver. After her nodded and pulled away, she tirned back to Leise. "Still good dreams?"

"The best," Leise mumbled. Then turned to Ari. "Oh, that reminds me. I forgot to tell Detective Westin about the man."

"What man?"

"Before we closed. An older gentleman came in just before we closed. He wanted to buy my necklace."

Leise couldn't seem to keep her hands off the thing. No wonder someone had noticed it. "Have you seen him before? What does he look like?"

"Sure, he's come in a few times before. He's an older man, salt and pepper hair, tall. Always in a nice suit."

"What did he say?"

"Nothing, really. He said he dealt with antiques and that he specialized in crystals." Then she cleared her throat and lowered her voice, "'And I will pay you handsomely for that little trinket.' I told him, no because it was a family heirloom. That was it."

Interesting, Ari thought.

The Uber dropped them off at a place that looked more like a junkyard than a secure police impound lot. It seemed to be about five acres surrounded by ten feet wire fencing with spiraled barb wire across the top. Only a few cars at the very front were on concrete, the other vehicles were lost in a sea of dirt and weeds.

It took only a few minutes for the young officer to find their cars. They signed the paperwork and officer took them to the concrete area where Tiffany and Leise's small black car waited.

In the light of day, Ari could see what had happened to Tiffany and cringed. The old BMW had seen better days. She tugged on the door handle, but it didn't budge. She moved around the vehicle, fingers dipping into each dent, hole and singe marks. The windshield laid halfway on the hood, halfway inside the car. "Poor girl. We'll get you out of here and fixed up."

Ari had called for a tow truck the moment they'd arrived. Tiffany might have only barely survived last night's encounter, but hopefully, the repair shop could work some magic and get her on the road again.

When it was all said and done, Ari couldn't watch them load Tiffany up. She grabbed Leise by the arm and walked towards a black Volkswagen GTI with dual red racing stripes spanning the entire car. As much as she hated how Leise drove, her best friend took her to the one place she needed to go.

)O(

"BOTTOMS UP." Leise lifted a shot glass, and the golden liquid sloshed over her fingers.

"Salute," Ari clinked her shot glass against Leise's.

Soothing lavender tea wasn't going to cut it today. Ari's heel clicked on the hardwood floors of her favorite fusion coffee shop.

The Hot Toddy.

The place exuded the intoxicating aroma of roasted coffee beans. Rumor has it this building used to be an old speakeasy with partial brick & stucco walls. The new owners remodeled the inside with small crystal chandeliers throughout, and vibrant red wallpaper with golden flourishes. There was even a small stage in the corner for open mic and karaoke. With a variety of liquors and craft beers, the bar rivaled that of any pub.

"Well, I have some info I didn't tell the illustrious Detective Westin," Ari said, then waved over the waitress.

"Why didn't you tell him?"

"Leise, whatever attacked you had magic. The police won't be able to catch it, let alone put it in jail."

When the waitress arrived, Ari ordered a whiskey on the rocks. "You want anything, Leise?"

"An Irish coffee."

Ari finished her story once the waitress walked away. "The thing that attacked you and Telly is looking for someone named Nyah."

"That name doesn't sound familiar at all."

"I don't know a Nyah either. But he's on a mission to find her."

They sat in a comfortable silence for a few minutes, when Leise reached into her purse. "Oh, yeah, I found these the other day." She flipped two tarot cards on the table. They landed face down.

Ari waved her hand above the cards. "Where did you find them?"

Energy hovered around the cards like a sticky, tangible web. She closed her eyes as she touched one card, then turned her head, like she was listening to a foreign language radio station.

Reading tarot had been Ari's only gift for many years, to her mother's dismay. During a reading or whenever she touched her tarot cards, they spoke to her with pictures in her mind.

She exhaled as fuzzy flashes of a place with purple hills and a dark sky, flickered through her mind. She couldn't figure out what place the cards was showing her. Then just as abruptly, everything went dark, before a lavender super-moon filled the darkened sky. Over the water, the moon was more massive than anything she'd ever seen in real life. It reminded her of a movie; it looked surreal. Ari's eyes snapped open.

The waitress placed the drinks on the table. Leise took a long sip from the Irish coffee before speaking. "On the floor…near the bed." She wiped the foam from her lip.

Ari nodded, and her entire demeanor became very serious. She turned over the first card.

The Star.

A shiver went up her spine, as feelings of hope and happiness overloaded her system. Endorphins flooded her body, and she shook with a love that touched her on a spiritual level.

"What is it?" Leise asked.

Ari couldn't answer. Her body felt like a live wire pulsing with energy, but she had to complete this unexpected reading. She turned over the next card.

The Hanged Man.

The electricity in her system ebbed as a dark figure flickered between Leise's bedroom and a darkened forest. Someone in limbo.

Never in her life had she felt power like this. Her fingers shook as she touched both cards. In the back of her mind, she could hear a drum thumping. She snatched her hands away.

Quiet.

She placed her hands more tentative this time, and again the drumbeat resounded in her mind. She let the sound settle over her and resonate through her. Then she heard it. It wasn't music, but a repeating pattern.

Much like the universal SOS, a call for help. Witches had their own version of this. Every child is taught this in case they got into trouble, and didn't have powers yet or were unable to use them. Bang it on anything and help would come. She'd never had to actually use the distress signal. No witch used the practice lightly. It had been passed down for generations, no one knew where it had begun, but every witch knew it like the back of their hand. *Tap…tap-tap, tap. About three-seconds passed, then four taps, in quick succession.*

"Leise, you are absolutely sure nothing happened to you the night we opened that present from your mom?" Ari's heart sped up. She wasn't in a panic, but she knew someone needed help. A supernatural mayday had been sent out, and she didn't have a coven to help. Nor did she have the first clue on where he was.

Leise's hand immediately went to her necklace. "No."

Ari's eyes followed her best friend's hands as she quickly put the necklace under her t-shirt. She knew Leise was lying but when her aura flashed black it was confirmed. She had no idea why her best friend would lie to her about something so inane. The cards told her bits and pieces of a story, but not the entire tale. She would find out soon enough.

"Why do you ask?" Leise's voice broke on the last word. She turned up the small glass mug and finished the now cold coffee in a two gulps.

Ari took her hands away from the cards as she tried to shake off her annoyance. The moment she removed her hands, the energy dissipated and the drum sounds faded from her consciousness.

Leise waved at the waitress near the bar, and a few moments later the young girl appeared.

"What can I get you?"

"Ice water for me." She looked across the table. "Ari, you want anything?"

"I would love a hot, jasmine tea." Ari needed the shot of tequila to take the edge off, but all in all, she had never been a big drinker. A drunk wielding magic is a deadly combination.

Once the waitress was out of earshot, Ari exhaled before she spoke. "When cards jump a deck, it's usually for a reason." She flipped the cards face down on the table. "But you said nothing happened. There's no new guy in your life. So…" She let that hang between them. Leise's aura flashed the smutty gray of guilt.

A guy.

Another piece fell into place. Ari would let Leise have her secrets…for now. The waitress brought their beverages, and they drank in companionable silence, but sometime soon they would have to have a serious talk about *sisters before misters.*

CHAPTER 12

A few hours later, Leise drove like a speed demon through the streets of Houston. Nearly dying gave her a new perspective on life. While Ari always had magic, she had only discovered her love of driving fast when she got her driver's license at seventeen. She wasn't an adrenaline junkie by any means, but there was something about shifting the gears and pressing the gas pedal all the way down that made her feel alive. She needed to know that feeling right now, Ari would just have to deal.

The light had changed from green as she cut a right turn a little too sharp. Leise pulled her handbrake causing the rear to drift a little bit around the corner. A laugh bubbled up out of nowhere. She'd been trying to do that move for months. Sure, she would need new tires sooner rather than later, but to feel the freedom when going around the corner unfettered was well worth it.

Ari threw her hands up, reaching for the non-existent 'Oh, shit' bar. "I'm pretty sure that was a red light."

"Nope, it was yellow," Leise smiled.

Leise whipped up into Ari's condo parking lot with a little more speed than necessary but hadn't parked in a spot. She cut the wheel hard performing a three-point turn without the pesky reversal part. The car faced the other direction when she came to a stop.

Leise had no intentions on talking about the 'dream guy' because there was nothing to tell. And she knew Ari well enough to know what she would say. 'It's dangerous, Leise.' Anything dealing with magic was perilous, but she hadn't got that kind of vibe from Brennan. Before, when she had insomnia, and the bad juju was running wild in her home, yeah, she had, but not now.

Leise nodded. "I'm off work tomorrow; you need me to drive you around?"

"Oh, no," Ari said, with her hands up. "I'm good."

Leise laughed. "Well, call me if you need me."

"I didn't say it sooner, but I'm sorry I didn't get there in time."

It was rare that Ari apologized, but the girl looked like someone had kicked her puppy, if she had a puppy. Leise touched her arm, waiting until her friend looked up. "It's not your fault. You had no way of knowing he would attack Telly and me. Wait, did you have a vision?"

"Girl, how many times do I have to tell you...I am not psychic."

"I know, but you never know with your wacky powers." She lifted her brows with a head tilt that said, you know I'm right. Ari nodded in agreement.

"Hey, I wasn't sure if you still wanted to volunteer at the Children's festival this weekend? I can call and cancel if—"

"No, no. We can do it." In all honesty, she'd forgotten about it. It wouldn't hurt to get out of the house.

"Okay." Ari leaned in for a hug. "Drive safe and call me when you get home."

When they pulled apart, she gave a two finger salute. "Yes, ma'am."

She waited until Ari went inside the building before she revved the gas with the brakes engaged, making the tires spin and squeal. A few seconds later her cell rang, she didn't need to answer it. Leise looked up towards Ari's balcony and saw her friend waving wildly. She released the clutch and burnt out in a cloud of smoke.

)O(

LEISE HAD DRIVEN home at a safe speed. The sun was still high in the sky, but that didn't stop her from crawling into bed. After Leise ran out of Otherworld the first night, she'd since returned. Every night, in fact. It couldn't be helped, every time she closed her eyes, she ended up there. Of course, she was annoyed when Brennan was around in the beginning, but over time she found him easy to talk to. She would tell Ari about him, just not yet.

She'd pulled the comforter up to her neck and snuggled deep onto her feather down pillows, then exhaled slowly before drifting off.

Leise moved, and a warmth rolled over her arms and legs. She opened her eyes, then blinked against the blinding sunlight. She squinted then lifted her arm to block the offending orb. When her eyes refocused, the first thing she saw were slow-moving clouds in the blue sky, but they reminded her more of fluffy cotton balls.

She lifted her hand towards the sky, and the sunshine's heat flowed through her fingertips, then up her arm. Usually, at home, the humidity would have had her arms sweaty and her hair in a huge poof ball — so not attractive. But in Otherworld, none of that had happened. Perfect California weather without the mudslides or earthquakes.

Finally, she raised up on her elbows. The blades of grass were soft under her hands. She wore a purple cotton sundress with tied spaghetti straps and eyelets of flowers along the bottom. Leise ran her hand over the soft material. It reminded her of an exceptionally comfortable broken-in tee.

When she looked at her hands, they were like foreign entities. All manicured with lavender polish. She quickly looked at her toes and moved them with excitement in white sandals — pedicured and polished as well. If she knew dreams could be like this, she would have been more gung-ho about having them sooner.

Did she catch his scent on the wind?

No, she felt him. It was like a vibration in her bones every time he was around. She didn't have any *witchy* mojo like Ari, but this place held an extraordinary power. Her heart sped up when she finally caught a whiff of him, wood smoke and pine. She closed her eyes and inhaled to savor the smell she thought of as strength and man. She would have never considered herself a girly-girl. She'd had boyfriends here and there, but something about this guy made all her girly parts tingle, and that hadn't happened before.

"A beautiful day, huh?" Brennan said in a low voice. He hadn't whispered, it was more like he was in church or a library.

Without opening her eyes, she said, "It's always beautiful here. Is that your doing?" Leise squinted one eye to look at the man standing above her blocking the sun.

Brennan moved to sit next to her, then laid on his elbows like her. He lifted his face towards the sun warming his pale skin. "No, that's all you."

Leise raised up, to talk to him. "You mean if I want a beach. It will appear?"

He watched her and smiled. His smile caused elephant sized butterflies to flutter around in her stomach. When he smiled, hell, even looked in her direction, she got warm all over. She tried to shake off whatever it was he was doing to her.

"Very interesting," she said softly as she wrapped her arms around her knees. How did he do this to her with just a smile?

Being here made her feel better. Made her feel safe. No one could rob her here or attack her. What happened to her was scary, she could have—. She clipped the negative word from her thoughts. Death wasn't something she wanted to entertain. She couldn't shut out the thought entirely because there was a man in a hospital bed because he protected her.

"What's wrong?" He touched her arm.

She hadn't realized she was crying until the cool droplets fell on her arm. "Nothing," she said as she quickly wiped her face.

"Please tell me. It breaks my heart to see you sad."

She looked into his lavender eyes. They held a concern and strength she couldn't muster up in that moment. She turned and wiped her nose with the bottom of her dress. She couldn't start the story with a snotty nose and puffy eyes. She sniffled one last time before she turned back to him.

She stood up and dusted the grass bits from her dress, and he stood right along with her. "Walk with me."

They walked in companionable silence for about five minutes before she started. "I was attacked last night at my job," she said with her head down.

She knew this horrible thing had happened to her, but it seemed more real now that she had said the words aloud.

He stood in front of her to stop her, then touched her arms. When she looked up, the tears were threatening to fall. She was fine until she looked into his eyes.

"Were you harmed?" He touched her cheek, then snatched his hand away.

She placed his hand back on her cheek. His warmth filled her, and she nodded. "I bumped my head." She had been knocked unconscious, but he didn't need to know that. "But my co-worker, he was with me." The tears fell as she stammered, "Protected me. He was badly hurt."

"What is your protector's name? We will say a prayer for him."

"His name is Sylvester, but I call him Telly."

"For the warrior, Telly." He grasped her hands and pressed his forehead to hers.

The prayer wasn't in English. Maybe it wasn't translatable. But his voice dipped and rose melodically. One day she would ask him to sing a song from his homeland. He squeezed her hand, then opened his eyes when he finished.

"We must keep the faith that he will return to you."

As they walked, the weather began to change. Maybe it was reflecting how she felt. The blue skies filled with more clouds as it blocked out the sun, before the entire sky went dark gray.

Brennan looked up, then grabbed her hand. "Come on." He took off running as the first cool drops of rain came down.

Unlike California, it rained in Otherworld.

)O(

IT TOOK mere minutes to cross the different lands. Brennan lead her from the rainy meadow, past a black sand beach that would rival any in Hawaii or Fiji, then slowed down once they cleared the redwood sized trees that extended into the clouds. If faery were a real place, this would be it. Butterflies hopped from yellow lantanas to blue thistles while the dragonflies and bees buzzed around nearby. Colors popped from every corner of this space. It could have been pulled straight from the pages of Home and Garden - UK edition.

A small cottage with a thatch roof was nestled just out of sight, behind a thicket of tall sunflowers. Brennan opened the rounded door, then stood to the side to allow her entrance. He didn't rush her. She could tell it was her choice to enter or not.

Upon entering, it was an explosion of color. Silks of purple, gold, and blue covered the walls of the one room cottage, making it look bigger than it actually appeared from outside. Brennan watched from the door as she walked around.

Her tour was quick: a fireplace, a pile of pillows under a small window, a small drum. It must have been his bedroom/living room. Leise didn't see a bathroom, but she did see something that looked suspiciously like a chamberpot in the corner. She didn't want to think about that too much.

Brennan finally closed the door and entered fully. "Would you like some tea?" Waving his hand towards the pillows, indicating she should sit.

She shook her head once as she sat down. "No, thank you." He nodded and took a seat across from her. "Explain to me what's happening here."

"I think there must be a lot of magic in your world because you are the first person to ever enter this realm. I had hoped someone would hear the drum, but no one ever showed up...until you. If you came in, then there has to be a way for me to get out."

"I don't understand how I got in, but when I leave, you can come with me," she told him.

He gave a huff of a laugh before he spoke. "It's not that simple. It was a spell that placed me here."

"Can you tell me how you got here?" Leise waved around the room.

"About ten years after my uncle's banishment, he returned because his wife had become deathly ill. He came to the family for help," he paused, "but my grandfather refused him. He was positive my uncle had been learning dark magic and wouldn't have anything to do with him."

He stopped talking for such a long time, Leise thought he wouldn't finish. She saw the fresh tears run down his face. He wiped them away and turned his back before he continued.

"After her death, my uncle killed everyone in our village. People he'd known his entire life." Brennan turned to her. "I was away but arrived just in time to see him begin a spell that would place his wife's soul in a young girl. I tried to stop him, and he stabbed me." He lifted his shirt to show a bright red wound that had never healed. "When my uncle cast the spell, my blood was on the knife."

He looked out the window, the bright moonlight illuminating him, but his eyes seemed to glaze over. Leise thought he must have been reliving it as he told it to her.

"I felt weightless, then like I was being crushed from the inside. I remember my mouth being dry like sand, then darkness. When I woke, I was here."

Leise thought of Telly, and it triggered a horrible thought. "What happened to your body?"

He blinked. "I don't… I don't know."

She had a morbid thought but didn't dwell on it. She quickly changed the subject. "You were saying a spell put you in here. Is there a way to get you out?"

"It would have to be a spell performed by a witch or druid."

"I can't say that I've ever met a druid." Leise tapped her chin with one finger. "I would have to ask Ari. She would know."

"Is she a witch?"

Everyone knew Ari read tarot in the park, but not everyone knew she was a real witch. Besides, he was trapped in this place, who could he tell? She needed to trust her instincts more. The first sign this guy was evil or said something weird, she would close her eyes, go home, and never come back. She hoped she wasn't making a mistake. "Yes. Yes, she is."

"What type of witch is she?" His eyes widened with so much hope.

"I don't know. Ari's not a psychic, but she reads tarot. She's also an herbalist." At his deer in the headlights stare, she added, "She works with plants and herbs in her magic."

"Sounds like she practices white magic."

Leise knew Ari's magic consisted of much more. "She can make things levitate, like in the movies."

That seemed to stump him. "What's a movie?" His head tilted like he was listening to the sky.

Leise smiled at the lost look. "Hopefully, when we get you out of here, you can go see one."

He looked down as an air of hopelessness seemed to engulf him.

"Hey." Leise touched his shoulder. When he looked up, haunted eyes met her own. In that moment, she knew...just knew, she had to help him. "What would she need to do to get you out of here?"

Although his eyes became glassy, no tears fell. She could tell he wanted to believe, but just as fast it disappeared. "Well, the crystal," he looked all around him and waved about the room, "there has to be a releasing spell. I never learned such magic. But, the curse was strong, it might need to be completed on a celestial event."

"What is that?"

"An equinox, Samhain, Beltane, I don't know maybe even two moon cycles might work." A small grin revealed deep dimples. "You think..." he took a deep breath. "You think this might be possible? You are here. It has to be."

She nodded.

"Even if it's not possible. I appreciate you visiting me. It's so quiet here."

Although he smiled, she could see the despair in his eyes. He had been alone for a very long time. "You know what? I'd like that tea now."

CHAPTER 13

*H*ot water sluiced through Ari's fingers as she waited for it to finish filling the tub. After Leise burnt out of the parking lot, she walked through her quiet condo. The silence just made the discord in her heart and mind roar that much louder. All she wanted to do was forget about it all for a little while. The airy suds from the bubble bath flowed up in high mounds in the tub. She waved her hand over the suds before turning the off the water. Her cellphone rang from the other room. She rushed to answer, and heard a voice she wasn't expecting to hear.

"Did I catch you at a bad time?" Heath's rich voice practically purred.

Ari sat on the edge of the tub. "Um, no. I was just about to get in the bath."

"Really?"

She didn't have to see him to hear the smile in his voice. "Yesterday was a long day," she said, with a light exhale.

"Can I help you with that?"

She lifted an eyebrow. "Excuse me."

He let out a rich, throaty laugh. "Not with the bath. With whatever made it a long day. Sometimes it helps to talk about things."

She was more than sure he was talking about more than sitting down having a friendly chit-chat. "Uh-huh. Well, this is something I have to work through on my own."

"Okay, while you are working on that. Maybe we could have coffee?"

"No, thank you."

"What? Wow, okay."

She wondered had anyone ever told him 'no' before. She was about to save him when he asked another question. This one didn't give up easily. She liked that.

"Can I ask why?"

"I'm not a big coffee fan. Now, if you would have said, 'tea'," she said smiling.

"All right then. Would you like to have a cuppa tea with me?"

She smiled at how his brogue thickened when he said, 'Cup of tea.' "You have my attention."

"I was hoping, maybe, after your bath, we could hang out," he stammered and his accent thickened. "I know a place that serves a blooming chrysanthemum tea."

If she wasn't mistaken, he was nervous. "Any other day I would. But I don't have a car right now."

"The long day?" he said knowingly.

"Yes."

"I'm sort of in between jobs right now. I could be your Uber."

"No, but thanks."

"Do you need a ride to get a rental. I can do that much for you, at least."

She opened her mouth to say no, but Tiffany wasn't going to be out of the shop anytime soon. Of course, him driving her around was out, but she needed to be at that coven meeting. She could imagine his face if she told him she was a witch and needed to be somewhere later for a gathering of more witches. "Blooming tea, huh?"

)O(

ABOUT AN HOUR LATER, Ari found herself inside a dessert bar and bakery. She cut her bath short in order to have more time to talk with Heath. Her place was just too quiet without Remy around. She missed him terribly, but it was nice to have male company as well.

The sweet scent of baked goods whooshed out the moment they opened the door. She closed her eyes as she inhaled the bold scent of fresh ground coffee. It actually made her want a cup. Now that was saying something.

"I know it's not fancy, but I promise you it's delicious." Heath's lips lightly grazed her ear as he whispered from behind her.

A chill zinged down her spine. She almost didn't hear what he'd said. "No, no. The place is cute."

And she meant it. She especially liked various French words written in calligraphy style alongside the black fleur de lis' of different sizes on tan wallpaper. She thought it looked like old vellum with burnt edges. The small bistro tables completed the French motif.

When they reached the counter Heath ordered the tea. "And could you add an order of madeleines," he added.

She had been eyeing the little shell-shaped cookies. "You didn't have to."

Heath took the black wire stand with their order number clipped to the top and placed his hand on her lower back to guide her away from the counter. "What's tea without a bit of cake?" He winked at her, and that glint in his eyes let her know this man could be downright sinful.

When they reached a small table near the back corner, she reached to pull her chair out, and his hand touched it as well. She snatched her hand back quickly, not from static electricity or anything, but a shock nonetheless. She couldn't remember the last time someone had pulled out her chair. If ever.

"Oh, sorry," Ari stepped aside as he pulled the chair out. She wondered if her cheeks were blazing a bright crimson. She wanted to fan herself with her hand or pour a glass of cold water over her head.

She watched him as he took his seat and thought his Paul

Bunyan red plaid shirt and well worn wranglers seemed a little out of place here. "This doesn't look like a place you'd," she thought about the correct word for a moment, "frequent."

He lowered his head with a smile. "Then you'd be right. It was an accident I assure you."

She was about to ask how when a petite, white-haired woman stood next to their table with a wooden tray. "Number 37, did you have the blooming mum?"

"Yes, ma'am," Heath answered.

The woman placed two clear teacups on the table. Then she set a clear teapot with a dry plant bulb of about three inches wide in the bottom, a metal pot, and a plate with four golden madeleines. The older woman sat the tray and their number stand on an empty table behind her, then reached for the metal pot.

Heath reached out and stilled the waitress' hand. "I'd like to do it if you don't mind."

She nodded with a soft smile, then said, "Enjoy," before walking away.

"You're probably wondering how I found this place. Well, I've worked lots of odd jobs around town." He took the top off the glass teapot, then placed the metal pot's spout over the opening. A nice plume of steam lifted from the pot as he poured. "I was hired as a PA, a Production Assistant on a commercial not too far from here. But I ended up driving the owner of the company around for the most part. I guess he loved the thought of making a commercial, but not actually being on set."

"What was the name of the company? Maybe I saw the commercial?"

He cleared his throat, then using his best announcer voice. "Destiny Organic Fertilizer. Fresh from the cow to your lawn." He said it with a straight face but couldn't hold it.

They both busted out laughing. The few people in the place cut their eyes toward them, but it didn't stop their giggles. "You can't be serious."

He crossed his heart with two fingers, then gave the scout's salute. "I swear."

"Scouts don't swear."

"Didn't say I was a scout." He lifted one brow, then the corner of his mouth rose in a slow smile.

It was like an ice cube slid down her back. She gave a full bodied shiver.

"Hey, are you cold?"

"No…no. I just caught a draft." She scooted her chair a little to the left. She felt so much like an awkward teen right now, it wasn't even funny. *Really Mason? A draft? That was the best you could come up with.*

He looked at the teapot. "Okay, now watch the magic."

The flower bud had swollen to twice its original size. Now, the thin leaves had enlarged and were beginning to unfurl, lying outstretched and encompassing the entire bottom of the pot. When all of the leaves laid wide in the pot, a bright red chrysanthemum floated along the bottom with small white and yellow bits of flower floating to the top of the hot water. "We just need to let it seep a few more minutes," he said.

"I was curious…wondering, if you believed in magic?" Ari lowered her voice on the last word. It was probably best to find out how he felt about magic before this went any further.

"Magic. Real magic?" he nodded like he was seriously considering it. "I think that if magicians could perform real magic—"

"Or witches," she interjected with a big smile.

"Witches. They would be cool to know." He picked up the teapot. "They could turn lead into gold."

Ari nibbled on the sweet, vanilla cake-like cookies. "I think that might be alchemy, not witchcraft."

He shrugged a shoulder. "No matter, magic would still be cool."

"Good to know," she said after she finished her cookie. She picked up her cup to blow on her tea. Small pieces of flower floated around the hot liquid.

"Why is that good?" he asked, before he took a sip.

She swallowed, then took a second sip to stall. This was the moment of truth. She wouldn't tell him everything, just enough to

see if he ran out the door. "I have a booth where I read tarot cards."
When he frowned, she added, "As a hobby."

"You know the future?"

"Not a psychic."

"Can you see the past?"

"That's not really my thing."

"But you read tarot in the park?"

"Yep. You weirded out yet?"

He poured himself another cup of tea, then waved the pot over
her cup. After she nodded, he poured her another cup. "In all
honesty, no. I like that you're unique."

They continued like that for a while, talking about odd jobs,
foods they liked, placed they wanted to visit, and tea. And for a little
while, she forgot all about the attack, the witch killer, and poor,
busted-up Tiffany. Heath didn't know it, but he *did* have magic.

He listened.

CHAPTER 14

The old adage, 'Time flies when you're having fun' was true, but it should include, 'Especially with great company.' Ari had glanced at her watch, only to realized she was late. And it would take too long to get an Uber. Heath ended up driving her to the White Cauldron instead.

"It looks closed. Are you sure this is the place?" Heath said as he looked out the passenger side window.

Ari nodded. "Look, I want to thank you. I haven't had that much fun in a while." She opened the door and got out. "And thanks for the ride."

"Maybe you can return the favor sometime," he said, with a wink.

"I will remember that." She shut the door and watched him drive away. She took a deep breath to clear her mind. She didn't know how to tell these witches that there was a killer in town and he could steal their magic. She lifted her fist to knock, but it opened before she had the chance.

"Merry meet, Ari," Elizabeth said at the door.

"Merry meet," Ari gave a slight nod.

"I hoped you would come by," Elizabeth stood aside with the door wider. "Please come in. The others are already here."

Great. Not only was she bringing bad news, but she was late to boot. "A lot has happened since we last spoke," Ari said as they walked through the darkened store.

Elizabeth stood at the back door. "Then, please tell us." She stepped through the door and held it from the other side. Waiting.

Ari looked at her feet with her heart thumping wildly in her chest. Her fear was palpable, but not stopping this monster wasn't an option. She had to do whatever it took because her being a little scared was a blip on the big scale of things. When she looked up and met the eyes of Elizabeth, she only saw understanding and acceptance. This woman had a quiet strength and intensity Ari wished to possess one day.

"I'm ready," Ari said as she stepped through the door. Elizabeth gave her a nod and smile.

Instead of stopping where they had had tea the other day, Elizabeth turned on the small platform and walked up the next flight of stairs. The next floor opened up to what could only be called a training room. But it sort of reminded her of a sports training facility, with the football blocking sled, small orange cones, and a speed chute, but witches used them entirely differently. Instead of running through, people and things floated around the room. The only thing that seemed familiar were how the two young girls worked with candles.

The shorter of the two flicked her wrist perfectly, and the candle whooshed to life. The tall, dark-haired girl frowned and looked really worried, but her friend encouraged her with a big smile and nods. The older female witch, presumably the teacher, stood nearby with a fire extinguisher behind her back. The young dark-haired girl flicked the wand and something closer to a torch than a match blasted out of it. Now she understood why the woman had the fire extinguisher.

"Everyone," Elizabeth clapped her hands with her voice still not much more than a whisper. "Please gather around."

The group of about ten young witches from ages eight to maybe sixteen, along with about five adults walked over. They were all dressed like they were going to a regular gym, shorts and t-shirts. During her training as a child in the coven, her mother had demanded everyone wear hooded black robes.

You are not an individual. You are coven. That saying was pounded into her as a child.

Seeing the witches train had brought it all back. Elizabeth had been speaking but Ari only heard the tail end of it. "She has come to bring us news."

"She's a black witch, why should we listen to anything she has to say?" an older bald man said while scowling in her direction.

Elizabeth reached out towards Ari, who walked towards the woman. "Signet, Ms. Mason is much more than her birthright, and she was kind enough to warn us about something that affects us all."

One of the young candle girls lifted her hand. Elizabeth nodded in their direction. "Oriana."

"I thought black witches were evil, she doesn't feel…" Oriana shook her head. "I don't know, she feels…different. May I?" Oriana looked at Ari's hands. Ari in turn, looked at Elizabeth.

Elizabeth's eyes widened as did everyone in the group. Ari got a feeling Oriana either hadn't talked much, used her power, or both. This was her chance to change a few of the suspicious minds in the room.

"Oriana is new to us. We are still trying to understand her gift," Elizabeth said.

"I don't mind," Ari said.

Oriana held her hands out, and Ari laid hers on top. The young girl closed her eyes and nothing happened.

"This is ridiculous," Signet yelled out. The crowd shushed him.

Ari got the feeling, whatever Oriana's power was, it must be interesting. Ari's hands warmed like her power was about to emerge. When her muscles tensed and she poised to move away, the girl's small hands clasped around her wrist like a vice grip. She was strong to be so small.

"Don't struggle, Ari, this is how her power works," Elizabeth said, even softer than usual. It almost sounded like she was in awe.

"I don't want to hurt her."

"You won't," Elizabeth said.

Ari wasn't so sure, but she stopped struggling and calmed her breathing.

Oriana spoke so softly, Ari could barely hear her. "Your power is fire. But there's more to it. I can't see it — because you haven't found it yet."

Then around the room, a 3-D holographic picture of fire filled the room. It wasn't a true depiction of Ari's fire, but more like how Oriana must perceive it. There were multiple bonfires.

The dark-haired girl's voice whispered from the crowd, "She's like me." And just as quick a woman's harsh response said she wasn't anything like Ari.

Oriana's head tilted from one side, then to the other, then she smiled. "You like plants. Only a good person grows things." The room looked more like the Amazon than a garden. Her breathing began to sound a little ragged.

"We can stop," Ari whispered.

"You are so interesting," Oriana said breathy. The picture around the room was a pocket watch swung like a pendulum, then the picture disappeared and Oriana fell backwards.

Ari grabbed the young girl's hands before she could hit the floor. Hands came from all around to help ease her to the floor. "I'm okay," Oriana said testily.

"Someone, get her some juice," a woman's voice yelled out.

"I don't need it," Oriana started.

"Hush child, let them help you," Elizabeth said with a raised brow.

"Fine." The teacher and dark haired girl walked her out of the crowd to sit down.

Elizabeth pulled Ari to the side. Ari's eyes kept flitting to the girl. "Was it me? Did I hurt her?" She wouldn't be able to live with herself if she had.

"No, she has only used her powers a few times. It takes a lot out of her," Elizabeth said.

"I've never seen anything like it. I didn't know a witch could do something like that," Ari said.

Elizabeth looked back, and the girl was on her feet again. "She is something special."

Ari heard the hesitation in the woman's voice, but also heard the pride. Maybe Oriana was something more than a witch. Interesting.

"Looks like we are ready." Elizabeth and Ari walked back to the head of the group.

Ari felt more calm than when she started this. If she didn't have any other fans, Oriana and her candle lighting friend were on her side. She began with what Lucas had told her, the attack at the senior facility, and the attack on Leise and Telly.

"Looks like trouble is following you," Signet chimed in.

Ari frowned, then exhaled. "Sir, I sit in a park three days a week. I'm not hard to find. It's attacking dismages and witches, indiscriminately. We all need to look out for each other."

Many of the older witches glared at her shaking their heads. "We can protect our own," Signet said. Then a small chorus of agreements followed.

"Well, I hope you have something that protects against lightning strikes because I was hit one time, and was knocked unconscious."

"Maybe you black witches don't know what you're doing."

And she was done here. There were asses in black witch covens and white witch covens. And this one was a supreme ass and there was no help for him. "Elizabeth, I don't think there's any more I can say."

"You've done all that you can, but if you don't mind may I have a word." In Elizabeth fashion, she walked to a corner without looking back to see if Ari followed. Once out of earshot, she began. "You said he struck you with lightning, did he call it from the sky?"

"No, I'm pretty sure he sent it from his staff from what I could tell. It happened so fast," Ari answered shaking her head.

"The protection you used. Do you have another on you now?"

Ari pulled the St. Brigit's cross from under her shirt. She went to take it off, but Elizabeth reached out. "No, leave it. I can get a better feel for it this way. May I?" She lifted her brows towards the necklace.

"Sure." Ari waved at it.

Elizabeth took the cross gently in her hand, then covered it with the other, as she closed her eyes. "You are lucky to be alive."

"I know," Ari said grimly.

Elizabeth let the necklace go. "The tiger's eye is good for protection, but lightning..." she thumped her lips with her forefinger, "I need to do some research. A shield or maybe something to absorb the power. I would like for you to come back by in a couple of days. Maybe we can create something stronger."

Ari looked behind her at the other witches. Old Baldie glared at them. She shook her head. "Maybe that's not such a good idea."

Elizabeth touched her hand, bringing her attention back to their conversation. "Don't worry about them. They had a son...he went down a bad path. They are good at heart. Just give them time, but we have to do something now."

Ari found herself nodding. "Okay."

"Also, we haven't been able to guide Drew with her power." Elizabeth looked behind Ari towards Oriana and her friend. "I was kind of hoping you could come and help her."

Ari was shaking her head. "I'm no teacher."

"Before her powers came in, everyone told her that fire wasn't a white witch's trait."

"That's not true," Ari said quickly. "Sure it's destructive, but it can also be beautiful too."

"She needs someone like you to tell her that."

Ari nibbled on her bottom lip, then she just said it. "Are you sure I'm the right person. I'm not exactly," she waved around the room, "one of you."

"Ms. Mason you are selling yourself short," Elizabeth said. "Think about it. But even if you don't join us, we must work on the protection bracelets. We have to protect as many people as possible until this threat is over."

"I'll think about it. Shield Bracelets. I could be like Wonder Woman, but...like a witch."

"Wonder...witch?" Elizabeth nodded slowly.

"Wonder witch, I like it!"

CHAPTER 15

A few days later, Ari knocked on Leise's door. She held a carrier with two large hot to-go cups in her left hand and banged on the door again with her right hand. When her best friend didn't answer, she yelled, "Annaleise!" *What was she doing in there?* Just as she lifted her fist to pound again, the door swung open.

"What?" Leise said testily, then held her hand up to block the morning sun from her eyes.

Ari lifted a brow at Leise's sleep ensemble. A picture of Einstein spanned the entire oversized t-shirt with beige and blue plaid boxers. She shook her head. "Were you still asleep?" She stepped inside the apartment.

Leise yawned, then wiped the sleep from her eyes. "What? No." She closed her eyes as she tried to flatten her wild hair.

Ari waved the cup under Leise's nose.

Leise's eyes immediately popped open as she snagged the cup with both hands. "Mmmmm. You went to the Hot Toddy." She grinned from ear to ear.

Ari nodded. "French creme, right?"

Leise took the top off and inhaled as the steam rose. Her eyes stayed closed through two swallows. "Thank you." She walked around Ari. "Why are you dressed like that?"

Ari held her leg out to admire her Timberland lace-up stiletto boots. They were not practical work boots, but she loved heels. She touched her khaki shorts, white cotton tee, and safari vest and frowned. "You forgot didn't you?"

Leise leaned against the futon. "What are you talking about?"

"Festival." Ari dragged out the word.

Leise blinked.

Ari shook her head in disappointment. "Volunteering...children's fest. Ringing any bells?"

Finally, Leise's eyes went wide, and she choked on a sip. "Geez." She put the cup on the side table. "You should've led with that. Are we late?"

"Just get dressed," Ari said.

"I bet we're late," Leise mumbled.

Ari didn't answer. Of course they were late, she was always late, but she needed some tea to clear her head before creating works of balloon art for the kids. She volunteered to work this festival because she thought it was important to support children.

No one ever really took the time with her as a child. She learned the basics from watching others. But mostly her skills came from a multitude of wrongly interpreted spells and mispronounced words before attending magic school. That's how Remy came into existence.

One day, she and Leise had hidden in the attic with one of her mother's grimoires. They were attempting to levitate a pocket watch they had found in an old trunk. Her Latin being what it was, words got mispronounced and before she knew what was happening Remy's spirit had lifted from the watch.

Of course, this wasn't magic school, but if she could bring a smile to a child's face today, she would be happy.

"Give me ten minutes," Leise yelled from upstairs.

Ari laughed. "You've never done anything in ten minutes."

Leise yelled from upstairs. "I heard that!"

Ari walked around the now spotless apartment. She sat on the futon, now clear of any clothes, pillow or blankets. She was happy her friend was getting some restful sleep.

Leise rushed downstairs twenty minutes later with her shorts unzipped, towel over her head and shoes hanging from two fingers. "Ummm…" Leise chewed her bottom lip, she sat down on the futon. "About that spell you worked on my necklace." She frowned, then gave her head a little shake. That thing people do when something is wrong, but they don't want to say what it is.

Ari leaned forward. "What about it? Did something happen?"

Leise slid on her shoes, but didn't tie them. Then exhaled loudly before half-heartedly rubbing the towel with one hand. "You know what…it's not important. Hey, since we'll be near the medical center, I was wondering if we could stop by the hospital to see Telly?"

Ari studied her friend like a hawk. Leise's aura fluctuated from her usual happy gold to purple - which meant she was hopeful about something. Then the light around her friend flickered blue. Sadness about something peppered her happiness and hope. Her friend was majorly conflicted about something. "Sure. We can go there first. We're only a little late."

$)O($

ONLY ONE LIGHT was lit in the room. The three other beds were empty. The privacy curtain was partially drawn near Telly's bed, but Ari and Leise could hear a man's voice with a Jamaican accent, talking, or maybe reading.

The man put the magazine down when Ari and Leise appeared at the foot of the bed.

"Oh, I'm sorry," Leise whispered. "I didn't know he'd have any visitors."

"No, chil'," the man said. His voice had a seductive contralto purr. He waved them both closer.

The thin, dark-skinned man stood about five-six with dreadlocks to his shoulders. He leaned into Telly's ear. "Sylvester, two beautiful young ladies have come to visit you."

Ari smiled at how he pronounced Telly's name. It came out more like Ceil-Vest-Staa. They stood on other side of the bed from the man.

"Nice of you to visit him." He extended his hand. "I'm Buster. Well, it's really Benedict but I no like that name."

"I'm Leise. Well, Annaleise." Leise smiled as she extended her hands, and when Buster's hand touched hers, the girl's eyes went wide, and the necklace under her shirt glowed a bright purple.

Ari could feel a low murmur of energy in the room before everything slowed down. The machine noises went quiet, and then a bright flash encircled them all. Flickers of thin streams of electricity stretched between Leise's and Buster's hands. The tip ends of Buster's dreadlock floated up and outward. For a moment she felt weightless. She thought this is what it must feel like in zero gravity. Then the world crashed back to normal. Leise and Buster fell backwards when he snatched his hand away.

"You have something serious going on right there." He cradled his right hand to his chest, and pointed towards Leise's necklace with his left.

Buster wasn't a witch. She hadn't felt any magic from him until he had touched Leise. A purple light swirled between Leise's gold and Buster's white aura. It was like their auras were one for a moment. She hadn't been around a lot of witches until recently, and none of them gave off an aura like Buster's. The bright white light surrounded him like a beacon.

Leise touched her necklace. A low purple light flickered between her fingers, then died out. "What?" Looking between Ari and Buster. "What did you just do to me?"

"Honeychil', I'm a medium. I didn't do anything."

"A medium? Kinda like you, Ari?"

Ari threw her hands up. "Girl, I read tarot. He talks to dead people."

"Um, you talk to Remy," Leise quipped.

"That is not the same thing," Ari retorted. Well, it kind of was, but they didn't have time to argue semantics.

"Not just dead people. In Ms. Annaleise's case…a trapped soul."

"Wait, wait," Leise said quickly. "You were there? You saw him? He's not dead then? He's not a spirit? Mostly, I thought I was going crazy." Leise mumbled that last part.

"Him? Him who?" Ari chimed in. She knew this was about the guy Leise had been keeping secret, but this sounded more complicated than she could have imagined. She'd just thought her friend had found a guy on a dating site or a chat room and was too embarrassed to say so.

"It's a long story, but I'll tell you. I promise." Leise turned back to the medium. "Buster?"

"Yes, and no. He's a spirit, but he's not dead," Buster said as he ran his thumb over his fingers like he was rubbing dried glue off of them. "That necklace holds some powerful old magic."

Leise gave him a pleading look. "Can you help him?"

"God, no." Buster stumbled. "Ooh, I need some orange juice. Anytime this happens, it zaps my energy." He rubbed the crease between his eyes as he moved past Ari, and bumped the edge of the bed. Ari reached out and caught him before he fell.

A jolt of electricity bolted up her arm and through her entire body. She couldn't remember when she had ever felt such excruciating pain. She wouldn't have been surprised if his magic singed every blood vessel in her body. Her body tightened, and her mouth froze open with a silent scream.

Those few seconds they were connected felt like a lifetime. Their hands fell away, and they both heaved loudly from the exertion.

"What...the hell...did you just do?" Ari gasped.

"I've never had that happen before." Buster fell back into an empty chair. "I would have never guessed you were a black witch."

"I'm not." Ari snapped.

"I did say *were*." Buster nodded with a frown. "You can deny what's in you all you want, but do you know what you are *now*?"

His eyes burned through her. He knew something she didn't. She moved her head slowly; petrified at his answer.

"Have you ever heard of a gray witch?"

She'd never heard of such a creature. That didn't even sound real. What was it about her that made him think she was this type of witch?

He squinted. "You have no idea what that is, do ya?"

Ari shook her head.

"Your innate darkness is battling with the white magic you are now performing." He stood and squeezed past Ari with his hands up. Making an effort not to touch her again. "I really do need that juice." He looked at Ari a minute longer and said, "Sylvester never told me he had such interesting friends." Buster excused himself, then stepped out of the room.

"Ari? What is going on?" Leise asked impatiently. "Are you okay? You look a little shell-shocked?"

"I'm fine." She felt more than a little shell-shocked. Almost like she didn't know herself. She put on a smile that didn't quite reach her eyes before she said, "Just not used to being electrocuted. Don't worry about me. Check on Telly." Ari stood at the end of Telly's bed.

She could tell Leise wanted to talk more, but she walked to the other side of Telly's bed instead.

"Hey, Telly. It's Annaleise." She patted his hand. "I brought my friend Ari. You remember her, right?"

"Of course I remember you," A deep male voice said.

Ari looked up, into the blue-gray eyes of Sylvester Telepsen. He stood just behind Leise, who couldn't see or hear him.

"You make the best Jack & Coke this side of Tennessee," Telly said.

Ari smiled. He looked more corporeal, more real than most ghosts she'd seen. Maybe because he wasn't quite dead, only in a coma.

"Don't tell her," he said, then his body flickered.

The heart rate monitor beeped louder.

He looked around. "Protect…" He flickered. "Trouble…" He faded away.

The monitor's alarm went off. "What's happening?" Leise asked.

The nurses and doctor rushed in. Ari pulled Leise out of the way. They stood outside of Telly's door.

Leise seemed anxious as she watched all the hospital staff go in and out of the room. "I hope he'll be okay."

"I'm sure he will," Ari said automatically, but she wasn't sure. That flickering had bothered her. She'd only seen that during an exorcism, just before the soul departed.

Buster met them at the door. "He will. This happens sometimes. He can hear us, you know?" He took a deep swallow of the bottled OJ. "Maybe it was just too much excitement." He patted Leise's hand. "He'll be fine. Just be sure to come back and visit him. I know he was happy to hear your voice."

Leise nodded. "We will."

Buster rummaged through his crossbody hobo bag and pulled out a business card. "Ari, maybe I can help you on this new path you are on."

Ari nodded as she took his card and Buster walked back inside. This was the second offer she'd had for help. Certainly, no one would help her if her soul was evil.

Maybe she wasn't as black inside as she'd previously thought. Maybe there was hope for her.

CHAPTER 16

*H*ermann park was hotter than sin. Ari took a deep breath and nearly coughed up a lung, as her nimble fingers twisted and turned the stretchy balloons. Leise pulled off her baseball cap, sopped her brow with a white cotton towel, then fanned the cap back and forth. Between the humidity, the goats, ponies, and bunnies from the petting zoo downwind from their animal balloon station, it was amazing that Ari and Leise were still on their feet and happy.

Ari admired her handiwork as she handed a blue balloon dog to the little boy on the other side of her table. His bright smile could have powered a small power plant.

"You made his day," Leise said with a smile.

"Yeah," Ari said wistfully. As a child, she wanted to go places and do things with her mother. But by the time she was eight, it was painfully clear her mother wanted nothing to do with her.

"Oh, my God, I thought we'd never slow down." Leise collapsed into one of the cushioned camp chairs behind them.

Ari leaned against the table. For the first time since they opened the table five hours ago, they didn't have any eager faces waiting. Leise snatched Ari's black hand fan from the other seat.

Ari nodded. "Yeah, I know, but did you see their little faces? Too freaking cute." She looked in the box under the table. "Hmmm. Looks like I gotta go get more balloons." Ari held a single red balloon up. "I'll be right back."

"Okay." Leise continued to fan herself.

On the way back, Ari juggled the unopened box of balloons between her hands, as she walked past the Cycle Ice Cream station. The kids stood in a long line to ride the stationary bicycles that powered the ice cream makers, ready to expend all that energy to make ice cream. If the reward was free ice cream, she would have ridden a bike too.

A little girl who looked five, six at the most, in a pink helmet, screamed at a man ten times her size. She flounced with anger, and her dress whipped back and forth when she stomped her foot and pouted. "I want a balloon flower."

"They're out of balloons, honey." A middle-aged man with a Barbie backpack tossed over one shoulder knelt before the little girl. "I got your favorite snow cone." He held out a red shaved ice in a paper cup. The little girl turned away.

Ari walked towards the two. "Excuse me." The man stood. He looked Ari eye to eye. "I'm the animal balloon maker. I just got more balloons. I can make whatever she wants."

The relief in his eyes was palpable, "Thank you," he mouthed. Then he squatted down. "Savannah? You hear that? This nice lady said she could make you a flower."

With her arms still folded, Savannah cut Ari the side eye, then to her dad, then back to Ari. This little girl was a hard customer, but in the end, she took the sno-cone, then slid her hand into her father's. "Okay."

When Ari arrived at the table with her mini entourage, Leise was fanning herself like she would melt at any moment. But she couldn't help the smile that blossomed on her face at the dark-haired man in her seat.

Heath looked fresh as a daisy in his clean white tee and dark camo cargo shorts. Even the man bun was tied neatly on top of his head, not a strand out of place. But the most disturbing thing, the man wasn't sweating. How was that even fair?

Ari couldn't stop smiling. "Heath, What are you doing here?"

"You'd mentioned this the other night. I thought I'd come see your handiwork."

Her heart swelled at his words. She had said she was volunteering to many guys before him and not one ever remembered, let alone showed up. "I'll make you something special little boy." She winked, then turned towards the small commotion on the other side of her table.

"Savannah? What did you do?" The dad took the slushy red mess from the little girl's hand and walked it to the trash.

"Was it good?" Ari asked.

Savannah gave a vigorous nod as a long stream of red sticky syrup painted her white dress, cheeks, and chin, Jackson Pollock style. Dad pulled out a wet wipe from the pink backpack to clean her mouth.

He was going to need a bigger wet wipe, Ari thought. "If you want to go clean her up, I'll work on her flower." Ari opened the box and pulled out a handful of green and yellow long, skinny balloons. The man nodded, then held Savannah's hand with a wet wipe as they walked away.

"She was just too cute," Leise said.

Ari stretched a green balloon twice its size a few times, before handing it to Leise, who stood at the air compressor. "She was throwing a fit. I guess after you told her we were out of balloons."

Leise attached the empty balloons to the compressor and hit a button. Air quickly filled the each balloon. They looked like extra long yellow and green bananas, squeaking when she handed them to Ari. "She was not happy."

Heath's hand touched Ari's lower back as he leaned in to whisper in her ear. "You need bottled water or anything?"

She pressed back into his large hand as she turned to look at him. "No, I'm fine."

His dimples appeared when he attempted to hold back a grin.

When he smiled like that, everything in her melted. "What were you just thinking?"

"Nothing," he said with an even bigger smile.

She stared at him and knew his thoughts were not PG. She stared at him a little too long, and all she wanted to do was fall into his multifaceted blue eyes. She'd noticed that sometimes if the light hit them just right, they took on a purplish hue. In her peripheral, she saw Leise lean in to look at them both.

"You guys really need to get a room," Leise said.

Ari looked at him a moment longer. "We were only admiring each other."

"You were doing more than that," Leise mumbled.

Heath laughed. "I'm going to get some ice cream before they close. Would you ladies care for one?"

"Yes, please," Ari said.

"Nope. I'm more of a brownie girl," Leise chimed in.

He kissed her cheek. "I'll be back."

Ari exhaled loudly and gave a little shake. She looked at the balloons, and she had forgotten what she was supposed to be doing.

"Flower," Leise said.

"Thank you." Ari smiled, as she twisted and knotted the yellow balloon.

"You like him. A lot," Leise said. She didn't ask, just stated a fact.

Ari's nimble fingers continued to attach the green balloon stem, twisting big leaves on the bottom. "Heath's different. He's not freaked out about the tarot stuff. He makes me feel..." Loved. "Precious."

"You going to tell him you're a witch?"

Ari let out a dry laugh. "I don't know. Kinda thinking about it." She admired her yellow balloon daisy, just as two people walked up.

"That's nice." Leise nodded in approval.

Ari nodded, then her face froze mid-smile when she looked up. She licked her dry lips and used all of her willpower to keep herself from screaming. "You changed clothes," she whispered.

The cherries on the little girl's clean tee reminded her of the worst day of her life. The day she realized her mother didn't have a heart. The day she walked away from her coven and her family.

"That's so purdy," Savannah cooed. Little outstretched fingers flexed, reaching for the flower.

A sharp pain hit her arm. Leise had given her a jab. "Ari," Leise whispered. Ari blinked and forced herself to hand over the balloon. When the little girl's hand touched Ari's, a bolt of electricity sparked between them. Savannah's smile died, along with the light in her soft brown eyes.

Everything happened so fast after that. Ari's finger trembled with power, and for the first time since she was a child, she honestly thought she wouldn't be able to control her abilities. Energy burned her palms like a brand. She screamed out incoherently as the little girl's body convulsed on the ground, the flower still clutched in her small hand.

"I'm so sorry. I'm so sorry. I'm so sorry," Ari said repeatedly. She wasn't sure if she was speaking out loud or not.

How dare the table not move out of her way? Why wouldn't her feet work? They were tripping over any and everything. An all-encompassing need took her over. She needed to see little Savannah. Needed to know she hadn't hurt her. It didn't matter that she couldn't touch the girl. She just needed to know she wasn't like her mother. *Goddess, please don't let me have condemned this precious child to a life of insanity.*

"I didn't mean to do it," Ari mumbled.

She could see the dad's mouth moving, but she couldn't hear over the keening. *Was that her?* He put something in Savannah's mouth, then lifted her and ran.

"Ari, listen to me. It wasn't your fault. She was having a seizure." Leise murmured.

Leise's small hands held Ari's face, but she couldn't see her friend. Barely even heard her.

"What happened?" a deep male voice asked.

Heath, she thought. He shouldn't be near me. I probably killed that little girl.

"Ari, can you hear me?" Heath shook her. "Give her to me."

Her body shifted from small arms to larger ones.

"Ari?" His warm fingers touched her face.

She didn't want to answer. She closed her eyes instead and let the darkness take her.

)O(

IT WASN'T every day that a girl woke up in the arms of a ghost. Remy laid behind her and his cold arms held her. Ari blink her eyes and looked around. She was in her bed, but she could hear Leise and Heath in the other room, presumably discussing her mental state. Closing her eyes didn't shield her from seeing Savannah's pink helmet hit the ground repeatedly or her face frozen in that grim smile. It shook her to the core.

"You alright, Cher?" Remy asked.

Pushing herself into a sitting position. "I've been better," Ari said in a raspy voice. She rubbed her throat. It wasn't logical, but she tried to rub the gritty feeling away.

She heard the front door close. Leise padded into the room in socks. "I didn't realize you were awake. Heath just left. You want me to—"

"No," Ari croaked. "How's the girl? Savannah? Is she—"

"No, no." Leise grabbed Ari's hands. "She's fine. She had a seizure, but her dad got her out of the park fast. The hospital was right down the street."

Ari exhaled. "Good. That's good. I thought I'd hurt her."

Leise grabbed a bottled water from the dresser. "Here." Then sat down next to her.

After she had a few swallows, she tried to speak again. "I need to tell you some things about why I left the coven."

Her life had changed drastically since leaving the coven. She looked around at the peach-painted walls. They didn't have any family portraits or a collage of happy times from her youth. There was only a picture next to the bed of Leise and her at the beach. That day, Leise had refused to take off her Chucks and full-length coverup with a hoodie. Ari smiled and nodded. These two people were her family and Leise deserved to know the entire truth about her.

She couldn't do this with Leise staring at her. She crawled out of her four-poster bed. When Leise moved to follow, she held her hand out. "No. Stay there. I won't be able to do this if you hold my hand."

Ari smiled as Leise and Remy mirrored each other and lay on the end of the bed like little kids watching TV. Leise nodded, rubbing her arm. Remy laid down next to her, chilling her with just his presence.

Ari exhaled, then paced and wrung her hands simultaneously. Flashes of every murder she had stood by and watched, every despicable spell she had performed rolled through her mind. When she finally stopped pacing, her hands were the only thing still moving, trembling actually. She tried to hold them still, but when she flipped them over, she could only see blood dripping from every finger. She closed her eyes against the mirage.

"Don't," Remy whispered. "It's not worth the pain."

"Ari, you don't have to," Leise said.

"That's the thing, Leise," Ari said. "I really do." She had been holding this for too long. She stilled herself, and took a deep breath, then began. "Remember when I met you, I kept trying to prove I was a witch."

Leise laughed. "Yeah, and nothing ever happened."

Remy jumped up. "Nothing happened! I'm sittin' right here."

Ari smiled, she couldn't help it. She remembered she'd wanted more than anything to make that pocket watch levitate, but she ended up lifting the spirit from it instead. That was the best thing that had ever happened to her. Her mother had locked up every grimoire in the house after a chilly run-in with Remy in the shower. Remy complained that he couldn't see for a month after that.

"Remy happened."

Leise looked at the empty spot next to her and smiled.

Ari felt her heart lighten and she started again. "I come from a long line of witches."

"Ari, I've known that for a long time."

"Black Witches. I didn't know the spells they were teaching me were…evil. For lack of a better word."

Leise covered her mouth with both hands but didn't say anything. She didn't have to. Her reaction said it all, shock and maybe pity. "I've met your cousin, even your mom. They didn't seem…all that bad."

"Erissa didn't like us being friends. She felt you were a bad influence on me."

"What? You for real?"

"Well, remember after Remy got released you couldn't come to my house anymore?" Leise nodded. "It started after that. She said that Remy would have never happened had you not been around. But I think it was because my mother began to teach me more advanced spells and those involved blood. I didn't want to learn those, but my mother made me."

"Blood? Did you have to ki..kill people?"

Ari stared at Leise. "I never killed anyone. But I have hurt people. Our coven mostly got hired to do…odd jobs."

"Like mercenaries?"

"No."

Remy said, "Exactement."

Ari gave him the side eye. "The last job before I left the coven, my mother demanded I go. Said I wasn't pulling my weight as her daughter." She rubbed her hands like she was trying to warm them. "The job happened to be a seven-year-old girl. My mother wanted me to wipe all her memories away, but this particular spell would slowly drive a person insane."

"You didn't?"

"I couldn't." Ari's eyes glazed over. "The little girl had blonde ringlets and a black sundress with bunches of cherries and a doll in her arms. Just like Savannah today, the spell coursed through her body. Her facial muscles seized all while her entire body twitched violently." She shook her head. The picture of the little girl never really left her. "My mother made it especially horrible, since I didn't do the job. She left the little girl's memories intact, but unable to speak."

"And you thought you did that? To Savannah?"

"By accident, of course. She had changed clothes. It shocked me. Please don't hate me." She sat back down on the bed. The silence stretched between them. If Leise hated her, she just might break.

"I don't hate you. Never that." Leise pulled her in for a hug. "If I know anything, I know you're a good person. I don't think you would ever knowingly hurt someone. But if you did, they probably deserved it."

"You sure?" Ari wiped her tears.

"Positive."

"My throat is still a little raw," Ari said.

"Yeah, you were screaming like a banshee."

"Shut up. That's not nice. I was traumatized."

"But you're okay now?" Leise held her face and stared in her eyes.

Ari's head nodded like she was a marionette. "I'm alright now."

"Good." Leise released her. "Now, how would you feel about some ice cream?"

"You read my mind."

"Not me. Heath."

"But he doesn't know my favorite ice cream." Ari stood up, and Leise followed.

"Oh, I don't know. He brought a half pint of something green…"

"Mint chocolate chip?" Ari cut her off. "That boy must have been fallen from the heavens."

CHAPTER 17

*T*here must have been something in the water. Everyone seemed to be in need of divine direction. After her last client, Ari slumped back in her chair.

"Hey Aramais, look at that," Topaz said as she walked over to stand next to her.

Ari wiped her tired eyes and stood to see a glorious piece of automobile history. A 1960, 4-door, navy and champagne Bentley with white-walled tires, and a long sleek nose that screamed old money. Going to car shows with Leise hadn't been a complete waste of time. Her best-friend would be so jealous right now. "What in the world?" Ari stood to get a better look. "Who could that be?"

The driver walked around to the passenger side back door. A man emerged in a dark gray, three-piece pinstriped suit, a red tie, and dark hat.

"A CEO? Or maybe even royalty? Whoever it is, they got money," Topaz said.

"True that."

Although Ari couldn't see his face, she could tell he was a sharp dressed man.

"Maybe he's here to buy a building," Ari sat back behind her table.

"Older men are incredibly sexy," Topaz said staring out. "Just saying."

"You're incorrigible."

"Easily corruptible, too. Oh my god, he's coming this way." Topaz walked back to her booth while touching her hair and fixing her clothes, and a little extra sway in her hips.

The man looked like he was on a mission as he stepped through the grass with purpose. When he didn't turn from the path to her booth, she realized she was his purpose. Her heart rate sped up just a bit when he stood before her without saying a word. He held his dark gray fedora in both hands. The man had to be at least six-three, well built, ebony hair with a little gray at the temple. She thought a man being driven around in that car would be much, much older, but this guy didn't look a day over forty. Even with the gray hair.

"May I help you?"

A gruff sound came from him as he cleared his throat. "Yes, I'm looking for an Ari Mason," he said.

His rich baritone voice felt like silk caressing her spine. His light accent encouraged the goosebumps that sprung up on both arms. His voice held its own particular kind of magic. She had to blink to come out of the fog. "You've found her."

"May I?" He indicated the chair with a nod. When she nodded, he sat. "I'm a neighbor of Eunice." At her continued silence, he added. "Mrs. Haversham."

Ari held her smile, but everything inside her stilled. "Mrs. Haversham is a nice lady. Is she doing okay?"

He nodded. "Yes, she's doing fine. She told me about," he leaned in and whispered, "what happened the other night."

"Mister...?" She paused.

"Drake," he supplied.

"Mr. Drake, I provide a special service to help people. So, if you're here to ridicule or..."

"No, no. I want you to help me...like you helped her."

"Oh, okay." She opened the wooden box that held her tarot cards. "I can read your cards."

Mr. Drake looked around. "Not here. Could you do the reading at my house? Or some place special to me, maybe?"

"Mr. Drake, I need for you to be honest. Is your home haunted?"

"No. I lost my wife some years back. I want to know if she's okay." His hands tightened on the hat, crushing it.

Ari wasn't sure how she could help. Sounded like he needed a medium. "Maybe, you need—"

"Please, Ms. Mason," he cut in, "if Eunice, Mrs. Haversham, trusts you, I know I'm in good hands. Won't you please try?"

Ari pursed her lips and thought of all the people she could have helped, and hadn't. This man needed closure. She could give that to him. "Okay."

"Thank you." He stood, then pulled a card from his pocket and handed it to her. "Call me when you are ready. I'm very eager to do this, Ms. Mason."

In other words, ASAP. Ari understood, but she wouldn't be caught off guard like at Mrs. Haversham's. She needed to prepare. "You have a good day, Mr. Drake."

"You could have sent him my way," Topaz called out after he left.

Ari looked over. Topaz looked like she had just come off a photo shoot. Who carried that much makeup with them? "I will remember that for the next time."

Ari laid back and closed her eyes. It couldn't have been more than a few minutes before she felt someone else standing in front of her. She opened her eyes to a pleasant and unexpected sight. A smile spread across her face.

A to-go cup.

The guy holding it wasn't bad either. Heath stood in a pair of dark denim jeans, and a black tee.

"What's this?"

He popped the top off. "It's not coffee." He waved it under her nose.

The steam and aroma of jasmine hit her like a champ. She knew that smell. She knew that tea. "Did you go to the—" He handed her the drink.

"Hot Toddy." They said at the same time.

"Yes, I did," Heath said. He took a seat at the table and sipped his own beverage.

Ari closed her eyes before taking a sip.

The rich aroma of his drink reached her as she sipped her own. Coffee. Black.

She took another sip of her tea before asking, "So, what brings you here this fine afternoon?"

"I found myself in the neighborhood."

Ari looked up towards the mirrored skyscrapers and concrete streets. Not a 'neighborhood' to be seen. "Hmmm," she smiled smugly around her to-go cup. "Really, why are you here?"

"I wanted to see how you were doing today?" He sat down in the chair across from her.

As happy as she was to see him, she didn't want to talk about it. "I'm sorry you had to see me like that."

"Ari, I'm happy you're okay. That's all that matters."

"Well, thank you and thank you for the ice cream, but how did you know my favorite?"

"I didn't. I just picked what I liked."

"Great minds and all that."

He smiled. "Great minds. I like that."

He looked into her eyes and held her there in that moment. He reached out, and she slid her hands into his. His warm touch felt like a balm to her fractured soul. She didn't know how long they stayed like that, but she heard someone clear their throat.

Insistently.

Ari smiled as she looked over to see Topaz lingering between their two booths. She slid her hand from his and turned to face her neighbor. "Topaz."

"Hey, Ari," Topaz said with a big smile. "Who's your friend?"

"Topaz. This is Heath." She smirked at Heath with brows lifted. "Heath. Topaz."

He moved towards the young woman. Topaz extended her hand. He grasped her fingers, but instead of shaking her hand - he turned it over, then softly pressed his lips to it. "A pleasure."

Ari shook her head at the blushing woman. She could have sworn she heard her squeal. He came back and took a seat across from Ari.

Ari spoke softly. "You know you made her day. I'm never gonna hear the end of it."

Heath's eyes gleamed with mischief. "Really? I can't help my natural charm."

Ari rolled her eyes. This man was nothing but trouble. Between those blue eyes and Irish accent, she would have to put an invisibility spell on him to keep women off him.

Heath looked over the items on her table. "You going to read my fortune?"

"You're as bad as Leise. Tarot is not fortune telling. It's more of a guide." She put her to-go cup at her feet and shuffled the cards. She placed the stack in front of him. "Cut the deck."

He eyed her suspiciously. But instead of cutting the deck, he made a circle with his index finger, then tapped it. A slow, crooked smile revealed those dimples.

She nibbled on her bottom lip. There was no missing the suggestive way he caressed her cards. She was happy this guy was not magical. The deck might have gone up in flames if he were. She spread the cards out in a half moon in front of him.

"Pick a card." Her voice came out huskier than she had intended. She had no doubt he could tell what kind of effect he was having on her.

With the same finger, he seemingly touched every card. She was sure it was all in her head, but it felt like that finger was caressing her, from her temple, over her lips, down her neck. She was anticipating where that finger would go next when a cool breeze flowed over them. As much as she wanted to finish, she knew who had caused that lovely change in weather. The next wave of biting winds felt more like a nor'easter.

The tarot cards fluttered and Ari's hand stop the cards from flying off of the table. "The weather is not cooperating today. Maybe I'll read your cards another day."

She quickly gathered the cards then boxed them up. "My next client should be here soon, maybe you should get going," she said abruptly.

Ari hadn't seen her cousin yet, but he couldn't be too far off. She moved around the table when the next breeze sent some of Topaz's art rolling down towards the reflecting pond.

"Where did that come from?" Heath asked as he looked around.

The words came out automatically, but she never stopped scanning the area. "You know how Texas weather is."

He stood up and looked around. "What's wrong?" His hands wrapped around her waist. "Ari, what is it?"

She shivered under his hands. Although she couldn't see Lucas - he was close. Knowing him, he'd want to meet Heath. Shake his hand, pull out a ruler. Boys were so stupid. She really liked this guy, and meeting anyone from her family before she kind of had a chance to explain things about herself could send him running for the hills. Just because he accepted the tarot reading didn't mean he was ready to hear she was a witch.

The light stubble on his face prickled her hands when she held his face and looked him dead in the eyes. "There are so many things about myself that I need to tell you, but not now. I really, really need for you to trust me and go."

He chuckled, then scrutinized her face and realized she was serious. "Go? Why? What did I do?"

"What? No?" She let go of his face and hugged him. When she pulled back, she said, "It's not you. I promise. I forgot I was supposed to meet with my cousin today." Her eyes flickered over his shoulder. No Lucas yet.

His creased browed morphed into a deep dimples and a bright smile. "I would love to..."

Her finger covered his lips before he could mention meeting her family. "No, you don't."

His lips spread into an even wider smile, if that were even possible and pulled her fingers from his lips, then kissed each one.

"Okay, fine. But soon," he lifted a brow. "I'd like to know where my girl comes from."

Did he say,'his girl'? "Excuse me?"

His voice lowered to a husky whisper. "You heard me."

She looked again, and sure enough, Lucas was coming across the grass. He had the worst timing. They would have to have a serious talk about him calling before visiting.

He folded his arm, "Ari."

"What? Yes?"

"I will get to meet them, right?"

"Absolutely I'll make sure we all get together," the words came out in a rush. Her cousin's smile was a little too bright. This was not going to end will if Heath didn't leave. "But please, you have to go."

He looked back following her eyes. "I'm going to hold you to that." He moved like he was about to leave, and she sagged with relief. But then Heath's big, warm hands cradled her face, much like how she had him a moment ago, and leaned in.

It all happened so fast she didn't get a chance to prepare for what happened next. His soft lips were on hers. His tongue moved back and forth gently coaxing her lips apart. She closed her eyes, took in his spicy scent, and allowed herself to fall into him. His arms wrapped around her tighter as he deepened the kiss with a light pull of her tongue.

Her heart pounded wildly, and the blood rushed to her head. When she opened her eyes Lucas stood inn front of her with a huge smile. "That good, huh?"

She looked around wild-eyed, walking in front of her booth, then Topaz's. He was gone. That kiss made her want to spin around with her arms wide and sing. She had faith that the hills were alive.

"So, who's the guy?" Lucas asked when she came back to her table.

She stopped her mental Sound of Music moment, but she could feel her cheeks warm, and a giggle bounced around in the back of the throat. Her cheeks hurt from trying to hold back her smile. She couldn't help it. *That kiss, oh that kiss.* "No one you need to concern yourself with." She flipped her hair as she walked past Lucas to sit down.

"You can stop smiling now," Lucas took the seat across from her.

"Shut up," she said with no real malice as she folded her arms. "And where the hell have you been. I called you like a week ago."

He held up a finger. "Ummm, it has only been three days, and it's chaos at the coven right now. Since the murders everyone is on high alert and the security force has to work longer shifts." He lifted his brows. "So, you see, it's not easy to get away. I'll have you know I'm at the dentist right now. So, speak fast."

Ari nodded and exhaled before she said, "My friends were attacked the other night?"

Lucas leaned forward with his hand extended. "Cuz, you okay? What the hell happened?"

"I'm okay," she squeezed his hand. "But Leise got knocked around pretty good, and her co-worker is still in a coma."

Lucas knocked the chair back when he stood abruptly. "Damn it!" Pockets of wind knocked over trash cans and the few people who were strolling by now walked against gale force winds. When they started to lose the fight against the elements and slide backwards, Ari touched his hand.

"Lucas," Ari watched as people were knocked around, and the small trash tornadoes. "Calm down."

Lucas looked around a bit wild eyed, then picked up the chair and sat back down. With the flick of his wrist, the winds died down. "I'm sorry. This is just," he closed his eyes, then exhaled, "just tell me what happened."

Ari told him about Nurse Francesca at the Ravenswood Arms, the attack in the Paper Trail parking lot, but left out her time with the white witches. "Remy hasn't been the same either. He said he felt like evil was pouring into him. Absorbing him."

"How's that even possible? He's already dead."

"Dead," she said at the same time. "Yeah, I know."

"And what is this thing, that can drain witches and kill ghosts?"

"Remy was positive it was male, but not much else. I can't be positive, but it looked like runes were carved into his staff."

"What if he comes after you again?" Lucas growled.

"Lucas," Ari groused. "I'm fine. I just have to be more careful. We all do."

"No, what you need to do is—"

"Don't," she held her hand out cutting him off. "Please don't say it. You know I'm never coming back."

"Fine." He threw up his hands in surrender. "But if you run across him — please, please don't try to take him on alone. I know you. Call Rum or me."

"What about Erissa? You could get shunned for talking to me - let alone helping me."

"Aramais, you're blood kin, even if you're not in the coven. You call me, I'll come. I'll keep my phone on me."

Ari could hear the truth in his words. Although Lucas stayed in the coven, she had never seen him kill with his power. He was so laid back, she didn't think he would be capable of hurting someone even if he had to. Whether he believed it or not, she needed to protect him as well.

CHAPTER 18

*A*ri stepped out the back door of the Cave, behind Bull. He stopped abruptly, and she almost ran into his massive back. "What?"

Bull turned his head slightly. "Stay right there, baby-girl." His hand reached towards the small of his back to touch his concealed weapon. His voice boomed through the night when he turned back around. "Can I help you?"

Ari could see the butt of the gun. She leaned to look around Bull's wide back to see who he was about to shoot.

Heath lifted his hands in surrender. "I just want to talk to her." He pointed towards Ari. "If I could?"

Ari patted the big man's shoulder. "It's okay, Bull. I know him."

"Well, tell him to use the front door like all the other creeps. I could have shot his ass." He gave Heath another look. "Night, baby-girl." He kissed her temple. "Be careful," he whispered before he walked away.

Ari watched Bull climb the steps into his big-wheeled monster truck. He made a point of revving the motor before burning out of the parking lot, leaving a trail of smoke as he sped away.

"Heath, what are you doing here?"

"I wanted to see you after our time got cut short earlier," Heath said.

Ari walked to her rental car and popped the trunk. "Well, I'm not free tonight either."

"Really? It's after two in the morning."

Ari nodded. "I'm aware."

"Another guy?" He crossed his arms.

"Yes. A huge group of them and a few women," Ari said. She leaned on the side of her rental car to unzip her wedge boots then put on some work boots.

Heath's eyes grew ten sizes. "Oh, wow. I didn't know you were into that kind of lifestyle."

She shook her head. "What? So, not what you're thinking. I'm doing a favor for some friends."

"Right now?" He looked up and around. "In the wee hours?"

"I say again, I am aware."

"I can't let you do this alone."

She laughed. "Fine. If you have to come, follow me."

)O(

"THIS IS A CEMETERY," Heath said.

Ari looked around as she closed the massive wrought iron gates behind them. Luckily, Heath wore a black sweater and dark jeans like he did most days, because he blended nicely in their stealth mission.

"Yes, it is. But not just any cemetery, one of the oldest in Houston," Ari said. Heath following her kind of put a crimp in her plans, but she was sure she could do this favor for the seniors and look for ghosts without Heath knowing.

She walked towards the huge, moss-riddled oak tree. The tree had to be at least three hundred years old, its trunk the size of a small Fiat. The auxiliary branches swept around in a craggy style, and those were about two feet wide. She held a small flashlight in her mouth and opened a large black duffle bag.

"Why?"

"There are a few people at the senior facility where I volunteer who are wheelchair users and can't come out here."

"And you do this for them?"

"Among other things." Ari lifted one shoulder.

"Now, look in the duffle bag. Sooner we get started, the sooner we can get out of here."

Heath squatted down and peered to look. His hand moved cautiously around the bag, moving like he thought there were snakes inside. "Goodness, Heath. I didn't bring you out here to kill you. Just pull it out."

He frowned, but when his hand emerged from the bag, with a handful of long-stemmed roses. Now, he had a smile as big as Texas. "But..." Then he looked around the cemetery. "All of them?"

"It's not that many." She pulled out a handful of roses.

"You volunteer at an old folks' home?" He placed a rose on the first headstone.

She frowned at him. "What? Oh, my goddess. Did you just say that?" she hissed. "I volunteer at an assisted living facility. I like to help those residents who don't have family." She laid a rose down, said a silent prayer and moved to the next.

"Sorry, I didn't mean anything by it."

"No worries, but you might want to speed up, we don't exactly have permission to be here."

"What else do you do there?"

"All sorts of things, dance partners on themed dance night, I read books for those who can't. Heck, sometimes they just need someone to talk to. I also make them special lotions and teas to help with whatever aches or ails them. It won't cure them, but it seems to help."

"You make your own teas? You are a woman of many secrets? Would you make me one of your special blends?"

Secrets? Me? "Sure. Whenever you come by my place, we can work on one for you?"

From the corner of her eye, something flickered. When she looked around, there was nothing there. Heath hadn't seemed to notice anything. There was another reason she was out here tonight that she hadn't told Heath about.

"Heath, I need to go back there," Ari said, pointing with her flashlight towards a small section of headstones, near a large tree.

"Be careful," he said before he moved to the next row.

Ari tripped over a substantial network of giant oak tree roots. She turned off her flashlight and stood still. When nothing happened, she called out. "I know you're here."

Nothing.

"I need some help. Please."

Taking advantage of the dark, she used her power to float the last five roses. The roses wobbled, then hit two headstones. She needed to work more on her telekinesis. She had all but given up hope, when a young girl of ten maybe, but no older than twelve, appeared on the wooden swing attached to the tree. To an average human, the swing would seem to move by itself.

"You're a witch," the young girl said. Her voice was nasal and high pitched. Very New York. She had light hair in a bob hairstyle, a dark dress with black Mary Janes.

"And you're a New Yorker. The Bronx?" Ari asked.

A smile crossed her face and Ari could see the braces. "See, you could tell. The rubes here know nothing. I'm Krista."

"Nice to meet you, I'm Ari. Are there lots of ghosts here?"

"Old ghosts, yeah," the girl said wrinkling her nose. "Like, um… why you here?"

"I have a ghost friend. Thought I'd…" Ari moved her head side to side. "Find him a friend."

Krista hopped from the swing. "A friend, huh? Is he cute?"

"He's too old for you."

"I'm older than I look," Krista said with her hands on her hips.

Ari lifted a brow.

"I'm thirteen!"

"Okay, okay. I believe you." Ari waved her hands. "Are you trapped here?"

Her smile died as she shook her head.

"Why not move on then?"

"I don't know. I only lived in this hick town a few months when I was in a car accident. I would like to see my Pop-Pop again before I go. I don't know, let him know it wasn't his fault." Krista seemed younger all of a sudden.

"What's your Pop-Pop's name, Krista?"

"Pop-Pop. I told you."

Ari smiled at her, then looked behind her. Heath was coming her way.

"You look for some friends for…my friend. I'll see about getting your Pop-Pop here to see you, or at least try to get a message to him."

"Really? Sweet."

"Now, go. My friend is just a human. He doesn't understand all of this," Ari said quickly.

Krista looked in Heath's direction, then frowned. "I don't know about him," she mumbled.

"Hurry," Ari said in a hushed tone.

"Who were you talking to?" Heath asked.

"What? No one." She looked around. "Just reading headstones." She moved to the one headstone she'd missed.

Krista Walker.

The girl had only been dead a few months. Ari laid her last rose down. "I'm all done," Ari said. "You?"

"I must say this was an interesting date, but maybe we can try a picnic or I don't know…a restaurant, next time."

"Ha, ha. Very funny. You're the one who invited yourself." In the distance, a flashlight moved back and forth. "I think our time's up."

CHAPTER 19

*A*n instrumental version of *Careless Whispers* played low throughout the Hot Toddy. Ari inhaled steam from an oversized mug before taking a sip of their signature drink, but she made the tea extra special with a double shot of Irish whiskey. "So, where were you last night?"

"I went to see Telly," Leise said, before making a face after taking a sip of her coffee. She quickly thumped a blue packet of sweetener and stirred it in. "Then I got to talking with Buster."

"How's Telly doing?"

"Not too good. Buster said, the doctor said he might want to get Telly's affairs in order." Leise lowered her head and wiped the tears she hadn't let fall.

"I'm sorry." Ari reached across the table to hold Leise's hand.

"I just wished I had been nicer to him. I knew he liked me, but I pretended like I didn't notice." Leise waved the waitress over.

"He's a fighter. We have to have a little faith that he'll come back to us," Ari said.

Faith was a new concept for Ari. She didn't grow up learning to pray or how religion worked. But since she'd been out on her own, she'd been reading different philosophies and learning what it truly meant to be a witch. Faith meant belief, and for most spells to work, you had to believe wholeheartedly. Otherwise, it might not work.

When the waitress arrived, "Could I get a cup of tea?"

"Hot or iced?" the waitress said.

"Hot, please." Leise spoke again after the waitress walked away. "I know you're right about Telly." Leise lowered her head, and her lips stretched into a thin line. Not exactly a smile or a grimace. "Um, Ari. I have something I need to talk about."

Finally, Ari thought, she's going to tell me about *him*.

Leise shifted in her seat, then sat up ram-rod straight and intertwined her fingers on the table. "After you did the spell on this." She touched the necklace and smiled. "I slept like a baby. Then…" she shook her head.

"The guy from your nightmares?"

Leise nodded. "I thought he'd be a demon or something hideous, there to Freddy Krueger me."

"But he wasn't. So, what happened? What is he?"

"His name is Brennan, and he's been trapped in this crystal for more than 300 years."

"Trapped or ? Maybe he's exactly where he's supposed to be."

Leise frowned. "He's a…" She stopped talking when the waitress placed the hot tea in front of her.

"I'm sorry. Can you take this back?" Leise handed the coffee back to the waitress. "He's the victim here. His uncle trapped him there when he tried to stop him from possessing a girl from their village." It all came out in a mad rush.

Ari held up her hands. "Hey, you know me. It had to be said. So this magic is coming from him. Why can't he get out?"

"A spell put him in, so he thinks a reversal spell will get him out. He said it might be best on a…what did he call it?" She took a sip with her brows drawn in consternation.

Ari watched Leise sip the cup a tea. The fact that she was drinking tea was amazing but without sugar — a miracle. What has caused this change? Who had caused this change?

"A celestial event or…" Leise finally said.

"A solstice," Ari supplied.

Leise nodded vigorously. "Yes."

"Sounds like you guys have talked...a lot." Ari wasn't jealous. Not really. Okay, well maybe a little. Her best friend didn't feel like she could come to her with this before now.

Leise's cheeks went bright pink, as she looked at the necklace. "Yeah. Almost every night."

She'd whispered it, and Ari heard why her friend hadn't told her about the guy. Leise was falling for him. Hell, she had fallen. Her aura fluctuated with various shades of pinks and purples. She'd come to realize the constant purple within Leise's aura was partly the necklace's magic and partly Brennan.

"Why didn't you come to me sooner?"

"I wanted to do this by myself. You can do anything, can fix anything. Me? It's never that easy for me, but for this guy, I kinda wanted him to see me the way I see you. A knight," she rolled her eyes, "or knightress in shining armor. I couldn't even do that right. I'm not you."

Ari reached across and grasped her hand. "You don't have to be me. Asking me for help is helping him. Not being able to do it all your own is not a sign of weakness. Knowing when to ask for help is a sign of strength." She had Leise's hand in a tight squeeze.

Leise looked up with tears in her eyes, "Thank you." She released Ari's hand before she wiped snot with the sleeve of her free arm. "You're the bestest."

"Yeah, yeah. I would hug you, but I'm steering clear of that arm of pestilence. Now, finish your tea."

Ari and Leise continued to sip their drinks. "We might be able to get your man out soon. May Day is right around the corner."

"I've never heard of May Day. What's that?"

"Sure you have, it's Beltane."

Leise smiled. "Oh, I know that one. That's when you witches run around half naked under a full moon, setting bonfires and stuff."

"I see you need more training on witch ritual etiquette. We do not run around naked. At least, not all the time." She quirked the corner of her mouth, then tapped in front of Leise's cup of tea.

"You donc? I'm gonna need some things if we're gonna get your man out."

"MAGIC IS ALL AROUND US, and can be found if you know where to look," Ari said as she and Leise walked down a sidewalk. They had to park on a side street because there wasn't any room on the two lane street.

Leise looked around. "There's nothing back here. Where are you taking me?"

Ari waved at the structure on her right. "Right here."

Lcise frowned as she looked the building up and down. "What kind of place is this again? I don't see a name."

"The White Cauldron."

"This one never came up on my search."

"Your internet search?" Ari moaned. "I should hope not."

Leise stared at the slender, filthy display window. She moved from side to side looking inside.

"What are you doing?" Ari asked.

"If I stand this way," Leise angled to the right, "there's this huge book in the window. When I turn this way," she angled to the left. "Nothing. Spiderwebs and dust." She repeated the turns a few more times. Then she put her face close, but not touching the glass, to look inside. "Are you sure this place is safe to enter?"

"Will you come on?" A bell chimed when Ari opened the weathered red door.

"No one's here," Leise whispered.

Ari walked around a table of leather-bound books. "She's here."

Leise slid her finger through a thin layer of dust on the same table.

Ari watched her surreptitiously as she walked the around the edge of the store. "Don't you dare write your name!" She turned around and said in a whisper yell.

Leise lifted both hands. "How do you do that?"

"She didn't need any special powers for that. It was written all over your face," Elizabeth said.

Leise jumped as she turned around. "Oh, my."

"I do apologize. I thought you heard me come in. I did not mean to scare you."

"Not scared. Just," Leise took a deep breath, "surprised."

The shop owner clasped her hands and gave a sage nod.

"Elizabeth, merry meet," Ari said.

Elizabeth greeted Ari with outstretched hands. "Merry meet."

"Elizabeth, this is my friend Leise." Ari waved towards her friend. "Leise. Elizabeth."

"Nice to meet you," Leise said with a nod.

"And you as well." Elizabeth nodded to Leise. "Now, is there anything I can help you ladies with?"

"Any tomes on old magic."

"How old?"

"Ancient. Three hundred years, give or take." Ari waved her hand back and forth. "And would you happen to know anything about crystals that could be used to imprison, I guess, a person's essence or even their soul?"

Elizabeth tapped two fingers on her lips for about a minute, then clapped her hands together. "I think I may have something in the library. Follow me." The floor-length skirt fluttered so quickly it gave the illusion that she was floating across the store.

By the time Ari and Leise reached her, Elizabeth was already up the step ladder with a huge book grasped in her arm. Ari lifted a hands to take the massive, leather-bound tome.

Leise stretched out a hand. "I'll take it."

"Okay, but be…"

Leise's hand dropped from the weight and quickly used her other hand to keep it from hitting the floor.

Ari laughed. "I was going to say, careful."

"Yeah."

Elizabeth smiled as Ari helped her off the last steps safely. "Those ancient texts are deceivingly heavy. Now, about crystals." She walked along the wall, and pulled a small, blue book from the bottom shelf and flipped through the pages. "There are a few crystals and stones that they said assisted in the rituals dealing with the spirit. There was one, much like the philosopher's stone, that was shrouded in legend. I remember it was an amethyst, but it had a morbid name. Ah, here it is. The gem of the tortured soul is rumored to transport wielder to another world, trap another's soul, immortality, even bring the dead to life." Her finger moved quickly through the text. "It says the necklace has been lost for more than two hundred years."

"Is there a picture?" Ari asked.

Elizabeth turned the book around and showed them a pencil sketch of a rough edged crystal partially inside a geode. Ari and Leise stared at the identical replica of Leise's family heirloom. Leise touched the lump under her shirt.

"Did that help?" Elizabeth looked at the two of them, then put the book back on the shelf.

"Yes. Thank you," Ari said quickly.

Elizabeth took the book from Leise as if it were light as a feather, and walked to the round table in the middle of the room. She rubbed her hand lightly over the cover. There was reverence in her touch.

"If you don't mind, why do you need this book?" Elizabeth didn't look up as she flipped through the book.

"It's to help a friend," Leise said.

The woman smiled and nodded her head in understanding. She stopped on a page near the middle of the book. Ari and Leise came closer to see the spell. The pages looked like they had been dipped in tea, then set out in the sun to dry without anything to straighten them.

"How old is this book...er...tome?" Leise asked.

"About a century, but it still may be able to help. Now, your friend. What exactly does he need?"

"How did you...?" Elizabeth lifted her brows in a knowing look. Leise nodded. "Never mind. He's been displaced and cursed."

"There are two spells here you could try."

"Great, we'll take it," Ari said.

There was no price on the book. The store never had prices on anything. Elizabeth had a way of knowing just what you could afford to spend. Ari looked in her purse, she had...

"Three hundred dollars," Elizabeth stated.

Ari laughed. That never got old. "Exactly." She laid two fifties and two hundred dollar bills on the counter.

Elizabeth wrapped the book in white silk material then placed it in a brown paper bag with handles. She glanced past Ari towards Leise, then back to Ari. "Ari, I hope you changed your mind about joining us tomorrow night," she whispered.

Ari looked behind her towards Leise, then spoke just as low. "I still don't think it's a good idea. Your people are never going to accept me."

"Don't worry about them. They'll come around. This is about protecting all of us and helping Drew."

"I'll do what I can to help the girl."

"Thank you, and I have a good idea on that protection shield." When Leise came to the counter, Elizabeth spoke louder. "I hope this will help your friend." She handed the bag to Ari. "If you need anything else, please come back."

Ari looked away for a moment when she handed the bag to Leise. When she turned back to say good-bye - Poof, Elizabeth was gone.

CHAPTER 20

*L*atin was a dead language for a reason. Ari thought this same sentiment every time she turned the page of the huge grimoire. Each spell was more confusing than the last. Ari and Leise went back to the condo after leaving the White Cauldron. She tried to explained to Leise that she had to decipher the two spells Elizabeth had suggested and get the ingredients together. Her best friend wanted to wait, then curled up on the couch and started a British car show on Netflix.

Ari didn't know what time it was when she lifted her head out of the book, but she was about ready to quit. She had tried a few spells; one even caused rainbows to sprout from her potted oxalis plants. The small weed looked a lot like a shamrock, but no pot of gold appeared. Failures like this had her questioning her magical prowess.

"Leise, you should go home. I'm not having much luck," Ari said as she closed the large book.

"Nothing?" Leise slid from under the blanket and walked towards her.

"Well, there was one spell that looked promising. But it required a house cleaning, then performing the spell at a place of power."

"You know I don't speak witch." She sat next to Ari.

"I need to make sure no other spirits are in your place before we start. Then perform the spell where ever you see him the most. And from what I read, I think I need Remy to pull it off."

"Okay, let's do it. I'm not tired, are you?"

Ari was exhausted, but seeing the hope and excitement in Leise's face, she gave in. "Sure. Let me grab a few things."

)O(

LESS THAN AN HOUR LATER, Ari had walked through every room in Leise's place with a sage smudge stick. "Okay, the cleansing is done. Now, I need to know where you see him most often?"

Leise lifted her brows, looked up, then blushed as she quickly looked at her hands.

Ari's eyes followed Leise's, and her eyes lit with understanding as her friend turned a new shade of red. "Right, come on then." She grabbed Leise's hand and led her upstairs.

Leise dropped to her bed like a rock, then fell back with her arms over her chest like an old style vampire. Ari sat on the edge of the bed next to her and gently unfolded her best friends arms. "That's just a little too Morticia Addams for my taste." Her fingers grazed Leise's cheeks, coaxing her to look at her.

Finally, she did.

"I need for you to relax. This isn't a root canal," Ari said with a smile. "Now let me see the necklace."

Leise sat up to pull it out of her t-shirt.

"Leave it." Ari reached out when Leise moved to pull it over her head.

The amethyst lit up in a purple brilliance when Ari's hand grazed it. She snatched her hand away quickly. The crystal's bright light died away. She waved her hand near it, and 'Hello, Las Vegas,' it lit up again. The crystal's beauty brought a smile to her face. Sure, she now knew it held a long list of nearly impossible properties, but sometimes a girl liked to appreciate something beautiful.

"Bren said that might happen." Leise lifted the crystal to look at it closer.

"Bren, huh?" Ari lifted her one imperious brow.

Leise blushed. "Shut up."

Ari's laughed died down to a giggle. "Okay, okay. What might happen?"

"That the crystal would illuminate when near strong magic." Leise rolled the crystal between two fingers, staring at it before she let it go.

Ari paced near the bed, nodding, then looked around the room. "Where is that boy?"

Leise looked around like she would spot Remy first.

"Remy! Get your invisible butt in here."

"Merde, Cher. You needn't yell," Remy said from the other side of the bed.

With hands on her hips, she said, "Could you just float inside her necklace please?"

Leise looked from Ari to the empty spot next to her.

Remy hovered over Leise's body.

Goosebumps raced up Leise's arm. "I take it Remy is just above me."

Ari nodded. "Well, give it a go."

Remy arced like he was taking a swan dive into a lake.

"Oh my God!" Leise gasped as her body spasmed. "So cold."

Ari watched Remy's ghostly form emerge back on the other side of the bed. "So that didn't work." Ari grabbed the afghan from the foot of the bed and wrapped her up.

When Leise finally stopped gasping for breath, Ari asked her how she usually visited Brennan.

"I don't know how I do it. I fall asleep, then wake up there." Leise shrugged off the afghan.

"Okay, let's try that then." Ari urged her to lie back.

"I'm not sleepy though." Leise pushed against Ari's hand.

"I understand, but if you want to help him. I need for you to do this. Lay back and close your eyes."

Once Leise complied, Ari grabbed her bag and sat with it on the bed. She rummaged through it and pulled out three small vials, and gave them each a shake. She pulled out a white sachet, then sniffed it, then snatched her face back from it. "Okay, not that one." She quickly dropped it back in her bag and rummaged around again. After a moment or two of digging, she pulled out a medicinal dropper and a purple sachet. She lifted the sachet to her nose and inhaled and smiled.

She put her bag on the floor and pulled the bulky tome out. "I'm going to do a betwixting spell."

This spell allowed a person to have one foot in this world and one in another. The vials contained a little something extra that would help Leise fall asleep. She flipped through the pages and read through the spell, then used the dropper to place three drops from each small container onto the sachet.

"A what?" Leise's eyes flitted between Ari and the vials in her hands.

"Betwixting. You will be half asleep and aware of this world while you are wide awake in the other. Kind of like a waking dream." Ari massaged the sachet, as she sat back next to Leise.

"Will it hurt? What's in it?"

"No, it won't hurt. It's just lavender, valerian, and other herbs. It'll just help you doze off, I promise. Now, lay back so we can try this again."

Once Leise laid back, Ari placed the sachet into a small bowl and struck a match. Instead of catching fire, the bag smoldered. "Remy, when she begins to doze, I need you to enter that crystal. Whatever magic that allows her in, should allow you in as well."

Remy gave her a stiff nod.

The dark gray smoke filled the bowl, and then slowly crept over the edges, like a low moving fog. Ari waited until the smoke reached the floor before she walked with the bowl around the peninsula of the bed and back.

Leise's nostrils flared as she inhaled the smoke surrounding her bed. "It smells kinda like a garden."

"Shhh. Sopor somnus."

Leise smiled and closed her eyes.

When Leise's breathing leveled off, Ari whispered. "Now."

WHATEVER ELSE WAS in that smoke, it made Leise feel like she had become cloud nine, not just floating on it. Leise heard Ari say, 'Now.' She wasn't sure who the girl was talking to because the next thing she saw was complete darkness.

Ari's spell was not gentle. She had hit the ground with a thud, and if this were her real body, she would've cracked her tailbone. She groggily moved as she sat up in a field of tall, feather-topped grass. This spell didn't quite have the same effect as natural sleep. Standing up felt like that first step when getting out of a pool, sluggish and heavy. But finally, she stood up. Not far from her stood a tall, dark-haired stranger, rubbing his hands back and forth over the feathery tops of the grass.

Instinctually she knew but asked anyway. "Remy? Is that you?" Never in her wildest dreams, did she think this day would happen. The spell had pulled him into the necklace with her. She began to walk towards him. He had to be at least six-three, a swimmer's build with slim shoulders, midnight hair and the clearest blue eyes she'd ever seen. Ari's description did him no justice. He stood firmly on this side of being a demi-god.

His head snapped up, and his eyes looked glassy. "C'est incroyables." He touched his chest, then face.

Leise's high-school French wouldn't help her if he said anymore, but she was pretty sure he said, "Incredible."

She held her arms wide. With his size, she braced for a bear hug. Instead, he fell to his knees and wrapped his arms around her waist. Strong but gentle arms held her firm. She came out of the hug and held both his hands, looking him over. "Remy, you really need to speak English." She lifted her brows, waiting.

He licked his lips. Opened his mouth, then closed it twice. "Annaleise, you're beautiful. I've always wanted to tell you that."

"Thank you." She gave his hands a strong shake before letting him go. "Now, come on. We need to find Brennan. I don't know how much time we have."

"This place is amazing." He snapped a blade of grass as he walked behind her.

Leise looked around them and as far as the eye could see, miles and miles of grass. "Remy." She spoke, still looking all around. "Remy, take my hand." She extended it to him.

When he didn't respond, she turned around to see him running a stem of grass over his cheek, with his eyes closed. She wanted to give him a minute, but they didn't have it. The smile on his face broke her heart, but they didn't have that luxury today. Maybe soon, he could come and hang out here. A tear rolled down his cheek.

"Oh, it's okay, Remy." She patted his shoulder. It had been more than a century since Remy had touched anything. "Remy," she spoke softer this time, "we really have to go." She held her hand out to him, and he took it.

Leise cleared her mind. Brennan had explained the power of this world. Instead of thinking of warmer temperatures or water-front property, she thought of him.

Brennan.

From one moment to the next, with Remy in tow, she stood in front of Brennan's cottage.

"What the hell! Annaleise, what did you just do?" Remy said as he leaned against a tree and dry heaved.

She hadn't been sure if she could teleport them to Brennan's place. "Pretty cool, huh?" She flexed her fingers. All there. Then she patted her body to make sure everything was where it should be.

"No, Leise. Not cool."

"Stop being a baby and come on." She walked quickly, not quite a run, but her muscles flexed involuntarily. Her impatient self must have been preparing to run. A small cottage with a thatched roof lay in the distance. The gentle breeze carried the fragrance of lavender and rose over her and through her senses, and she knew she was home.

The door flew open before she even touched the knob. The first thing she saw was his smiling eyes, then his oh-so-kissable lips. That smile that said he'd missed her too. Just as quickly, his smile turned into a scowl, when his eyes lifted over her shoulder. In a flash, he snatched her behind him. She didn't know he could move so fast.

Leise had been fairly sure Brennan didn't have a weapon, but wouldn't have staked her life, or Remy's on it. She felt a rush of giddiness at his protectiveness but pushed that down quick when she felt her cheeks warm. With a mental shake, she opened her mouth to explain, but Brennan began to bellow.

"Who are you? How did you get here?"

Remy lifted his eyebrows towards Leise, who blushed again. "Leise?"

"Annaleise, you know him?" Brennan turned back to look at her.

His angry eyes snapped her out of her schoolgirl lust. She ducked under Brennan's arm to move to stand next to Remy, grabbing his arm to bring the two guys closer. "Yes, yes. This is Remy. You remember I told you about him." She waved towards Remy. "Remy, meet Brennan. Remy entered with me," she said proudly.

Brennan's eyes went from deep slits, where it was clear he was measuring the man up, to wide-eyed surprise, when he looked at her. So wide in fact, for the first time, she saw flecks of deep blue she'd never seen before.

"The ghost?" Brennan's brogue became thicker, and the words started to run together. "He doesn't look like a specter to me."

"I know. Ari did a spell and surprise, Remy's not quite invisible."

Brennan grabbed her by the face and gave her a big kiss. "You wonderful girl. You finally asked your friend Aramais to help me? Is Buster helping her? I met him as well. Now, he appeared very ghostlike."

Her heart tightened at the joy she had brought him.

"Why didn't Ari come?" He rubbed his hand up and down her arms a few times mindlessly before he removed them altogether.

"She hadn't figured out how to yet, but she sent Remy in her stead. To see if he could enter." Her eyes cut to Remy.

Remy extended his hand. "Remy-Pierre Arceneaux. Enchanté."

Brennan grasped the outstretched hand firmly. "Brennan Drake of the Clan Dubhghall and for a ghost, you feel very real."

Remy smiled. "In the real world, this is not how I appear." He touched his chest. "This place," he looked around, "is amazing." No one could mistake the level of awe in his voice.

"After a few hundred years or so of solitude, 'Amazing,' is not the word that comes to mind when I think of it."

"Je comprende," Remy said with a smile and nodded.

Brennan turned to Leise, who stood nearby, and asked, "Does your witch have a plan?"

She had opened her mouth, to answer when she lifted her eyes towards the sky. "Did you hear that?"

Brennan looked at Remy, who shook his head as he walked to stand beside them. They both stared at Leise.

"Hear what, Annaleise?" Brennan looked up, then at her with concern.

"Ari," she said absently, then held up a finger to stall any more questions. "She wants to know if we made it okay." Louder, she said, "Yes, we are all here. What do you want us to do?" She spoke to the sky.

"Uh-huh. Yeah. Got it." Leise looked into the expectant eyes of the men near her and wished she had better news. "No exit strategy yet, but the sleep spell should wear off in five minutes or so." She looked at Remy, "Ari thinks we should be touching when that happens. She's not quite sure, but thinks you guys will become roomies if I leave without you touching me."

"Je comprende. I will let you two say your goodbyes." Remy gave a slight bow to Brennan, "Until next time." He turned to walk on the far side of the cottage, towards the gardens.

Brennan watched until Remy disappeared, then grabbed Leise's hands. "Thank you so much. This is the first time I've ever had any hope of getting out of here, and it's all because of you."

Leise could feel her cheeks heating up. When he ran his fingers over them, then back and forth on her bottom lip, she thought she would explode from just those small things. What would it be like to make love to this man? Dangerous. She tried to shake off what he was doing to her. Her words were a bit breathy when she finally spoke. "It's what anybody would do."

She looked at the ground when she spoke. The words embarrassed her somehow. Brennan took her chin between two fingers to make Leise look him in the eyes. "I've been in here a long time." She tried to look away. He placed both palms against her cheeks, then continued, "From my limited knowledge of the crystal, each possessor should have the power to enter, and in all my time here, I have not seen a soul. So, thank you."

His powerful hands tilted her head slightly, as his lips lightly brushed against hers. When her arms moved around his neck, that seemed to be the green light, and the kiss deepened. Leise was happy to discover kissing hadn't changed much in 300 years. Although Brennan nipped her bottom lip when they came up for air, she suspected that was his own unique twist, and it made her toes curl.

On an exhale, he finally released her mouth. His forehead touched hers, "I know, love." He growled. She pulled away from him still keeping contact with his arm, then elbow, then fingers. With a light shake from Brennan, she let his fingers go as well.

"Remy. Come on, it's time to go," Leise called out.

Remy walked out from around the cottage sniffing a rose. "Already?"

Leise nodded. "I know. I know, but maybe when we get Brennan out, you can come back." She held her hand out, and Remy's fingers intertwined with hers. She didn't miss the frown Brennan gave when she touched the other man. She told him in her sweetest voice that she would see him later, just to break his glare. She closed her eyes, and when she opened them a second later, she was staring into the gorgeous hazel eyes of her best friend.

"Welcome back," Ari said, with a huge smile.

Leise slowly moved into a sitting position, when Ari moved from lingering over her. "I feel like I slept a week." She massaged her neck and rolled her shoulders.

"Yeah, side effects, sorry about that. So it worked," Ari beamed. "How's your boyfriend?" Ari asked in a sing-song voice.

Leise rolled her eyes. She knew better to engage her friend when she asked questions, which were not really questions, in that annoying voice. "I saw Remy."

"I figured you would," Ari shrugged a shoulder.

"What? Why didn't you tell me?"

"The supernatural is a strange thing. I wasn't sure exactly how he would appear to you, so I thought it best not to even go into it," Ari said.

Leise spoke softly, "What did Remy tell you?"

"Nothing, oddly enough. Any other day he's a Cajun Chatty Cathy. He seemed...I don't know...solemn, then he disappeared. What happened to him in there?"

"In that world, he's corporeal. He touched my hand, we hugged, and I swear I saw a tear roll down his face."

"Wow, I never expected that. That had to be a shock." Ari looked around the room. "No wonder he left without a word."

"Since that worked, you have any ideas on how to get Brennan out?" Leise asked hopefully.

"Some, but nothing to talk about yet."

"When can we try again?"

"May Day is in a couple of days, plus it's a full moon. A lot of magical energy will be swirling around. That should be the best night for it."

"Okay." Leise stared at Ari. "I'll be ready."

Ari began to pack up her stuff and the book. "Why are you staring at me like that?"

"What? No, I was just thinking."

"About what?" Ari pulled her bag over her shoulder.

"So, um...what's up with you and Heath?"

"What?" Ari tried to hide her smile. "I don't know what you mean."

"So, it's getting serious, huh?"

"I don't know about all that, but..." Ari paused like she was choosing her words carefully. "I think I'm ready to tell him...about me."

Leise's eyes widened. "Really? You think he's the one?"

"I think he's special and different. So, yeah, maybe." Ari patted

Leise's leg. "Give me a hug." She stood with her arms wide. "I won't be around tomorrow; I've decided to help a young white witch with her firepower."

"At that magic store?"

Ari nodded. "I'm so nervous. I'm not a teacher."

"Think about what makes you happy," Leise said when they pulled apart. "If magic makes you feel free and brings you joy - tell them about that."

"Sage advice. Thanks," Ari said.

"That's just what my mom used to say when I couldn't figure out what to write for school papers. 'Find the joy in whatever you do.'"

"Your mom was a smart woman."

This was the first time in a long while that Leise didn't want to cry after thinking about her mom. Her heart tightened, but it was from joy. "She was."

"Okay, I'm outta here, but I'll send Remy to hang with you. If there's trouble, he can find me fast."

"As long as he doesn't go through me again, he can hang out all he wants." Leise rubbed her arms.

"I'll let him know."

CHAPTER 21

"Fire!" Elizabeth yelled from the middle of the training room.

Ari launched two baseball sized fireballs towards the petite woman. Elizabeth seemed smaller than normal as she stood with her arm across her body. Ari imagined under the woman's long, flowy skirt, she had squat in a defensive stance, bracing for the hit in case their latest shield bracelet incarnation didn't work.

They had been working on different runes and spells over the last hour. Something that would protect better than Ari's St. Brigit's cross. They tried necklaces and rings to find what would give the wearer the most protection. They settled on a copper bracelet with two rune carved crystals.

Before the blast hit, Elizabeth was snatched up unceremoniously from behind and thrown behind Old Baldie. He extended his blue and white marble wand as he spoke and a wall of water tall as himself formed washing out the small balls of flame. Then just as fast, tennis balls sized water blasted out like shots from a gun.

Ari had taken off her protection cross when they started testing the bracelet, so she had no defense against the first few water blasts.

They knocked her back but not down. Piercing her skin like bee stings.

"Stop this, this instant," Elizabeth yelled. "Marjorie, let me go." She broke the hold from the large woman standing behind her, presumably protecting her. She touched the water witch's shoulder, "Signet, stand down."

The man looked around wild-eyed, but the water shots had ceased. "What are you talking about, this black witch attacked you? You know they can't be trusted."

"I asked her to," Elizabeth spoke in her regular tone now. A chorus of what and why came from Majorie and Signet. "We were testing out this new protection bracelet." She lifted her right arm. "What you did was uncalled for."

"How was he to know?" Marjorie went to the man and put her arm around his waist.

"I've already explained that Ms. Mason would be coming to our meetings."

Marjorie looked back at Ari, then towards Elizabeth. She tried to whisper, but she couldn't disguise the hate in her voice. "You can't trust them. No matter what they say."

Elizabeth's lips tightened. "I understand you have your reasons for feeling this way, but I have looked into Ari and I trust her. Also, Marjorie, I meant to say something sooner but Ari will be taking over Drusilla's training."

"What?" The woman moved out of Signet's arm. "We can't expose our children to her type."

"I think it's for the best."

Marjorie huffed before she stomped out. Signet followed behind her.

Ari walked over to Elizabeth. "I didn't mean to cause a rift."

Elizabeth waved her hand. "It had been building for some time. She'll be back, if only to say I told you so."

Ari didn't say anything, but she could see that the older woman had that way about her. "We've all taken turns trying to help Drew, but she has been particularly harsh with the girl. But I'm sure you are exactly what she needs." She took off the bracelet and handed it to Ari. "I think this is ready. Mind that it doesn't seal you in a bubble, but a shield."

Ari felt the magic the moment the metal made contact with her skin. It had a light touch, like fluttering butterfly wings. "Normally, my magic doesn't react well to metal. What kind of metal is this?"

"It's an infused copper."

"Ms. Elizabeth!" The young girls screamed when they entered the training room. She wrapped her arms around them.

Ari wanted to yell, infused with what? But the room was filling up, and Elizabeth had already moved away.

"Come on in everyone. I have some news."

)O(

"LIGG-NIA!" A young woman's voice rang out throughout the training room. It wasn't a 'ki-ai' yell, like from a karate class, but it sounded like it for a minute. Ari watched the teenager's lips move and could faintly hear the girl recite a spell, before thrusting her wand outward. "Abscindo ligna!" The six foot wooden board about ten feet from her only cracked. "Dammit."

"Language," Marjorie said.

"Sorry, Mrs. Guilderoy."

Marjorie clapped her hands. "Now, try again."

Ari had been surprised that Signet and Marjorie came back, but Elizabeth said that they would. Needless to say, that when Elizabeth announced that we had created a stronger shield to protect them, they were the first to decree they would never wear anything created by a black witch. That didn't deter Elizabeth, she forged ahead with the introductions. Most of the witches were very welcoming, and it made Ari feel better about her decision to be there.

Not too far from Ari, Drew and Oriana worked on lighting the candle again. Drew's face fell when the candle looked exactly the same - the wick unlit and smoke rose from her wand.

"It's either," Elizabeth said from next to Ari. "She burns everything to a crisp or nothing at all."

Ari took a deep breath to calm her thumping heart. Of course, the woman's sudden appearance didn't frighten her, just startled her a bit. *How does she do that?*

Drew flicked the wand up and down, while her mouth moved in a fierce litany of words. Ari could hear the spell but could see it wasn't working.

"Are you ready?" Elizabeth stepped out, and Ari nodded before she followed.

When they reached the girls, Oriana had lit three candles and had made them levitate. Drew didn't look jealous or even mad, just sad when she whispered, "You are so talented."

"Hello," Elizabeth said. "Well done, Oriana. Now, you remember Ms. Mason." The girls vigorously nodded as Ari cringed at being called *Ms. Mason*. "She's here to help Drew with her fire powers."

Drew's eyes widened to encompass her entire face at those words and her smile was just as wide. "Really?"

Ari smiled at the girl's reaction. Seeing Drew's face was the same reason she volunteered with the seniors and with the children's festival. Helping others is what brought her joy. "Yes."

"I will leave you to it. Come along Oriana." Elizabeth extended her hand to lead the young girl away.

Oriana's lips pouted as she looked between her friend, Ari, and Elizabeth, then crossed her arms. "I want to stay with Drew."

"But this lesson is for Drusilla," Elizabeth said.

"But, but…" The girl looked even younger as her bottom lip went out a little further.

Ari's heart broke because she knew this feeling. When they put Lucas in guard training; they wouldn't take her. She must have cried a month. "It's okay. She can stay."

Elizabeth stepped closer and lowered her voice. "Are you sure?"

Ari looked at the girls who clutched each others' arms. "Positive. We won't be doing anything too strenuous today. It'll be fine."

Elizabeth gave a nod before she glided away.

Ari turned back to the two glowing faces. *Was she ever this young and innocent? This impressionable?* She would do for them what no one did for her. She reached out her hands. "Come along ladies." She led them away from the candles to a quiet corner.

All three sat cross-legged on the floor away from everyone else. "Tell me about your power," Ari said.

Drew frowned. "I don't understand what you mean."

"Do your hands feel hot when you try to use your power? Does it only work right when you're mad or scared?"

Her face lit up then. "Oh, well," she tapped her chin, "my momma sent me to bed early once, and I burned my comforter. I was mad, but my hands didn't get hot or anything."

"And you Oriana, how does your magic feel?"

The girl didn't speak for a while. She had a faraway look like she was concentrating on a truthful answer. "When I touch a person, it's like putting my hands into warm oil, I guess, then whatever they're feeling rushes through me as the pictures appear in my head. Also, my magic seems to work better at night. I find it hard to concentrate during the day."

Ari hadn't expected that much information but found it interesting all the same. As Oriana spoke, Drew picked at her shoelaces, then glanced up occasionally as she fidgeted, but hadn't said a word.

"Drew, you want to ask me something?"

Drew looked at Oriana, who nodded slowly, then back towards her shoes. "We were wondering if you would…if it's not too much trouble. Would you show us your power?" She didn't look up as she fumbled through asking.

Ari's heart tightened as she listened to the girl. "Sure. You ready?"

They both looked at her and nodded eagerly. Ari placed her hand in the center of their tight circle. She closed her eyes, and her power churned at her core. In her mind's eye, her core was a lake of fire, and she placed her hand in it for just a little. When she opened her eyes, a quarter-sized ball of golden flame had formed, then it increased into a baseball size.

"How did you do that?" Drew asked almost wistfully.

"And without a wand?" Oriana had asked at the same time.

It had been a while since she had to think about how her powers worked, it was kind of refreshing. She closed her hand and the fire went out.

"When I first came into my power, the only way I could get a fire to start was to imagine myself striking a match."

Drew pointed her wand in the middle of their group. Ari quickly grabbed the tip of the wooden stick with two fingers. "Why don't we try it without the wand first?"

"But, but all witches…" Drew started.

"Let's try this first." Ari cut in with a smile. "You should get a feel for your power. If you really want to use a wand later, we will. Alright?" When Drew nodded and relinquished the wand, Ari continued, "Hold out your hand and close your eyes." She had only been speaking to Drew, but both of the girls did as she asked.

Ari lowered her voice, but not as low as a whisper. "Think of a box of matches. You have that?" They both nodded. "Now, take a match from the box and pulls it across the striker."

The girls didn't have to say if they had done it or not. The evidence was before her eyes. A small flame flickered in the palm of Drew's hand. Then a life-sized hologram of Oriana unsuccessfully striking a match over and over appeared around them.

"Whatever you are feeling now, hold on to it, and open your eyes."

When Oriana opened her eyes, the virtual version of herself held up a lit match. Drew pulled her hand closer to her face and smiled at the tiny fire. It wasn't much bigger than a dime.

"I did it. I did it," Drew said. Her flame mimicked her excitement and began to grow. "Ari." The ball of fire was a little bigger than a baseball. "Ari, help me please."

"Calm down." Ari took Drew's other hand and put it over the now soccer sized flame and pressed it down until the girl's hand touched and the fire had gone out. The girl's eyes were wide with shock, fear, a bit of exhilaration. "You okay?"

The corner of Drew's lips quirked up, then her eyes focused on Ari's as a real smile spread across her face. Before she could say what her face expressed, a nasty snarl rang out from across the room.

"That's why she needs a wand," Marjorie said, pointing an accusing finger at Ari.

Drew's smile fell, and she lost her glow with those words. She looked back at the woman, then to Ari with tears in her eyes.

"Don't listen to her, you did great," Ari said, as she patted the girl's cheek and wiped away the tears.

Drew looked younger than her thirteen years when her bottom lip quivered. "You sure? She's an adult witch. She should know."

"Fire is hard to contain and control. Others don't understand that."

Oriana pulled her into a hug. "Yes. Mrs. Guilderoy is a mean woman."

"You hear me, witch. You shouldn't even be near our children." Majorie stomped over towards them. Her husband moved like a caged tiger behind her. But it seemed like he was content with letting his woman take the lead.

The girls moved to get up, but Ari touched their shoulders to keep them seated as she got up. "Stay here girls," Ari whispered.

Ari tightened her lips as she kept a lid on all the feelings churning inside of her. She was aware that everyone in the training room had stopped talking, she could've heard a pin drop. She held her fist tight as she walked towards the older woman.

"What is wrong with you?" Ari whispered angrily. "She's a child."

Marjorie did not attempt to lower her voice. "Do you even know the first thing about teaching young witches?" Her face scrunched up in accusation.

"I know what it's like to be a young witch with fire powers, do you?"

She flinched like Ari had slapped her, then spoke with even more vileness. "I know that black witches are born evil. Do not come here and taint our children with your darkness."

It was Ari's time to step back like she had been slapped. Her mouth had dropped open, and she really looked at the woman before her. How could a person have this much nastiness in them? She focused on the aura around the woman before her and there it was as clear as the woman's snarling lips. "What are you so afraid of?"

A cool smoke rose from Majorie's clenched fists.

"Ladies," Elizabeth's voice was faint as she called out from a few feet away.

"Heavens forbid they learn something from me." Ari knew those were the wrong words to say the moment she uttered them. She'd braced herself for an attack, but instead, she felt two warm bodies move between her and Marjorie.

A virtual picture of a dark-haired, green-eyed boy swirled around them.

"Kellan," Signet said reverently. "Oriana, don't do this."

Kellan kissed a younger, happier version of Marjorie, then hugged a man with a full head of dark brown hair. Signet's smile was just as bright as the boy's.

Marjorie looked at the picture with tears streaming down her face. Then her head began to move back and forth. "No, no." She slapped Oriana's hand away and knocked the girl to the floor. She walked through the face of the smiling boy before the image faded away. Signet ran after his wife.

"Are you okay?" Ari helped ease Oriana up.

"Oriana, don't move too fast," Elizabeth said, as she helped steady the girl as well.

"Please say you're okay. I told you not to do it," Drew said.

"I know," Oriana said, as she pushed to get up.

"What did I just see?" Ari asked no one in particular.

"Her son went over to the dark side," Oriana said. "No offense."

"None taken," Ari said with a smile.

"You are okay, though?" Elizabeth touched the young girl's cheek. Once Oriana nodded, Elizabeth smiled, then clapped, and said in a louder voice, "Everyone, I think we'll shut down for the evening." Elizabeth walked towards the exit.

Ari followed Elizabeth. "I didn't mean for that to happen. I mean, she just..." she bit her bottom lip. "They're children. We should be encouraging them. It made me so mad that she would say such hurtful things."

"She's had a hard time since Kellan left," Elizabeth said.

Ari quirked her lip with one lifted eyebrow, that screamed, Really?

Elizabeth waved her hands in surrender. "I know, I know. That's no excuse for her behavior. She's…" Elizabeth's eyebrows scrunched together like she was searching for the right word.

"A bitch," Ari supplied.

"Complicated," Elizabeth said with a smile, but she hadn't disagreed with Ari's stellar assessment of Mrs. Guilderoy.

When Ari walked out of the building, Oriana and Drew were standing next to a man and a woman. Just great, another set of mad parents, she thought. Maybe this gig wasn't worth it.

The girls ran to her, and each grabbed a hand. "Hey, girls, what's going on?"

"We showed our mom what you taught us and she wanted to meet you," Drew said without taking a breath.

"I didn't know you were sisters."

"We are adopting her," Drew supplied. "We're sisters already though."

"Good to know," Ari said, before they stopped at the mid-sized car. Two people got out of the car and met them on the sidewalk.

"Mom, Dad, this is Ms. Ari. She's teaching me to be a good witch with firepower," Drew said, excitedly.

"Ari is fine." She extended her hand.

The parents looked at each other, and then the father shook her hand. "A pleasure. I'm Charles, and this is my wife, Blossom."

The wife extended her hand and Ari shook it. "It's nice to meet you."

"When Elizabeth said a black witch would be helping train our girls, we were naturally skeptical," Charles said.

"True, I was born a black witch, I can't help that. I would hope you guys wouldn't hold that against me. But I'm more than that." Ari realized by she had so much to offer these girls. She wasn't just a black witch learning white magic. She was both. Her knowledge of both witch cultures gave her an advantage and made her stronger than most.

"I believe you," Charles said.

"Drusilla's power—"

"Mom," Drew whined, "It's Drew."

"Drew's power," Blossom continued, "has always been unpredictable. But from what she's shown us tonight. You might be able to help her control it."

"That's the plan. I want you to know - I only have the best intentions where Drew and Oriana are concerned."

Both parents nodded. "We appreciate you helping our girls," Charles said, before they all loaded into the car and drove away.

Ari had a skip in her step after that. This job was worth doing. For the first time, Ari understood who and what she was. She was put on this planet to help others. She was a gray witch - not wholly bad and not entirely good, but just enough of each to understand and control the powers she wielded, and put them to good use.

Now, if she could get Leise's boyfriend out of magical prison, she'd be a rock star.

CHAPTER 22

*A*n avian concerto woke Ari the next day. The birds chirped and tweeted out a cheerful melody. She wiped the sleep out of her half opened eyes. She expended a large amount of magic yesterday, and all she wanted to do was sleep. Unfortunately, the birds took that option off the table. She rolled out of bed and stumbled to the bathroom for a shower. She didn't have anything to do today, with that in mind, she didn't bother fixing her hair and dressed in her most comfortable outfit. She thought of the holes like a self-air-conditioning system in the t-shirt and cut-off shorts.

She stumbled to the kitchen and put the kettle on. She needed something to get her going to tackle the large book on her prep table. She had pulled a few herbs and placed them on the table, then picked a few faint pink rose petals from the bush on her balcony.

The teapot whistled at the same time there was a knock on the door. "Coming."

She wasn't expecting anyone. The wards on her place were strong, and wouldn't let just anyone in, but she checked the peep hole anyway.

"What are you doing here?" Her back slammed against the door as she touched her hair, then her clothes.

There was a protocol to visiting a lady at her home. Just dropping by wasn't it. Today's men needed to read Emily Post's book on etiquette.

Heath's rich voice laughed. "You said I could come over and you'd make me tea and read my cards."

"But not today," she squealed.

"Ari, are we going to have this entire conversation through the door? Open up."

"But, but…you can't see me like this."

"Are you dressed?"

"Yes."

"Then open the door."

This was the first time she wished she had a glamour like in those vampire romances or a fairy godmother. She wouldn't let the man of her dreams see her looking like this. But in the end, she whispered the words that released the wards and hid behind the door as she held it open for him.

The first thing through the door wasn't the tall figure of Irish manliness, but a large wicker picnic basket.

"You brought lunch?"

When Heath walked in, he flinched. Flinched! If she had blinked, she would have missed the subtle movement.

"Oh, interesting look you have there."

"Whatever." She rolled her eyes as she closed the door. "Now, why are you here so early?"

"I wanted to make tea with you. And I as I recall, you promised me a reading."

She really didn't expect that. "Seriously?"

"Of course. Where can I put this?"

Ari held her hand out. "Do I need to refrigerate it?"

"Sure," he said when he gave it to her.

"Have a seat," she said as she walked into the kitchen and placed the basket in the fridge. "You want something to drink?"

"No, I'm okay," he called from the living room.

When she returned to the main room, Heath was looking at the plants on the balcony. She stood in the sliding door watching as he touched the petals and leaves of different plants. "You like plants?"

"This one reminds me of home." He touched the shamrock shaped plant.

"That's an oxalis," Ari said. She was about to talk about the plant when a flicker of golden sparks floated down like snowflakes near Heath's hand. "Come on in," she waved her hand insistently, "we can do that reading now if you want?"

"But," Heath moved to turn back.

"No worries," Ari grabbed his free hand and moved him away from the potted plants, "you can look at those later."

Ari hustled him off the balcony without him seeing the remnants of magic below him. She looked back, and a small rainbow had just blossom from the plant in a high curving arc, spanning the entire balcony. There would have been no way he would have missed the colorful display.

Once inside, Ari had paused near the couch, but Heath had moved straight to the leather tome on her country prep table.

"We can do the reading over here," Ari called out.

"What's this?" He turned the pages. "I didn't know you knew Latin?"

His impromptu visit threw her off her game, she'd forgotten all about the grimoire. She rushed over and moved the book away from his fingers.

"I speak a little," she said as she wrapped the book back in its white silk material.

"It looks like an antique."

"It is. I was helping my friend Leise with some research." Ari moved towards her bedroom.

"Ari, wait." He followed her. "You don't have to hide who you are with me." He placed his hand on the book. "I know that you read tarot cards. I see your gypsy style of clothes and your home is full of plants and crystals. You even wear a St. Brigit's cross. I see you, Ari Mason."

She nibbled her bottom lip. It was all she could do not to blurt

out what she was. He had no idea what he was offering her. His eyes
bore into hers as he waited. This may be the first time, in a long
time, she was speechless. She had waited for so long for someone to
say those words to her. She wasn't sure why she wasn't yelling out
that she was a witch.

"I know what you are and you don't have to be ashamed."
Heath's hands moved slowly towards her face and cupped her
cheeks.

She froze under his touch. *How did he know? And for how long?* A
croak of barely audible words came from Ari. "You do?"

"You practically wear it on your sleeves. You're Wiccan."

She'd let out a breath she hadn't realized she was holding.
"Wiccan?"

"It's pretty obvious, and you know what? I'm okay with it."

Wow! He was okay with her being Wiccan, she thought. She nodded
but didn't confirm or deny his assessment of her nature.

Heath pointed at her book with a smile when she had stayed
silent. "I'm not much for Latin, but I can Google like nobody's
business."

They both laughed, then Ari said, "Thank you, Heath. You're
an amazing individual. I will certainly keep your Googling prowess
in mind on my next project, but I think I got this for right now." She
tapped the book. "Take a seat at the table. I'll put this up, and we'll
get started."

)O(

WHEN ARI WALKED BACK into the living room, dressed in a hole-free
t-shirt and yoga pants, Heath had cleared the plants from the bench
side of the table. She couldn't remember the last time there had
been a man in her place. She'd grabbed a set of tarot cards from her
bedroom.

"Are you ready?" Ari took a seat in front of Heath.

He looked at her curiously. "Not really. You know you didn't
have to change on account of me. I'm the one who just
showed up."

"I was going to have to put on some decent clothes at some point." She shuffled the cards. "Have you done this before?"

"I've seen it done." He couldn't figure out where to put his hands. On the table folded, then off the table.

She got the vibe he was nervous. His body moved like he was thumping his leg like a rabbit. She decided not to do a full reading. For all his gusto, it didn't look like he would make it that long. She decided to do a three-card spread. This reading was just to get a feeling of what he needed in his life.

Heath didn't cut the deck, only tapped the top card. Ari spread the cards out in a long line straight across. "Don't look so nervous. I'm not pulling teeth." She extended her hand across the table, palm up.

He pulled his hand from under the table, and his incessant bobbing stopped. His hand was moist as he slid it into hers. The touch seemed to calm him. He let out a long exhale. She wondered why he would subject himself to this if he was this nervous?

"Now, pick three cards."

He held her fingers tighter in one hand as he pointed to three cards. She wanted to tell him that wasn't how a reading worked. He needed to touch the cards, and put his energy into them. But she didn't want him any more distressed than he already was.

She released his hand and slid the cards in front of her before flipping them over.

Ari looked at the cards and smiled. They read like a timeless fairy tale: a knight in shining armor, a guy and a girl, rainbows with a happy ending.

"Well, what does it say?" Heath's voice strained out.

"Heath, you are a romantic. Everything here is about you finding love and happiness."

"Really?"

"I would have never guessed," Ari smirked. "Come on, let's get your ingredients."

He followed her to the balcony where they picked some lavender and red rose petals. She grabbed some dried ginger and pome-granate from the kitchen, along with a few other things for taste, then they got to work. She showed him how to use the pestle and mortar. After ten minutes, the frown on his face told her he wouldn't make it much longer.

A few hours later, they had a taste-worthy tea. It was more pomegranate than anything else, but as long as the customer liked it, that was all that matters. Ari and Heath were cleaning up when a rumble sounded through the dining room. It sounded like the neighbors were moving furniture.

"I guess you're hungry," Heath said with a laugh.

Ari wanted to fall into a hole, never to be seen again. But with her luck, he'd still be able to hear her tummy growl. "I'm feeling a bit peckish."

"I'm on it." Heath grabbed the picnic basket from the kitchen. Then opened her fridge to retrieve the wine.

Ari liked him all the more when he didn't comment on her lack of food in the refrigerator. Milk, eggs, and bread were her staples. If she wanted anything else, she'd just order take out. She had yet to find the joy of cooking.

She'd put the last few dishes into the drain board. When she stepped out of the kitchen, she didn't see Heath. She'd assumed they would go to the park since they were having a picnic. He must have been downstairs already. Her keys rattled as she headed towards the door.

Heath popped up from behind the sofa. "Where are you going?"

"Aren't we having a picnic?" She walked back towards him.

"Yes." Heath reached out for her. She laid her keys and purse on the sofa before she took his hand. "Right here."

Heath led her to the red gingham tablecloth; it took up the entire area between her couch and wall.

Ari looked at the spread and nearly cried. The cards were right; he was a romantic at heart. She leaned over and admired Heath's attention to detail. The sesame crackers were in a circle on an actual plate. Three different types of meat and three different kinds of cheese lay alternated on a wooden chopping block.

He stood and handed her a glass of white wine. There were no words, but apparently tears. He wiped under both her eyes. "Hey, hey. Why are you crying?"

"I'm just happy." No one had ever done something like this for her. She wiped her face and sniffled. She was happy she hadn't put on any makeup. This would have gotten real ugly, real quick. She turned her head to wipe her face, but Heath didn't let her move away from him. His firms hands held her by the waist until she stopped fidgeting.

"No more tears, okay?" His thumb wiped the tears from both cheeks.

She nodded and stepped out of his grasp, then took a seat on the corner of the tablecloth and looked at everything. "What do we have here?" She needed for him to stop looking at her like that.

He parked it next to her. "Try this." He picked a large strawberry from the bowl of colorful grapes and golf ball sized strawberries, then put it to her lips.

Never taking her eyes from his, she leaned in, slowly took it into her mouth and bit down. She felt the juices burst from the fruit, sweet on her tongue. She felt sexy. She wanted the moment to be sensual. Well, the fruit had other ideas. When she bit into it, juice went everywhere. Down his hand, across her face. She had to admit that was the sweetest and juiciest strawberry she'd ever had. He grabbed a napkin and wiped juice from both cheeks and even up over her eye. She spoke after swallowing the mouthful. "Oh, yeah. That was good."

They talked and nibbled on meat and cheese until it was all gone. He cleaned away the small dishes. *This guy was a keeper.*

"And for dessert." He pulled out a small box and sat it in front of her.

She knew that pink box, a little french bakery a couple of blocks away. She shimmied the top off and her mouth watered at the sight of four petit fours. Each small cake was covered in white frosting, with a strand of pearl candy under a red rose. They were like little works of art. She almost couldn't eat them. Almost.

Ari picked up the little cake between two fingers, but instead of taking a bite, she held it to Heath's lips. His eyes held hers as he took the entire cake into his mouth.

She gasped, but his firm grip held her fingers in place. He drew each finger into his hot, moist mouth. She closed her eyes to the sensation. It had been a long time since any of her girl parts had lifted their heads and said, "Hello."

When he wrapped his strong hands around the nape of her neck and pulled her in, she didn't resist. His lips pressed against hers. She never thought his lips would be so soft. He pulled back and smiled before he lightly nipped her bottom lip. When he moved in again, his lips were more insistent. Strong hands pulled her into him.

Bam. Bam. Bam.

Ari would like to think she was so caught up that she didn't hear someone knocking on her door. She kept kissing, hoping the person would go away.

"Ari? You home?"

Ari pulled back but gave him one last peck on the lips. "Sorry." She crawled up on weak legs. Yes, that boy could kiss. She opened the door without looking through the peep hole because she already knew who it was.

Leise rushed in. "What's wrong with your phone? I tried to call you. Buster called…"

Heath stood and waved. "Hello, Leise."

Leise's mouth dropped open as she looked between Ari at the door and Heath shaking out napkins. "Oh, Ari, I am so sorry. It's just, it's important."

"Okay, give me a second to clean up, then you can tell me," Ari said.

Heath had just folded the tablecloth and placed it under the basket. "There nothing to clean. I packed it all up. These are for you." He handed her the pink box.

She took it from him, then wrapped her arms around his neck. "Thank you. This had to be the best picnic, hands down."

"I enjoyed myself." He leaned into the hug more, lips touching her ear. "Maybe we can finish what we started soon."

Ari didn't think her dark skin could blush a bright pink, but her entire face warmed at his words. She put her face down to hide the look she knew he'd be able to read.

He lifted her chin. "Look at that." He kissed the apple of both her cheeks. "You're blushing. I'll keep that in mind. My girl likes dirty talk."

That made her blush even more. The way he said, 'dirty' made it sound positively filthy. She pulled away. "Shut up and go. I'll call you tomorrow."

"You better." He pulled her in for one more kiss, fast and hard.

Ari closed the door and exhaled loudly.

"Wow." Leise shook her head. "Aramais Mason is in love."

"Am not." Ari touched her cheeks. She couldn't stop from smiling, and the little flutter in her heart told her that maybe Heath could be the one. "Now, tell me what happened?"

"Telly possessed Buster and left us a message."

CHAPTER 23

*A*ri, Leise, and Remy stood in front of an all-night washateria. Ari opened, then closed her mouth, before she finally said, "A washateria."

Bust-a-Sud buzzed in baby blue neon, with white neon suds bubbling up. Although, the 'u' and 'd' had burned out, leaving the word, Bust-a-S.

"Buster lives in a washateria?" Ari looked around in astonishment. The laundry-mat was sandwiched between a Zumba studio and a Chinese food restaurant in a small strip mall.

Leise frowned. "I think it's more above the washateria. But yeah..." She looked at the piece of paper in her hands. "This is it." She walked forward and opened the door.

A bell chimed as they entered. Inside, a young woman in cut-off jean shorts and a midriff-showing red tee flipped through a fashion magazine across from the two orange-brown dryers - the only ones spinning. A middle-aged woman in a multicolored muu-muu that reached her ankles stood at the folding table. Her pink satin hair bonnet revealed a few pink foam rollers underneath, and a cigarette bobbed from the corner of her mouth. She moved back and forth as she folded clothes, and the ash extended the long length of the cigarette without disintegrating. A little boy about seven ran around with a plane in his hand.

"Ladies," Buster called, as he waved to them from the back corner.

He stood in front of a heavy metal door that read, Employees Only. He wore black parachute pants; a red, green, and gold Baja style hoodie; and a crocheted slouch beanie in the same colors. The beanie expanded to about four times its size, and held his headful of dreads.

Ari spoke when they reached him. "Buster, interesting place you have here."

"It's a living." He opened the door. "Matilda!" He yelled to the muu-muu wearing woman. "What have I said about you smoking in here?"

The yell must have startled the woman, and the long line of ash fell onto the stack of clean white clothes, just before she pulled the cigarette butt out of her mouth.

"Sorry about that, ladies. Right this way."

Ari and Leise walked in. When Remy followed Buster rubbed his arms like he was cold, but didn't say anything.

"You own this place," Leise asked as they followed him up one flight of stairs.

"Yes," he replied. "Living the American dream." They walked down a short, dingy brown hallway. Ari couldn't help holding her arms tight to keep from touching the walls. As she walked behind Buster, she got a nose full of his natural, woodsy scent mixed with patchouli oil, but there was a scent of something else that filled the narrow hallway. The smell flowed over and through her, and before she knew it, her entire body felt loose and relaxed. Before long it didn't matter if she touched the wall or not. She was at peace with herself and the world around her.

Buster entered a gray door, and Leise followed him. Ari and Remy looked around the doorframe. A light wave of energy pulsed. It reminded her of heat rising off the scalding hot asphalt.

Leise turned back when Ari hadn't come in. "What's wrong?"

"He has a ward, and Remy and I can't enter."

Remy had floated past the door just as Buster came back and his eyes went wide. "I thought I felt some-ting downstairs, but that door is by an air vent. I can feel his presence, now." His Jamaican accent was more pronounced as he spoke.

"Sorry, Buster. I forgot to tell you my friend, Remy, would be joining us. Could you lower the ward so we can enter?"

"Give me a minute." Buster moved inside. A moment later the pulse died away.

"Welcome," Buster said, with a flourish.

Leise stopped abruptly, and Ari bumped into her. The scent of sulfur dioxide gas rent the air, just before a small flame lit a taper candle. The soft, buttery light made Buster seem to glow as he walked from the back room.

"That light has been acting weird all week," Buster said.

He stood in a doorway with enough illumination from the candle to brighten their area. Ari looked around. The small room would be called a foyer in a large house, but this tight space could be called an anteroom. No chairs but a small, half-moon wooden table with a wicker bowl and a tall coat rack.

"Oh," Leise said.

Buster started laughing. "You thought it was some mystical reason for the dark room and candles." They moved through the beaded doorway, and he put the candle down on a table to the right, then clapped his hands. The lamps and overhead light sprang to life. "That's the extent of my powers."

Ari smiled, and Leise laughed outright, then she covered her mouth as if she had surprised herself. Ari liked hearing Leise make that sound. Her friend had been extremely solemn as of late. The robust scent of patchouli incense permeated the air, along with the soothing smell of something else. Now, she understood why she felt so relaxed. Cannabis. Maybe Leise's outburst had been herbally induced.

A large round table took up the center of the room. No Celtic banners or silk material stapled to the ceiling, just a living room. There was nothing that screamed, 'Psychic works here' but the room had the ominous feeling of mysticism.

Buster waved towards the two chairs across from him. "Ladies, please sit."

Remy smiled as he floated near the table but stayed near Ari.

"Ari, what is he? He has a white light inside of him that calls to me," Remy stared from across the table.

For the first time, Ari felt comfortable answering Remy in public. She didn't have to hide who she was with the people in this room. "Buster's a medium."

"Interesting. Then I could..." He lifted his brows and waved over Buster's body.

"Yes, you could, but you would never. It's rude."

"Oui. Non, jamais." Remy nodded.

Buster lifted his brows. "What did he say?"

"He just finds what you are interesting. Over the years, I've kept him away from magical beings as much as I could." Ari protected him, but he was a ghost.

"You'll have to tell me the story one day on how you two got together. He feels like a happy guy though," Buster said as he took the seat across from Ari and Leise.

"He is, for the most part." Ari looked at the table. "I feel like you are about to give me a reading."

"From time to time, I use this room to do readings," he said.

"Please, how is Telly? This is about him, right?" Leise asked.

"In part, yes." Buster unzipped a pocket from his parachute pants and pulled out a piece of paper. Nothing big, it looked like it had been torn from a notepad. "The doctor don't think Sylvester is going to come out of the coma. They are going to give him one more week. If he doesn't wake up..."

His emotions made it difficult to understand his Jamaican accented English as the words ran together. But they got the gist of what he was saying. The hospital was going to pull the plug on Telly. Leise gasped, Ari put an arm around her.

"Is there anything we can do?" Ari said from over Leise's head.

"Pray." Buster shook his head. After a moment, he said, "That brings us to this letter. Sylvester knows what I am, but in all the time I've visited him in the hospital, he never once took me over, 'til this morning. I think he knows his time is...maybe...well, he wrote this." He slid the paper towards them.

Neither girl touched it. Ari leaned in to read it. The lines were thin and thick scribbles. Much like kindergarten art, but she could make out a few words.

"Leise. Protect. Stalker. Kill."

"What does that say? I can't read it," Leise squinted, turning her from head side to side. "All I can make out is my name."

Ari could read it fine, but couldn't decipher the word after, Kill. It could have been many things: Killer, kill her or killed me. No matter, it all spelled terrible news for Leise.

"Leise, have you noticed anyone watching you?" Ari asked.

"No. No more than normal. I mean that guy still comes to the store asking to buy my necklace." Leise's voice went up an octave. "Why? What does that say?"

Ari turned in her chair to face Leise. "Telly wants us to look out for you." She turned back to Buster. "Before Telly's attack did he say anything?"

"No, not really. I realize now, the girl he always talked about was Annaleise. He would make sure you got home okay at night after work. He said that you lived alone and your neighborhood was not the best."

Leise nodded, her hand trembled over her mouth. "It's true."

"You okay?" Ari asked.

"Not really." She looked up, and her blue eyes were swimming in unshed tears. "I don't understand what's happening." Leise pushed out of her seat. "I'm going to go sit downstairs." She walked away without waiting for Ari.

Ari nodded to Remy, and he followed Leise out.

"Keep her safe. She's in real trouble," Buster said.

Ari nodded again. "I will." She stood to leave.

"Before you go, did Leise ever tell you about the guy trapped inside her necklace?"

"She did, and I have no clue how to help him."

"Have faith. Remember, if you need me, I will help."

She knocked her knuckles on the table. "Thanks." From his lips to God's ears. And the goddess', as well. She needed all the help she could get.

CHAPTER 24

The next night, after witch training, Ari stayed behind to speak to Elizabeth. Their conversation was quick and she ran downstairs to catch the girls before they went home. She heard Drew the moment she stepped into the library.

"OMG! Did you see that? First, I lit the candle, and then I made a freaking fire whip." Drew hopped around in a circle as she and Oriana walked through the White Cauldron. "I have a fire whip! I can't wait to tell mom and dad." Drew was ecstatic as she shot out of the front door like a bullet.

"Wait." Ari stopped Oriana at the door. "I wanted to give you guys this, but you two ran out so fast."

"Yeah, Drew's really excited about her powers, now," Oriana said with a huge smile.

"I'm glad I was able to help you guys." Ari held out a bracelet. "Here you go."

The girl didn't take the bracelet at first. She waved her hand above it with her eyes closed. "What is this? It pulses…like a heart-beat." Oriana opened her eyes and smiled. "That's so cool." She took it from Ari's hand and put it on.

"The bracelet draws from your power. It will protect you, but if you are tired or pass out, the shield will go down. We tried to figure a way around that, but no luck yet."

"I don't care. The blue is pretty and is the other obsidian?" She turned it to get a better look.

"No, the darker one is hematite, and the blue is sodalite. Wear it at all times. It should protect you if you are attacked, but run or hide if you can. Okay?" Ari patted her shoulder. "Do whatever it takes to survive."

Ari pulled out the other bracelet to give to her for Drew when something that sounded like a bomb exploded outside. Glass went everywhere when the storefront window blew in. A gut-wrenching scream echoed at the same time. The sharp glass shards cut Ari's arm and back when she wrapped Oriana up, protecting her. They both moved to the yawning hole in the front of the building and leaned to look out. Ari quickly turned Oriana's face away from the fire and bodies laid out in the street. She wasn't sure if they were dead, but no one was moving.

"Oriana, I need for you to stay in here."

"But, but...Drew's out there," Oriana said through tears.

"I'll find her, but I can't worry about you too. Okay?" The girl nodded and grabbed Ari around the waist. For such a petite girl, she had a firm grip. It took a moment before she wrapped her arms around the little girl in a tight embrace. It was a quick hug, but it only took a moment for Ari to realize she needed it just as much as the girl.

Glass crunched under Ari's feet when she stepped out of the busted door onto the sidewalk. It was strewn about the street from busted car windows and maybe part of the front window. She looked down the sidewalk and Drew was nowhere to be seen. But the street was by no means empty. The hooded figure stood in the middle of the street with a stream of water bombs being tossed in his direction. Signet held the crumpled body of Marjorie in one arm as he launched his water bomb attack. Ari was sure he had no idea what it meant when the runes along the staff began to pulse with bright orange light. But she did.

Ari's feet were moving before she assessed her own safety in the situation. She ran just as the lightning strike headed for Signet. When Elizabeth offered the protection bracelets, Signet and his wife had refused rather adamantly. It was along the lines of 'We'd rather die than have anything from that black witch.'

If Signet had ever paid any attention to anything she had said about the attacks, he would know being a water user in a puddle made him the perfect target. Ari jumped in front of Mr. Guilderoy just as the lightning reached him. Sparks flew over her head, and the shield looked as if she were behind a clear umbrella. The shield lit in an iridescent glow of pinks, purples, and baby blues as the force of the lightning strike knocked her to the ground. She wasn't unconscious this time, so that was a win. Her happiness was short lived. Out of the corner of her eye, a petite figure rose from the side of a nearly flattened car.

"Dear goddess, no," Ari whispered.

Drew's steps were rigid and determined, almost zombie-like in her stiffness. "Drew, no!" Ari screamed but was still pinned down by the lightning attack. If she moved, Signet would be burned to a crisp.

"Drusilla," Oriana cried out.

Drew's hand flicked out, and a long cord uncoiled like a snake. "You hurt my dad!" A blaze of white fire flowed down the length of the six-foot whip.

The lightning retracted from Ari's shield as the figure turned towards Drew. The outline of the runes began to glow a bright white this time instead of the orange. Ari wasn't sure what that meant, but she moved to get to the girl before he launched another attack. A bright light blasted out of the staff much faster than the last attack. Ari felt a little woozy from the bracelet's power drain. She had pumped enough power into the shield to protect her, Signet, and Marjorie. She jumped up a little too fast and found herself face first in the filthy water around her. All she could do was watch as the line of electricity zig-zagged its way towards a defenseless Drew.

An illusion of a jungle sprung up around all of them. If Ari didn't know any better, she would have thought they had been transported to the Amazon. Oriana's bright pink dress whipped past her and then disappeared into the illusion. The bolt didn't stop as moved through the trees towards where Drew last stood. Ari held her breath, not knowing if Oriana made it to Drew. Then sparks flew above the trees and shrubbery, lighting up the jungle and Ari exhaled the breath she'd been holding.

The illusion began to melt away, much like a film burning from the middle out. When the illusion had fully dissipated, Drew and Oriana were on their knees as Oriana heaved. It must have taken everything in her to maintain the illusion and protect both of them with the shield.

Ari began to launch baseball sized fireballs in the figure's direction, but the empty sleeve waved in an arc, diverting the shots. His interest was solely for the girls now. "Girls, run!"

Before they could turn their heads, the figure had wrapped them into the wide gaping sleeves of his robe. A faint picture of a smiling, beautiful black woman with green eyes filled the air around them, then the purple edges of an amethyst flickered, before dirt, glass, and bits of asphalt kicked up creating a tornado. Ari blinked and they were all gone.

A keening noise cut through the now sudden silence. Drew's mother held the bloody body of her husband. She had lost her husband and both daughters in one night. This couldn't be happening. She looked around the disaster area: busted windows, destroyed cars, Charles was unconscious (goddess, she hoped he was unconscious), Marjorie was dead, Signet and Blossom were injured, two other dead bodies of people she didn't know on the street, and two missing girls. She hoped she hadn't brought death and destruction to their doorsteps.

The place looked like a war zone. At some point, someone must have called the police. Ari sat with her arm around Blossom, who sobbed uncontrollably on her shoulder when the red and blue flashing lights flooded their end of the block. "It's going to be all right," Ari said into Blossom's hair.

"But the girls," Blossom said between sobs.

Anything Ari said might send this poor mother over the edge.

But she owed the woman the truth. "He could have killed them, but he didn't." Ari tried to rush to the point when a groan rumbled from the woman. "He must want them for something. I'm sure they are still alive, and we will find them."

))(C

"Ms. MASON, why am I not surprised?" Detective Westin said from above Ari.

Ari had remained sitting long after Blossom went to the hospital with Charles. Thankfully, he had been only knocked unconscious when he was tossed into the family car.

Ari hadn't even attempted to dust herself off when she stood up. Her outfit needed to be burned. Not for any ritual, but the blood-stained and battle worn clothes now held horrendous memories. "Detective Westin," she said wearily.

"Do you go out looking for trouble or does it just follow you around?" He pulled out his notepad and pen from his inner jacket pocket.

Too tired to orally spar, Ari waited.

"Can you tell me what happened?"

She exhaled. "I don't know." Before the police showed up, Signet and Blossom agreed to say that whatever happened on the streets was over when they arrived. After what they'd witnessed they knew the cops were ill-equipped to handle this monster. And frankly, so were they.

Detective Westin closed his pad and stared at her, brows drawn together and mouth quirked before he finally spoke. Guess he figured out his stare wasn't going to intimidate her. "Ms. Mason, if you want me to help you, I need for you to tell me the truth."

"Detective, what you see here is what I walked out into. People down, cars destroyed."

"You didn't hear all of this," he waved around with his pen, "being destroyed? You didn't hear any screams?"

Her head moved back and forth before answering, "Inside training. The room's padded, so maybe it's soundproof. I don't know."

He nodded and mumbled in agreement as he wrote down something in his little pad. "What kind of training? Like jiujitsu or something?"

"Something like that."

"What does that mean?"

"I train my mind, body, and soul to be in balance and work as one," Ari said.

He rolled his eyes, then caught himself. "Why do I feel like you are not telling me everything? None of you are." The last he more mumbled to himself, then closed his notepad.

"Are we done here? Because I don't know what you want from me. I can't help you." Her voice hadn't sounded defensive, just resigned.

"Ms. Mason, I'm going to find out the truth. And if I find out that you've had anything to do with these murders," he moved closer, looming over her. "Under the prison will be too good for you."

"Happy hunting, detective." Ari was over this entire conversation and gave him a two finger salute before walking away.

She was tired of trying to answer his questions. She and the other witches needed to figure out how to get the girls back. Only they could save the girls and they would. She wouldn't stop until she got them back.

She pulled out her phone and swiped Leise's picture. The phone rang more than five times then went to voice mail.

"Remy," she called as she walked back inside the metaphysical store.

"Yea, Cher," he answered when he appeared walking in step with her. "You okay?"

She stopped and looked at him, he looked good. Well, good for a ghost anyway. "Can you please check on Leise? Just let me know that she's okay."

He stopped in front of her. "Cher? What's going on?"

"I'm not sure, yet. But do this for me, please." He disappeared without another word.

She pulled out her cell phone and dialed a number she knew by heart. She waited for the music to finish before leaving a message. "Lucas, call me as soon as you get this. I have something that will help protect you. No, better yet…meet me at my place tomorrow afternoon. It's been a crazy night." She swiped the phone off.

"Elizabeth, you still here?" Ari called as she walked around the store. There should be a sheet or something around there to cover that big hole. "Woman, where are you?"

Still no answer.

She pulled out her phone and pressed the number of someone she was starting to trust. "Hey, Heath. Can you do me a favor?"

CHAPTER 25

$\mathcal{A}$ny other time, Elizabeth would appear out of thin air. Except for tonight. Ari thought the woman would've appeared when the window exploded. She walked all around the shop, stepping over broken bottles of herbs and books that fell off the shelves during the attack.

Ari leaned into the stairwell. "Elizabeth!"

Nothing.

She walked up to the training room.

Empty.

On the way downstairs, she knocked on the door to Elizabeth's private quarters. The door creaked open. "Elizabeth? You in here?"

She had only taken a few steps inside when she saw two button-up boots on the floor near the fireplace. "Elizabeth!"

She wasn't ready for what she saw. Elizabeth's body had a large hole in the center of her chest. Ari touched Elizabeth's wrist, and it was ice-cold under her fingers. Ari said a prayer as she waited for a pulse to kick in, but she knew nothing was going to change. Then the woman gasped, and her eyes popped open.

"Wha…?" Elizabeth's eyes looked to Ari, then side to side. She flinched when she moved to get up.

Two hands pressed her back. "Stay still. You're badly hurt." Well, that was an understatement. How was she even still alive? And moving?

Although the hole encompassed her entire chest, there wasn't any blood on the rug. *What was she?* "What do you need me to do?" She didn't think calling 9-1-1 was a good idea for this.

"Must...heal this body." Elizabeth pushed up again. Ari's hands supported her back and helped ease her against the leg of the nearby wingback chair.

Within the hole, white wisps moved around in circles then exited the shop owner's body. Ari couldn't take her eyes off the display, and before she knew it, she blurted out, "What are you?"

"The house," she said with a weak smile. Her skin color seemed to pale, despite there not being any blood loss.

"But I can touch you. You aren't a ghost."

Elizabeth inhaled deeply before continuing. "I wouldn't be so sure," she said with a smirk. "I was murdered here. My husband had been dabbling in the dark arts, then blood magic. The more power he attained, the more he wanted, and over time it drove him mad. When he killed me, my spirit didn't ascend. The house had somehow contained my soul and preserved my body."

"I'm so sorry." Ari looked around the room with new eyes.

"This building is full of wild magic. I've keep it warded, but I don't know what will happen if too much escapes. I'm not strong enough to re-ward and perform the ritual to fix the building. I need your help."

"You would think I would be the last person you would ask for help, given my ancestry. You sure you don't want me to call the other witches?"

"We don't have that kind of time. May Day is tomorrow, and we need to do this now." She patted Ari's hand. "Ari, you are nothing like my husband. I could feel your intentions, your inner struggle and your potential for goodness the moment you walked into the building. So what do you say? You'll help me?"

What could she say to that? "Yeah. What do you need me to do?"

Elizabeth lifted her head. "Over there. On the shelf. Small leather bound journal and the decanter next to it."

Ari thought they both needed a good, stiff drink before they started this craziness. She preferred whiskey to red wine, but anything would do right now. Ari placed the items on the table next to the chair. "Now what?"

Elizabeth wheezed out a dry cough before she gently patted the rug she was sitting on. "Gotta move this."

Ari scooted the woman off to the edge, before moving the chairs and rolling the large Native American inspired rug out of the way. A large ceremonial circle with a five-pointed star had been carved into the hardwood floor. At each point, a rune had been etched in as well. Her fingers followed one of the rune pattern, it was for protection, but she didn't know the other four. Power pulsed from the circle. "What is this?"

Elizabeth used her upper body to pull her body into the circle. "This is where I died."

That would explain the wood's deep red color within the circle.

She had to catch her breath before she spoke again. "I need one of those dolls from over there."

Dolls, in general, creeped Ari out. She tried not to look at them the first time she entered the home. Their vacant eyes had always sent a chill up her spine. Of course, this was an irrational fear. She knew they couldn't hurt her, but that had never stopped the sense of dread that rolled over her in their presence.

She grabbed the first one she came to, a three-foot blonde with tight curls, round glasses, white shirt and long dark skirt. The doll looked very much like a Victorian-era librarian. She placed it inside the circle.

"What kind of spell are we doing?"

"A transference spell. I can't stay in this body much longer."

Elizabeth's arms shook as she pushed herself up inside the circle. She worked the stopper back and forth to open the crystal decanter. The woman seemed to be losing strength quickly. She tilted the bottle, and a poured a small amount of the red liquid into the deep groove of the circle. A rich, coppery scent reached Ari's nose, and she knew instantly that it wasn't a Merlot.

The blood rolled through the circle, star, and runes, and when it completed the round - a flash of red illuminated the room. Almost every witch can feel or sense magic. It's rare to actually see it.

"I will need some help with this part." She swayed.

Ari thought the woman would pass out before they finished the spell. "I don't know the spell."

"Repeat…after me. Say it, five times." Elizabeth sounded like she had run a marathon. She laid down and began the spell.

Elizabeth said it twice before Ari got the words correct and repeated them. By the forth time, they were in sync. Her body went limp, and Ari thought the woman looked very much dead. The hole in Elizabeth's chest no longer had the flowing white wisps.

"Elizabeth?" Power still emanated from the circle. The spell wasn't complete. But if this woman died, Ari was sure Detective Westin would blame her for this and every other recent murder.

The room had gone quiet. Too quiet. Ari's inhales and exhales seemed to resound off the walls. Then the doll raised up like 'The Undertaker' from wrestling.

Ari fumbled backwards on her butt getting away from the circle. "Elizabeth?"

The doll's head turned in her direction, then the light blue, glass eyes blinked. "Yes, Ms. Mason." The doll's voice squeaked, but the prim and proper cadence of Elizabeth's speech was still there.

"I don't know what I was expecting when you said 'transference spell' but it wasn't this." Ari stared in awe.

The doll stood up, running her fingers over her skirt and wiping dust from her shoulder. "This reminds me, I should dust the others off more often." She straightened the frames on her nose as she stepped out of the circle. "We need to get started."

CHAPTER 26

*C*arrying a doll around was strange. Carrying a somewhat sentient being, in doll form is a whole other bag of beans, Ari thought as they moved through the store.

"We need to set up a ward that extends past the curb," Doll Elizabeth said.

"I've only made small wards, shields. Personal sized necklaces, you know. At the most, apartment sized." Ari shook her head back and forth. She had no idea how to make wards for large empty outdoor spaces.

"Ward stones." Doll-sized Elizabeth pointed to a line of large river rocks.

Ari put the doll down and walked over to the large window. She waved her hand above the rocks. Some emitted a coldness and others a little bit of heat. They had been infused with magic. The things took two hands to pick up and weighed at least anywhere from two to five pounds each.

"What are the runes on them?"

"They basically create a varied protection ward. You might feel a difference in the power they emit." She stood next to Ari. "As you can see, I am not equipped to handle these behemoths." She held out her hands. "And I can't leave the building. So you, my dear, will have to do the heavy lifting."

"Why can't you leave?"

"I'm not a ghost. I'm more…smoke and particles. The building's magic is what keeps me together."

"You think you will blow away if you leave it? Even in your current form?"

uhj All I know is I tried once, and my body felt like it was being torn apart. Very similar to what just happened. Not fun at all. Now…" She pointed her small hand towards the stones. "I'd like to get back into my body, sooner rather than later."

Ari picked up the stone that the Doll-sized Elizabeth had touched and placed it at the curb.

Ari went back and forth with three more stones. "All done."

Doll-sized Elizabeth and Ari moved to the busted front of the building. When she touched the door, it dropped down barely holding on by one hinge.

"We only need to power the stones, the spell to veil the building is already in place." The doll bent down to a fist-sized obsidian crystal Ari had always thought was a doorstop. "This starts the spell. Put your hand here and release your magic."

"That's it?" Ari cut her eyes towards the doll.

Doll-sized Elizabeth smiled as she placed her hand on the dark crystal. A thin, pale blue line of power wavered, then jumped from stone to stone. Ari placed her hand on the obsidian and released a torrent of golden firepower. The ward flared to life in an ombré of orange and yellow. Her power entwined itself with the thin, blue line of power. This building's magic was unlike anything Ari had seen before.

A spirit appeared in front of the store and moved back and forth along the ward line. "Cher, I can't enter."

"Can we stop the ward from forming? For just for a minute," Ari said.

"I'm sorry. Once it begins we can't stop it. We might finish by dawn," Doll Elizabeth said.

"Is she okay?" Ari yelled out to Remy as she walked along the large opening.

"She's fine. She's asleep."

"Could you stay with her anyway? If you have any trouble, find Lucas. I'm going to be here at least until morning." Seeing the amethyst when the girls disappeared made her apprehensive about Leise's family heirloom.

He nodded, then disappeared. The ward completed with a pop, then all traces of the orange and blue light disappeared.

Doll-sized Elizabeth stood next to her. "He is a handsome one."

Ari denoted something in the doll's voice she had never heard in the real woman's voice. When Ari looked down, Elizabeth was still staring out to where Remy had been standing. "He's single."

When the doll looked up, she had fixed her frames and cleared her throat or whatever she had down the plastic neck. "Pish-Posh, I don't have time for that. Now, the ritual isn't difficult; it shouldn't take too long. We will have to wake the house and repair the damages."

)O(

PURPLE MOONLIGHT STREAMED through the small window of Brennan's cottage. Leise pulled her feet under her on the large, colorful, silk pillow pallets he had on the floor. Brennan handed her a cup of tea in a dainty floral patterned teacup. He usually served tea in cups that looked like small stone bowls, but after he explained that she could control some of the aspects of this world, she gave it a try. She wanted something that reminded her of home, and of her mother. It took a bit of concentration, but she created a set of teacups and saucers with pink flowers and light green leaves.

Leise had never been a fan of tea. Iced, sweet, hot, or cold, but especially not the loose leaf kind. They always seemed to be bitter, and those floaty bits freaked her out. Not to mention Ari kept trying to hone her divination skills — to which she had none, by her own admission. Brennan must do something different because his tea was smooth and pleasant. She actually looked forward to having it, and that was saying something. This entire scene might leave Ari speech-less. That would be worth seeing.

"How does everything fare in your world?" Brennan asked after he sat down across from her. "Any progress?"

Leise took a deep sip of the warm, sweet liquid. She had closed her eyes as she savored the flavors. What makes this tea so good? A deeper part of her answered that he makes it with love.

Her eyes snapped open. Where had that come from?

Brennan touched her arm. "Hey, are you all right?"

When she looked up, Brennan was staring at her. Those lavender eyes seemed to sear her clean to her soul. She placed her cup on the floor. "I'm fine. Sorry, I zoned out for a minute. What did you ask me?"

"How are things going?"

"Oh, we've tried lots of spells, so I'm not sure, but Ari said since tomorrow is Beltane she's going to try something different. She's confident it'll work."

"Is she preparing for that now?"

"Um, I doubt it. She said something about training some young witches. I'm not sure what, then probably hanging out with her new boyfriend, Heath."

"Boy...friend?" he said the word slowly. Rolling it around in his mouth like he was trying it out. "What is a boy-friend?" He stretched each word out.

"Surely, there was dating back in your day." When he still looked stumped, she said, "When a guy likes a girl, I don't know, gives her flowers, kisses her." Her cheeks went red with thinking about the next step. She refused to explain how sex and hooking up worked. When his eyes went wide with understanding, she let out a sigh of relief.

"Parents choose our mates at birth and arrange the marriage. Sometimes within the clan or with a nearby clan in an effort to avert war, settle land issues, or grow a clan."

This time Leise's eyes went wide. "Excuse me?" She couldn't believe what she'd just heard. "That's barbaric. Settle land issues? Oh, my." Lord, she needed strength. "You didn't get a say in the matter? What if you and the girl don't click?" He gave her the deer in the headlights stare. She took a breath and spoke slower. Not for his benefit, but to calm her own nerves. "What if they don't like each other?"

"That is not possible," he said with a straight, no-nonsense face. "They are chosen by the position of the moon and stars upon birth."

Witches, Leise thought. They couldn't just meet around the campfire with a pint of witch's brew and talk. No, their fates were written in the stars.

She wanted to argue but what could she say to hundreds of years of tradition. They probably never even heard of the word divorce.

"Well, that's not how it's done now. We choose our own mates, then go out on dates, eat dinner, or see a movie, to see if we make a good match."

"And Ari is doing this *dating*?"

"Sure," Leise answered quickly.

He looked down at his teacup. His words came out soft and hesitant, "And are you doing this dating?"

His question shocked her. "Me? Um, no." She touched her cheeks. She needed a glass of ice water. Ice water would be good now. She had to be twenty shades of red now. Her blood seemed to pump loudly through her ears, but she could have sworn she heard him whisper, 'Good,' after she had answered.

Leise needed to stop this conversation. She got off the pillows and took her stone cold tea to the kitchen-esque area. She placed the cup on a short wooden table. Unlike a regular prison, this magical world gave the inhabitant items to make and create things. His woodwork rivaled anything she'd seen in an antique store.

When she returned to him, her cheeks felt only a tad warm, but her breathing was back to normal. She had made a point of not sitting next to him again. She stood by a what she thought was a writing table. The short table had ornate flowers carved into each corner with some sort of light beige parchment in the middle. A feathered quill laid atop it with a seashell next to it.

"Does your language have letters or characters? Could you show me, so when I go back I can look it up, then, maybe I can figure out where you come from."

He jumped up. "Good idea. That never crossed my mind." He sat on a wooden mushroom-shaped tree stump at the table. He poured a dark, grainy substance from a small bottle into the empty seashell.

"What's that?"

"Part of a burnt log. I use it to write." He poured a little bit of his cold tea into the mixture. "It's not as good as from home, but it works."

His letters were rounded with serifs, but not overly flourished with long stroke curves, like some capital words in calligraphy. Some of the alphabets looked familiar, but the words were definitely not English. Along the edge, he made a daisy chain.

"That's so cute. I have a tattoo of that." She pointed to the flowers.

He put the quill down. "What's a ta-two?"

She'd remembered trying to explain the same thing to her mom when she had decided to get a tattoo when she graduated from high school, but found the direct way was always best. "It's body art, created with ink and needles." She lifted the hem of her dress to show the daisy chain around her ankle. "See."

His cheeks flushed a bright crimson. "That is beautiful. We had these tattoos in my time as well." He cleared his throat. "I have an entire grove of those out back." He held his hands in a tight grasp.

She could tell he wanted to touch it. "You can touch it. It doesn't hurt."

"In my time, ladies did not show their ankles."

"Thank God, we are no longer in your time." She allowed the dress to fall back into place, hiding her tattoo again.

"Do you have, like a family crest or a signature?"

"Of course," he turned back and began to draw. Before he completed it, the picture had three interlocking circles. It looked a lot like a pointy shamrock and flourishes around it and through it.

"I've seen something like that recently. Can I try?"

He moved out of the seat and waved to it with a slight bow while holding the quill out to her.

She took the quill and the vacant seat. "What do I do?"

"Oh, it's easy," he said as he moved behind her.

Apparently, this move hadn't gone out of style, she thought. When all of a sudden he leaned in behind her and clasped his right hand over hers. She closed her eyes when his warm breath tickled her ear. The tingle went down her spine and to her toes.

"Just dip it in," he moved her hand up and down, "then slide it off the edge. You don't want to drip ink everywhere."

Leise turned her head slightly, and his lips were right there. All she had to do was lean in a smidge. She looked down and admired the curve of his bottom lip. It made her want to taste them. Her tongue darted out to moisten her own lips. He must have noticed because they parted on his sharp intake. Everything that was woman in her craved this man. Her heart ramped up as she nibbled lightly on her bottom lip. She had no experience being the temptress or the seducer, but she was ready to give it a whirl.

"You don't want the ink to dry," he said softly, breaking the spell.

She blinked then nodded her head, "Yeah, sure." She moved her hand over the parchment like she was sketching a picture. Instead of curving broad strokes, she made thin, rigid lines and zigzagged circles, before she could start the small line patterns through the middle, Brennan stilled her hand.

Leise looked back at him. "What? What's wrong?"

"Do you realize what you're drawing?"

"Yeah, I was drawing Heath's tattoo."

"No, you were drawing the sign of a dark druid."

He moved her parchment and started on a new one. His arms moved quickly up and down in broad strokes. Drizzling ink on the material as he frantically created a picture. Leise walked up behind him.

"Is that it?" He pointed at the drawing. "Is that what Ari's Heath has?"

Leise couldn't believe her eyes, as she picked it up. Brennan's drawing looked exactly like Heath's tattoo. Within the three circles, three jagged bolts cut vertically through the middle of it. "What's it called?"

"It's a perversion of the sign of Awen. It had once meant your life was in balance. That you would always search for truth and live by it and have an eternal thirst for knowledge and that knowledge would be passed on. You see this..." He pointed to the lines in the middle. "You see how they go outside of the circle. The circle is our lifespan. The bolts are the sign of The Order."

"The people of the Order seemed to live outside the normal lifespan. Oh, they are immortal?"

"Maybe not immortal, but the thought was they would live a long time. My Uncle Haviland had joined an Order that wore that symbol." Brennan began to pace.

Leise shook her head. "I'm sure Heath just picked that symbol off the wall. Your uncle died hundreds of years ago." She touched his shoulder, and he stopped pacing.

He shook his head. "I wouldn't be so sure. Those dark druids claimed that if you joined, they would show you the path to enlightenment, illumination, and eternal life."

"You know how crazy this sounds?"

"I know. But Haviland was powerful, even before the dark magic. If there were a way to survive, he would have figured it out. Tell me, what color are his eyes?"

Leise frowned as she thought about it. She'd never seen lavender eyes before Brennan. Then her eyes opened wide. "Blue, I think," she answered automatically, then paused, "But nowadays you can change your eye color very easily."

"Magic."

"Contacts," she responded before she sat back down.

He closed his eyes at this news, then spoke under his breath. "So, it could be him." He knelt before her and held both her hands. "Annaleise, he's very dangerous. I need for you to stay away from him. At least until we know for sure if he's the one who trapped me in here."

She'd heard what he'd mumbled to himself, and that worried her, but him telling her what to do went a little too far. She squinted her eyes at his dictate. "If he's as dangerous as you say, I have to tell Ari."

"I'm trapped in here, and I can't help you fight him." He ran in hands over his face and through his hair. "Out there you're on your own." He waved his hand in no particular direction. "I had some magic a long time ago, but still, not like my uncle."

"Brennan." She held her hand out to him. "Please, come talk to me." Hand still extended.

Finally, he took it and sat down next to her, but that didn't stop his restlessness. Looking up, he slid his hand from hers to rub them on his pants. She knelt in front of him and grasped both of his hands.

"Calm down. Breathe." She watched him until he exhaled. When his eyes met hers, she continued. "I need for you to tell me whatever you can remember, weaknesses."

"My," he paused as if to find the right words. "Haviland was the most powerful in our clan. You say witches now, but we are druids. Simple people really, we lived off the land. Kept to ourselves."

She tried not to bring up his family after he told her how he was imprisoned, but it seemed important now. She didn't want to say anything that would stop him from talking now.

"But my uncle always ventured off our island. He would be gone for days at a time. Sometime later, we found out he was learning other clans' magic. And at some point, in secret, he started practicing the dark ways. Blood magic. But it was when he brought home a foreigner as a bride," he shook his head. "He was shunned because of it."

"Why? Was she the one teaching him the blood magic?"

His brow creased as he seemed to concentrate. "I was only ten or eleven at the time, so I don't remember everything, but I remember her. His wife, Nyah, was different but beautiful. Her skin was a rich, dark brown. Sun-kissed is what we called it, and her eyes were a vivid green. Very unique. My grandfather said she came from the savage lands and nothing good would come from mixing with her kind."

Leise could not believe what she was hearing. "Your people were racist!"

He frowned as he shook his head.

She could tell he didn't understand. "It's when one set of people hate or feel superior to another race of people. Most of the time it's because of the color of their skin."

Brennan nodded thoughtfully, "Yes. I believe they were then."

"And are you? Will you hate Ari when you meet her? She's mixed race." He looked bewildered. "She's part African American, part Native American, and few other things. Point being, she has dark skin."

"No, I could never. I would not. I feel I know Ari from your stories. How could I ever hate someone, who, without knowing me, has tried to help me? And one you love so much?"

Leise knew those were rhetorical questions, and didn't try to answer but just sighed in relief. If this boy had said anything else, she would have left his butt right there and put the necklace back in the safe deposit box.

"Wait. What did you say her name was?"

"Nyah."

Leise had heard that name before. This wasn't good. "What do we need to do to stop your uncle?"

"I'm not sure he can be. A powerful witch or a coven, maybe. To bind him or place in a prison, like this one."

"I hope so, after what he did to you," Leise said with such savagery it shocked her.

"It might not be possible." Brennan sounded grim.

She knew that couldn't be right, but didn't comment on it. "Okay, I have to get back. I need to try and find Ari before he does." She rose to leave.

He followed her to the door and held her face between his hands. "Please be careful. I...," he bit his lip, "just come back to me."

She could see he wanted to say more, but she wasn't sure if she was ready to hear it. She touched his hand. "I will." She closed her eyes, and he leaned in, then she woke up in her bed.

CHAPTER 27

*W*hen Leise woke, it was well after two in the afternoon. She got dressed and rushed out the front door. She had her phone in her hand, looking down to call Ari, only to bump into something hard.

Heath.

In the span of four-seconds, her emotions took a quick ride, from shock to fear. She took a step back, putting space between them.

"What are you doing here?" Leise's voice quivered.

"Looking for you actually," Heath said with a grin.

Many thoughts ran through her mind. One, how did he know where she lived?

He took a step, closing the space between them. "Ari sent me."

After all she had just learned, she needed to get as much space between them as possible. She took a step back, thumping her back against the now locked door. She looked left, then right, but the walkway was regretfully clear.

"Oh, I'm good. I was just on my way out." Leise attempted to move past him.

Heath lifted his hand, blocking her path. Shuffling back, she moved until her head hit the door.

"Leise, why are you so skittish? I was sent here to protect you."

"I don't need protection."

His fingers caressed her cheek. She cringed at his touch. "On the contrary, you do. When Ari sent me to you, she had no idea you had something I needed."

He gently ran his finger under the silver chain beneath her shirt, revealing the amethyst. She quickly snatched it out of his hand. He waved his other hand, and the air around Leise seemed too thin.

Leise's hand went cold, and she couldn't control it as it peeled away from the crystal, then pinned itself to the door above her head. She couldn't move her head, but the glow from the amethyst illuminated them like a purple sun.

A laugh emanated from him. "I've searched a long time for this." He closed his hand around it, then snatched it back quickly.

The scent of burning flesh prickled her nose. "It's mine, and apparently it doesn't like you." The smack against her cheek rattled her teeth. Pain blossomed and numbed the left side of her face. Before she could cradle the cheek, he snatched her free hand.

"I was going to spare you, but you can die along with your best friend."

Leise's hand tingled where Heath gripped her. It felt like a light electrical current was running through every vein and every finger. Her mouth opened to scream, but only silence emerged. Her legs felt like they were going to melt under her.

Dark spots formed in front of her eyes. She tried to fight through the fog, she didn't want to lose consciousness. A deep chill ran through her, not once but twice. Remy's otherworldly coldness numbed the pain. In the back of her mind, she thought, it was nice to know she wouldn't die alone.

The more logical part of her mind reminded her that Remy would tell Ari. She just had to hold on until then. All wasn't lost. At least, not yet. Her mind began to slip into a fog. She couldn't grasp ahold of any one thought, but for one moment she had become lucid enough to see a mass of dark clouds and lightning swirl around her before complete darkness consumed her.

CHAPTER 28

"'It won't take long,' she said. 'The ritual's not too difficult,' she said," Ari said as she grabbed her bag, and walked through the now clean and restored White Cauldron building.

The truth was, it did take a long time, nearly twenty hours. It was almost six in the evening, and she didn't have enough time to go home and change for her job in an hour. The restoration spell had been more complicated and exhausting than anything she'd ever attempted before. She'd poured a lot of her power into the ritual. In a way, she was the battery that powered the building until it got on its feet.

She was supposed to do a reading for Mr. Drake. She wanted to help him find closure, but it wouldn't be tonight. She'd pulled out her phone to call and cancel when a full-sized Elizabeth appeared next to her. Still quiet as ever.

"Ari, I want to thank you. I couldn't have done this without you." Elizabeth looked around the room.

Ari looked at the place with new eyes and smiled. During the spell, Elizabeth had explained to her how to make improvements to the building. More seating, a fireplace, and shelves in the library, and a large bay window for the storefront. The hardwood floors looked like they had just been buff shined, and the dirty threadbare rugs looked brand new. "You're welcome."

"And for saving my body. I could feel myself floating away into the aether," Elizabeth said as she touched her stomach.

"I'm sure the building would have protected you."

"You're probably correct, but with my luck, I'd end up being an air spirit who couldn't talk. I'd be floating around here shaking the chandelier, and flickering candles every time someone came in."

That made Ari smile. Elizabeth was always so serious, this was the first hint of actual humor. She liked this Elizabeth. Maybe in time, she'd be able to call her Lizzy or El. They weren't there yet, but she could sense a real friendship forming.

"I'd like to see that," Ari said.

When she opened the spanking brand new red door, she didn't expect to see Signet, Blossom, a few other witches she hadn't seen before, and a bandaged up Charles on crutches. She stood to the side as they all walked in, then turned around to leave.

"Please don't go. We'd like to speak to you," Signet said solemnly.

She looked back at the man who'd spoken and the crowd behind him. They looked as grave as Signet sounded. But each person's eyes bore into her with sorrow. It tugged at her soul.

For all of them to come here and see her, she knew it was important. "Before we start, could you give me a sec? I need to make a call."

She stayed near the front door as Elizabeth, and the other witches moved towards the two new wingback chairs in the library.

The phone rang two times before a distinguished voice answered. "Hello, Mr. Drake, this is Ari Mason."

"Ms. Mason, how are you this evening?" Mr. Drake asked.

Ari cleared her throat. She was tempted to cough like she was sick, but contained it. "Sir, I know we're supposed to have your reading this evening, but I need to reschedule. A few things have come up that require my attention."

He stayed quiet for nearly a minute.

"Mr. Drake?"

"Ms. Mason, is it possible for me to change your mind? I'm sure what we need to do won't take long," Mr. Drake said.

"Sir, I would rather come to you at full strength to get the best reading possible," Ari said.

"Yes, I would rather that. I will see you soon then," Mr. Drake said.

They hung up after that, and then she quickly tapped out a text to Leise.

No response.

Last night, she had asked Heath to check on her best friend this morning. She texted him.

No response.

"Ari," Elizabeth called from the library, "we're ready when you are?"

"Here I come," Ari said. She stared at her phone for a moment.

She wasn't worried, just found it odd neither had picked up. She'd called them both and had left a messages. One of them would call her back, she was sure of it.

Ari slid her phone into her bag and walked to the back of the store. All of the witches stopped talking and stood up when she entered the small library area. Okay, now they were making her nervous.

Signet moved towards her. She braced for the accusations and blame and how his wife's death was her fault.

"Ms. Mason, I want to apologize," Signet said looking her square in the eyes.

She wasn't expecting that. "Oh." She wanted to say more but didn't know what to say. She didn't have to when he held up his hand.

"Please let me finish." She closed her mouth, and he continued. "You were," he cleared his throat, "right."

Ari got the feeling he hadn't made the admission often.

"That monster is strong. Stronger than I could have ever imagined. He kill...killed—" Signet fiercely wiped away the tears. "He killed my Marj in a matter of seconds. I only stayed behind for a few

minutes and…" He took deep breaths to stop the tears, but ulti-
mately the tears won out.

A tall, dark-haired man patted his shoulder. Signet gave a tight
nod, then moved back into the small crowd.

Blossom stepped forward. "My girls are in this thing's hands.
What are we going to do to get them back?" She looked poignantly
at Ari.

Ari's eyes widened a fraction. Then she looked at the small
crowd. Everyone was staring at her. She didn't know the first thing
about launching a rescue mission. But she knew plenty about assault
missions. She thought of how they would go about finding a target.
They had witches with special skills in the coven. She was working
with a lot less here.

"What were your ideas?" Ari finally broke the silence. "Do you
guys know how to scry or do a locator spell?" She looked around
the group.

The red-headed girl whipped up her hand. "I totally know how
to scry."

"And there's a scrying mirror in my place," Elizabeth said.

"Great," Ari said. "Elizabeth, if you can try a locator spell as
well, that doubles the chances of finding the girls."

"Don't we need something of theirs for that?" Signet said.

"Totally, like I've used head-bands before. But, ew, hair or
fingernails work too," the red-headed girl said.

A light giggle went through the crowd. Even the men chuckled
behind their hands.

"Sutton, I'm sure we can come up with something." Blossom
smiled, and Charles nodded at the teen with a smirk.

"Just curious, of the witches you know, does anyone have an
affinity for finding things?"

They all looked at each other, then shook their heads.

"But you haven't addressed the real problem," Signet said.
"What do we do when we find them…find him? After last night, it's
obvious we aren't strong enough."

"You're right. We aren't strong enough by ourselves." Ari moved
into the center of the group and made sure she looked at every face

in the room. "But together, we might be able to beat him back. Together, I believe we can save our girls. He's looking for someone named Nyah. He killed a young witch with the power to find anything. If we find this Nyah, maybe she can stop him."

"You're grasping at straws." Signet shook his head.

"Actually, I think Oriana gave us a clue before they were taken. I know a lot was going on, but do any of you remember the last image she showed?"

"Kinda," Blossom said. "There was a bright, purple light, then a woman. It was...I remember now, she had beautiful light brown skin, a lot of hair." She held out her hand to indicate more of an afro and not long hair. "And haunting green eyes." She stared at Ari.

Blossom's unwavering stare lasted long enough that it made Ari uncomfortable. Ari wanted to check her teeth to see if something was stuck in there. "Yes, maybe this is all about her. If we find her, we could end this."

An unfamiliar ring tone blared. It went on for a while then started ringing again. Everyone looked at Ari.

"I think that's you," Sutton said.

"I'm sorry, guys." Ari opened her messenger bag to a lit up phone. "Hello."

"Oh, thank God. Where have you been?" Heath panted.

"Heath? What's wrong?"

"I went over to Leise's place, and when I got there, some guy grabbed her."

"What?" Ari yelled into her phone. "What happened?"

"He threw her in a car?"

"A car?" That didn't sound like the guy who took the girls. "You sure?"

"Yes, I'm sure. I followed it."

"Where are you?" Ari could hear rustling. Like he was running through underbrush or grass.

"I don't know where he took her exactly. There are so many trees out here. Shit. I think they saw me."

"Heath! Focus. Where are you?"

"Harris County Arbore—"

He didn't finish the last word, but she'd heard enough to guess where he might be. Then she heard rustling, a volley of grunts and moans. It went quiet, then a long scream. After that nothing. "Heath. Heath!"

Ari had already started moving towards the front door when Elizabeth yelled out. "Ari, you need our help?"

"No, no. I can handle this. Give everyone protection bracelets and find the girls. Call me when you do." Ari ran out the door without another word. The old man was a dismage. She could handle one man. She just prayed it wasn't too late.

CHAPTER 29

fter driving through a wrought iron and stone gate into a heavily wooded area, Ari found it hard to believe she was still inside the city limits, but she was. She drove about a half mile on the path lit with small lights, it led her to a small white brick building.

"I guess this is as good a place as any to start." Ari drove cautiously with the lights out as she pulled into a small parking lot.

The moon cast a beautiful, soft white light through the tall trees, and bathed the stark building and parking lot in such a way that made it look like it was glowing. Just this side of ethereal.

The door was open. She stepped inside cautiously. When her stilettos thundered on the tile floor, she hopped from one foot to the other to pulled them off. You would fail miserably as a spy, she thought.

She crept along the hallway, the bank of windows on her right had closed micro-blinds and two locked doors on her right. The hall only turned to the right. She walked stealthily through the large, open french doors. It opened up into a solarium, but tonight it was illuminated by a full moon.

Ari walked into a room made entirely of glass. When she looked

up, the ceiling must have been nearly forty feet up. Revealing silhou-
ettes of the trees, stars, and the moon. The soft scent of moonflower
hung in the air. As she moved around the mostly circular room, she
noticed a bevy of night-blooming flowers. She closed her eyes and
leaned in to sniff a humongous white rose. She didn't have time for
this, she had to find Leise and Heath.

"Beautiful, isn't it?" A familiar voice said from behind her.

Ari turned around quickly. "Mr. Drake? What are you
doing here?"

"Waiting for you, of course," he said as he moved closer. Ari
stepped back wearily. "Naturally, when you canceled our appointment I had to make other arrangements to get you here."

He kidnapped Leise. "Where is she?"

"Safe. For now."

"You didn't have to do this? I can do the reading now, just let
her go."

Mr. Drake chuckled. "Oh, you will do the reading, but Ms.
Morgan has something I need. And she was being so difficult about
selling it."

"The necklace," Ari mumbled to herself. But apparently, he still
heard her.

"Yes, I've been searching for that little trinket for some time."

"It's just a crystal. You can go to any store and buy one. Hell,
you can order it online. You didn't need to kidnap her for it."

"That is no dime store piece, Ms. Mason. Now, if we can get
started." He waved her towards a round table with two chairs in the
middle of the room. "If you try anything, your friend is dead." His
wolfish smile sent a chill up her spine, and she believed he would
do it.

She pulled her messenger bag over her head. She pulled out a
white silk runner, then pulled a unique deck from a purple silk bag.
She only used them during special occasions. This year, Beltane
happened to have a full moon. He sat in front of her without a
weapon. If she knew where Leise was being held, she could take this
old man. *And what about Heath?* A deeper voice asked. He could be
getting tortured right now. All because you asked him to do you a

favor and he was kind enough to do it. The blood on her hands was stacking up. First Telly, now Heath. And in the back of her mind, she was positive Oriana and Drew fell into that category as well.

"Ms. Mason, are you with me?" Mr. Drake snapped his fingers in front of her eyes.

She blinked wildly. "Yes, let's get started."

"What do I need to do?"

"Do you have something of hers?" She shuffled her tarot cards.

He loosened his tie and pulled a necklace from inside his shirt. It was a small corked bottle, containing a thick blue liquid and dangling from a silver chain.

"Place it on the table." Once he laid it in the center of the table, she placed a tarot card face down in front of him, then created a circle of twelve cards around the necklace. "Tell me about her."

She turned over the first card. A mermaid wrapped in a blue sash, near the sea where a ship was setting sail. Around her, a snake completed a circle by devouring its own body. At her feet, sat two beasts as she seemingly floated above.

The World.

This card's meaning could vary from deck to deck, but in this particular deck, the mermaid had completed a long, hard-fought journey. This could mean various things, good and bad. Mr. Drake would have to answer more questions.

Ari had a list of questions she would typically ask, and between the cards and their aura, she could find what the person most desired. She had never performed a reading like this before. She had brought a Ouija board in case she made contact. She hadn't held out much hope, until she felt a light pulse of magic from the necklace.

Mr. Drake kept talking about his life with his wife, seemingly answering every question without her asking.

"Have you done this before?" Ari asked as she turned over the sixth card.

"Once or twice," he said. "But never with someone as strong as you."

She turned over another card. "Tell me about her death." Her heart tightened on the last. She could see the pain in his eyes.

Mr. Drake cringed, then looked away. "That's why we're here." He looked at Ari a long time before he started.

Ari felt like the man was looking through her as he started his tale. She took a deep breath to try and shake off the melancholy emanating from the man.

"She'd contracted something, while we were traveling. I brought her home, thinking my family would help us." He went very quiet.

"What's your wife's name?"

He let out a slow exhale. Ari looked up when he still hadn't said her name after a minute or two. The crease between his eyes became more pronounced, and the tight line of his lips hadn't opened. Ari suspected he might not have said her name in a long time.

"Nyah," he finally whispered.

Ari stiffened. It couldn't be a coincidence that he was looking for a Nyah as well. This man wasn't what he'd been pretending to be. She knew with glaring certainty she couldn't defeat him. She needed to get out of here, and that started with finishing this reading.

She touched the last card. "Nyah, if you are here, you have heard the words from your love. Now, do you have any last words for him?"

The corked bottle trembled and the scent of flowers blossomed. It smelled very similar to her own perfume. Ari pulled her hand away from the table. The necklace stopped moving abruptly. Then every card began to turn over, starting with the one nearest Mr. Drake.

"Nyah? Is that you?" He waved his hand above the cards. He closed his eyes to inhale. "She's here. I smell her. Lilacs," he inhaled deeply, "she always smelled of lilacs."

Each card had flipped over by then, but the twelfth card lifted in front of Ari's eyes. It slowly turned, revealing itself only to her. The sun at the bottom, the cup's contents pouring out, the sea where the sky should be.

The Knight of Cups, in reverse.

In any deck, the knight is a messenger and usually brought good news. But this was in reverse. And judging by the other cards, even more sinister. Nyah did have some last words, but they were not for her husband. Nyah had sent Ari a warning. Mr. Drake was dangerous.

She had never really looked at Mr. Drake before. She let her eyes drift into the unfocused place as she looked around him to view his aura. What she saw or better yet, what she didn't see, disturbed her. Instead of colors ranging from one end of the spectrum to the other. There was nothing. No light. No color. Just a deep, all-consuming darkness. His aura was a like a black hole. She had never seen anything like it.

"What does the card say? What did *she* say?"

His outburst brought her back, and she pulled the Knight card from the air.

"Dammit, girl!" He slammed the table and the cards scattered. "Tell me."

Right then, she felt it. His control had slipped and black magic pulsed around them in his anger. Ari took the opportunity to switch the knight card amongst the scattered ones on the table. There was no way she was telling him what his wife had actually revealed.

"She said." She held up a card with a couple locked in a passionate embrace by a lake. The full moon smiled as it cast a hypnotic trance on them. "She will love you forever."

The Lovers.

He exhaled a sigh of relief. "Thank you. I knew you were the one."

The cards remained in a small heap as she pulled them towards her. They were not cooperating as she tried to straighten them. By the end, she wrapped them in the white silk and shoved them in her bag.

"Where is she? I want to see her."

All Ari wanted was to get out. She hadn't felt that level of darkness since she left the coven - if ever. Her bag was packed and it was all she could do to hold herself still, and not run from the building screaming.

"I am a man of my word. I will let you see her."

)O(

ARI FOLLOWED HIM. She hadn't noticed much on the way in. There were a few doors on the way to the solarium, but they had all been closed. The place was as quiet as a tomb, but then she heard it.

A moan.

He waved her towards a closed door. Ari eyed his suspiciously as she moved past him. She wanted to burst into the room. But she remembered her training from the coven. Always check for traps and wards when entering an unknown place. She waved her hand a few inches from the door. She felt very much like a mime and probably looked just as silly. Better safe than sorry.

"There are no wards, child."

"I'd just like to check for myself, thank you very much," she snapped back before thinking.

No wards like he said, then she turned the doorknob and pushed the door open slowly. She half expected it to creak like in a horror movie, but instead, a whoosh of coldness chilled her to the bone when she stepped inside a few feet.

A chair or something scraped along the floor in the darkened room.

Her hand pushed the door open slowly. "Hello," she whispered. "Leise? You in here?"

She closed her eyes, and let the tingle of magic roll over her skin. The room was full of it. Goosebumps filled her arms and legs, and she could see puffs of smoke as she breathed. The temperature had to be at least thirty degrees colder inside the room. She could smell soil. Maybe this room had been used for potting plants at some point.

It crossed her mind that this could be a trap. She knew it, but that didn't stop her from walking in to save her friend. Two candles came to life when she made it about halfway through the room, and revealed a dark figure near the back of the room. She knew this was a real person and not a ghost. Ari stopped when the person began to moan and rock violently.

Ari touched her protection bracelet, and the light prickle of magic let her know it was working fine. She formed a small ball of fire in case this was a trap and lifted it to see the face of the person in the chair. The light revealed the scared eyes of her best friend.

"Leise."

Leise's eyes went wide and frantic, but her body stayed put, and her jaw moved, but her lips remained shut tight. Magic had been used to seal her mouth and arms.

Ari didn't need extensive magic for this. "Don't overthink this Leise. I need to break the spell."

She thought deeply about where she needed to culminate her powers. Her entire face warmed like she had leaned into a sauna. The necklace around Leise's neck lit up.

"That doesn't ever get old," Ari whispered before she pressed her lips to Leise's. The kiss wasn't romantic and certainly not French, but it was hot. Literally. Ari had to send a fraction of her power towards her mouth.

Leise smacked her lips together before she spoke. "I think you burned my lips."

"I'm so sure I didn't," Ari said. She sent power to her hands to burn through the ropes that bound Leise's hands behind her back.

Nothing.

"You sure took your time rescuing me."

Ari tried again, but the arm bindings stayed in place. "Are your legs bound?"

Leise kicked them out, then stood up.

"I didn't even know you were here until Heath told me," Ari said while looking around the room. "Come on." Ari began walking towards the door.

Leise jumped in front of her best friend. "About him. I have to tell you something."

A whoosh of brightness lit the room behind them. The wicks of the candles flared two feet into the air. "I can't have you spoil everything, dear Annaleise," Mr. Drake said from the door.

The girls stumbled back into the small room when the older man appeared in front of them. Ari pulled her friend behind her.

Leise whispered. "He's the one who kept trying to buy my necklace."

Ari nodded. "He kind of let the cat out of the bag earlier," she whispered back, never taking her eyes off of the older man. Then she spoke to Mr. Drake. "Where's Heath? You said I could see them?"

"I said I would let you see her and you have," Mr. Drake said.

"Where is he!"

"Heath is here." He patted his chest.

A sick feeling rolled through Ari. She didn't like how smug the old man looked.

"Because I am feeling so benevolent tonight, it being May Day and all, I'll let you see him."

Her eyes searched the room.

Mr. Drake gave Ari a slight nod, then with the wave of his hand he phased away, and Heath appeared.

Ari's mouth opened then closed, her mind couldn't form any words. What could she say? How could she not know?

"Yeah, that's what I was trying to tell you," Leise whispered.

"I know what you're thinking, 'He's a witch, how could I not feel his magic?'" He did a slow pace in front of her. "I'm not quite a witch. Surprise. I'm a druid, and I know more magic than you can conceive of in that little brain of yours."

She tried to recall all the times they had spent together. Why hadn't she felt his magic? She had, the first time they met. The electricity. And then later, as they'd grown closer, he would just kiss her to throw her off her game.

He answered as if she had spoken aloud. "Oh, you weren't too hard to distract. You wanted someone to love you so desperately," Heath said snidely. "But that guy who used to follow Annaleise home and watch her. He was harder to get rid of."

"Who? Telly?" Leise asked.

"Yes, your co-worker. He was a stalker. I saved you," Heath announced.

"You have any idea what you did?"

"I know exactly what I did. He had more spirit than I antici-pated though." Heath hunched his shoulders. "No matter, he will die soon enough."

Leise moved forward. "You're a monster."

"Leise stay back." Ari held her arm out. Her entire body vibrated with anger. Her nails dug into her palms and hot, blood pooled in her tight fists.

"Ari. Your eyes," Leise said from next to her.

Ari finally took her eyes off Heath to look at her friend. Leise didn't look horrified. "I'm okay. Trust me." She knew her eyes had taken on that golden hue.

Power rushed through her body like molten lava. She opened and closed both hands trying to expel the crackling energy. Her fingertips felt like they were on fire. When she looked down, her hands were engulfed up to her wrist in blue flames. This had never happened before, she had no idea how to control it. A stream of blue fire blazed at him. It was like it had a mind of its own.

Heath phased out of the way, and the blue flame stopped mid-air. Floating like it was waiting on a command.

Mr. Drake appeared in a new spot behind Leise. "Now, now. None of that." He opened and closed his hands like he was calling an animal. The waiting blue flames floated to his hand. "Try it again, and your friend dies." He rubbed his fingers through the blue fire until only smoke and embers floated away.

"Why are you doing this? Why bring her into this? It's me you want, right?"

"Don't you see? It was always about her. Well, her necklace anyway," Mr. Drake said.

"Why go through all the deception, you could have just taken it from her."

"He can't," Leise said. "I have to give it to him."

He squeezed. "You talk too much. As far as deception, I wouldn't call it that - I just thought it prudent to meet the woman whom I would spend an eternity with."

Ari frowned. "Mr. Drake, I don't understand."

"Please, call me Haviland. I feel we are closer than that now."
He laughed.

She ground her teeth, before starting again. "Haviland, I'll do
whatever you want. Just let her go."

"Afraid I can't do that. I need your friend's necklace, you, and
my other guests. You have no idea what that purple crystal can do.
Immortality for one, but also resurrection. It will bring my Nyah
back to life."

Ari knew precisely who his two other guests were. "Why do you
need the girls?"

"I've learned many things since my Nyah left this world. But in
all my years, I have never seen an ability like that little one's." He
snapped his fingers and looked around. "What is her name?
Olive...Orin."

"Oriana," Ari whispered, not meaning for him to hear.

"Yes, her. She is amazing," Haviland said with a gleaming smile.
"Her power will be a gift for my love."

"She's a child. You can't do this."

Mr. Drake hunched a shoulder. It didn't matter to him. "It's
been fun, but it's time."

Ari opened her mouth to speak.

"Enough," Haviland said with one finger whipping through
the air.

Ari touched her mouth then throat. Opening her mouth, but no
words came out. Her eyes bulged with panic.

"There's nothing more to say. Still." Haviland picked the phone
from Ari's bag. "Can't have you calling 9-1-1 again."

Ari's eyes moved between Leise and Haviland, she couldn't
move anything else. Not even a muscle twitch, she felt like a living
statue.

Haviland turned Leise towards him. "You, my dear." He
snapped his fingers, and Leise moved both arms from behind her
back. Released from her bindings.

Ari heard Leise sigh as she rolled her shoulders and flexed her
fingers.

"I need for you to give me that necklace now," Haviland said with his hand out.

Ari's eyes widened and moved back and forth before they met Leise's. Ari wanted to scream for Leise to run. To get away. In the end, all she could do was watch.

Leise's head moved back and forth. "No."

Haviland shook his head. "I'm disappointed in you, but that is your choice. I really would hate to have something happen to…" He ran his fingers into Ari's braids then snatched.

Tears ran down her cheeks. He hadn't released her from the paralysis curse.

"Let her go!" Leise yelled.

Haviland's grip moved towards Ari's throat, and his other arm snaked around her waist. "Feel me," he whispered. A tingle went through Ari's body and then she could feel him. Although she was still unable to move, she felt how excited this all made him, and it sickened her.

He began to rub his cheek against hers. "You feel so good. I can't wait until my Nyah has this body," he whispered so that only Ari could hear.

Ari found it hard to concentrate but had to try something. A hodgepodge of spells filled her mind — nothing made sense though. Then the first spell she successfully learned gleamed brightly in her memory. Candles began to levitate. He stilled behind her, looking around the room.

"Sleep," he whispered in her ear.

Every part of Ari's body felt like lead weights. She wondered how only one word could do this to her, then succumbed to the darkness.

)O(

THE CANDLES HIT THE FLOOR, and Ari's body slumped forward. Haviland held her limp body, not allowing her to fall.

"Did you…did you kill her?" Leise yelled.

"No. But I could wake her and give her a heart attack," Haviland said.

"You wouldn't." He needed her, right? Leise didn't know what to think.

Haviland opened his arms, and Ari's limp body crumpled onto the floor. Ari didn't wake. He leaned over her body with his hand over her heart and murmured some words she couldn't understand. Ari's body began to convulse. Leise thought Ari was having a seizure.

"Stop it! Just stop it." Leise cried.

He did, and Ari's body quit writhing. He stood with his hand extended. Leise knew what he wanted and only in this moment did she feel hopeless. She would do anything for Ari, even give up the man she loved. Leise whispered something into the amethyst then kissed it. She carefully pulled the chain over her head, and threw it at him. Leise closed her eyes to the brisk coldness she felt at the loss of the necklace.

The crystal flew through the air, and he caught it. "Thank you."

"Fuck you. I hope you burn in…"

"Enough. Sleep." Haviland waved his hand.

Coolness washed over Leise's body; then it suddenly felt like it had been weighed down by blocks of concrete. She couldn't keep her eyes open. All she wanted to do was sleep, and finally, she embraced it.

CHAPTER 30

*L*eise sputtered, then coughed up salt water.

"Leise," Buster said. "You okay?"

Hands helped her turn. She coughed up more water. She gasped when she tried to speak. "What...what was that?" She spat, then wiped her mouth.

"You wouldn't wake up. I didn't know what else to do. Salt can sometimes break a spell." Buster said.

Leise looked at the other person in the room, then wiped her eyes. "What are you guys doing here?"

Buster shook his head. "Honeychil', I have no idea. I suspect Ari's ghost snatched me so he could bring the cavalry." He waved behind him. "I had just stepped out of my place to grab a bottle of wine, and then I woke up driving on the highway. I nearly took out a semi and a guardrail at some point."

Leise leaned forward to look around Buster. Lucas she knew, but the woman next to him she didn't. The amazon had to be about six-one with long, brown wavy hair. She looked so much like Lucas, she had to be his sister.

"Remy informed us through Buster here that you were in trouble and Ari was unavailable. I don't know if you ever met my twin sister, Luca Bea, but we just call her Rum. She tagged along."

Leise looked around the empty room. "Thank you, Remy," she said softly. She reached out. "Help me up, please." Buster and Lucas each grabbed a hand and pulled her up.

Rum walked around the room holding her hand above various items: the chair, candles, the door. "What happened? This place reeks of black magic?"

"Ari's psychotic, transforming boyfriend, Heath, that's what happened. We need to find her. She's in serious trouble. He was talking about using Ari to bring his dead wife back."

"Wait. First, tell us what happened. We need to know what type of powers he has. It does us no good to run out there and die. Does he only transform?"

Leise shook her head. She told them what Brennan had said and concluded with how she was kidnapped, and Ari's blue fire.

"Goddess above." Lucas covered his face with both hands. "Do you guys realize who this Heath is?"

"It's him, isn't it? The guy who's been draining the witches of their powers and killing them?" Rum said softly.

"Wha...wha...what? Whatchu talkin' bout?" Buster chimed in, with his hands waving in a 'stop the presses' action.

"Someone has been killing witches and taking their powers," Lucas said.

"You said witches, but could it be regular humans as well?" Leise asked.

"Sure, there have been a few reports of attacks on dismages."

"Telly," Leise whispered, and she heard Buster whisper, "Sylvester" at the same time.

"We need the entire coven," Rum stated.

"There's not enough time. For all we know, he could have already drained and body swapped her. But he's strong, we can't attack him head on," Lucas said.

"Sneak attack. Not my forte, but okay." Rum flexed her fingers, and the building shook.

"What. The. Hell?" Leise grabbed the doorframe.

"Sorry." Rum took a deep breath, and the mini earthquake stopped.

"You can cause freaking earthquakes?" Leise took a deep breath. She was kind of freaking out. She was accustomed to Ari's tarot cards and overall 'woogieness,' but this was on a whole other level.

"Rum, you okay?" When the woman nodded, Lucas asked, "Buster, no other powers?"

Buster's accent thickened when he answered a little too quickly. "No, no. Just a medium, man."

Lucas looked at Leise. "Where are they now?"

Leise shook her head. "I don't know. Out there somewhere, I suspect. He said some words and I passed out."

"Ok, you guys are going to have to stay here." When Leise protested, Lucas held up his hand. "I can't fight him and protect you."

"I'm not asking you to. She's my friend. Hell, the only family I've got since my mom passed away. I have to go. She'd do it for me."

Buster went very still next to her, and then his eyes rolled up in his head. When he finally looked at Leise, she took a step back.

Buster held his palms out. "Annaleise, it's me." The Jamaican accent was gone, replaced by a Cajun one.

"Remy?"

He nodded. "I know where Ari is and he has two little girls. They are through the woods that way," he pointed behind the building, "but we need to hurry."

Headlights blinded the small group as they rushed out of the building. The wind picked up and the ground rumbled a little. The witches were on edge, and she couldn't blame them. She didn't recognize any of these people when they emerged from the car but doubted them showing up right now was a coincidence.

A bald, older man; a tall, dark-haired woman; a red-haired teenaged girl; and two well built, tall men in their thirties climbed out of the car.

Buster/Remy held up a hand. "These are the witches that Ari has been training with. They are white witches."

"Geez, just what we need. A bunch of goodie-two-shoes," Lucas said under his breath.

"Hello, my name is Blossom," the woman said as she walked towards them, "we are searching for…"

"Two girls?" Leise cut in.

"Yes, my daughters, Oriana and Drew," Blossom said enthusiastically.

The others from the car moved closer. Their excitement showed on their faces. "You've seen them?" The bald man asked.

Leise shook her head. "No, but I think I know where they are."

The teen girl seemed oblivious to them as she looked down at a paper map in her hands, then pointed towards a path that led into the trees. "I think they are that way."

"Ok, Sutton," Blossom looked at the teenager, "but call Ms. Mason and tell her where we are?"

Sutton pulled her phone from her back pocket and dialed.

"You really know my cousin?" Lucas stepped up next to Leise.

"Sure, she's been helping my girls with their powers."

"That sounds like her," Lucas mumbled. "But no need to call her."

"Why not? She wanted to know when we found the girls," Blossom said.

"Because," Leise cut in. "The same man that has your girls, kidnapped me, now has Ari. I don't think they have much time."

A purple beam of light shot straight into the air from within the trees.

Remy/Buster took off running towards the light. "We're out of time."

)O(

REMY LED the rag-tag cavalry to Ari. He ran the half mile in about sixty-seconds flat. The men kept up with him, but Leise and Blossom were happy Sutton had a map. Leise, Buster, and the twins stopped just outside a clearing, where they witnessed Ari's body rise about twenty feet in the air into a silver stream of moonlight. The others moved to the other side, closer to the girls.

Buster fell to his knees, and dry heaved. "I hope he never does that again."

"What? Possess you?" Leise whispered.

"No. Running. This temple was not cut out for that nonsense." Buster took deep breaths as he spoke.

Ari was still under a spell, her head bobbed limply and legs swayed. The girls floated on the edge of the circle of moonlight, much in the same fashion as Ari. They hadn't moved, yelled, or anything, even though Haviland had his back to them.

Leise heard the witches discuss something about water, earth, and wind power. But to be honest, she didn't understand much of what they were talking about. Her blood had been pumping so loud through her ears as they jogged through the forest, she could barely concentrate on anything. She saw the white witches move to the other side when they arrived. Closer to the girls from what she could tell.

"My God," Leise whispered.

"What is he doing to her?" Buster swallowed hard.

Ari's limp body lowered, then stopped in front of Haviland. The amethyst began to flicker with a low light. "I think he's starting the ritual," Leise whispered. She looked over to Lucas and Rum, "Hey, this is the magic free zone. You guys need to get in there and save her."

"Wait a minute. We got a plan. Not a great one but we got something. Look…" Lucas pointed. "Blossom and Signet have started."

Vines moved through the dirt like serpents on a mission for Haviland's legs. Various sized pools of water began to form around the circle. Then Leise spotted the woman and the bald man. That must have been Blossom and Signet, they were waving their wands on the other side of the clearing. She wasn't magical by any stretch of the imagination, but the hairs on her arm stood from all the magical energy in the air. She didn't understand why Haviland wasn't reacting to the witches. He had to know they were there.

"Big sis, you ready?" Lucas walked past her when she said, "Do it."

"Hey! I don't appreciate what you're doing to my cousin." Lucas entered the circle of light.

"He's so arrogant. He didn't even draw a protection circle," Rum whispered.

Leise remembered Ari explaining how protection circles worked. It was a way to shield or block external forces while you worked magic. This guy didn't think anyone would attack him. She watched how Haviland moved, unconcerned that Lucas had shown up.

Haviland held her necklace out over Ari's heart and recited words in Latin. An instant later thunder resounded in the distance.

"Now!" Lucas yelled.

Everything happened so fast after that. The witches came out from around the edges with their wands drawn. The vines worked up Haviland's legs to his arms. His arms snapped to his body, knocking the necklace out of his hand.

Well, that did it. Knocking away the amethyst seemed to snap Haviland out of his trance. He flexed his arms outward, snapping the vines from around his arms. He bent over to reach for the long stick at his feet.

"Don't let him reach that staff!" Signet yelled as he launched soccer ball sized water projectiles from the puddles.

The vines doubled around Haviland's body, restraining the arms so that he looked like a green leaf mummy. For a moment, it seemed like the witches had the upper hand, then the sounds of thunder began in the distance. Leise thought it was just random thunder, but then she heard a pattern.

"Is the thunder coming this way?" Leise said between the noise.

Lucas looked up then at the mummy. "Dammit, he's doing a spell. Signet, Rum. Do it now!" He yelled.

The man whipped his wand around and down, then all the balls of water fell at Haviland's feet. Rum knelt down and pushed the fingers of one hand into the ground. Leise fell forward from trembling earth beneath her feet. Ari's body floated above the mini earthquake. Dirt, rocks, and leaves bumbled and thumped around, but it all moved to the puddles under the bound man. It all seemed to melt into the water as it formed a circle around Haviland. The wet earth rose from the ground in a spiral working up his body.

Rum pushed her hands into the thick, rich earth in front of her, moving her hands as if she were working with wet clay. Molding and directing the soil in a cylinder shape. Even without the pottery wheel, she looked like she was making a thin handleless mug. Leise looked up to see the life-sized cylinder enclosing Haviland.

When Rum finished creating her oblong mug, Haviland's body had been completely covered in wet mud, resembling something close to an obelisk. Once he was completely covered, the thunder stopped, and Ari's body fell. The girls fell as well. Blossom and one of the men picked the girls up and carried them to the clearing's edge.

Leise and Buster had moved when cracks in the ground began to form around them. From their new location at the far end of the clearing, she had been watching the rest of the witches gather around the seven-foot tower of packed earth. Leise turned when she heard a noise to her left. A large man emerged from the trees.

"Detective Westin," Leise walked towards him. "You really shouldn't be here."

"I shouldn't..." The detective pointed, opened his mouth then closed it. It took a moment before he actually spoke. "What the hell did I just witness?"

She looked to Buster, who backed away with his hands up. He was no help at all. But before she could come up with a plausible lie, purple light flooded the area. She looked back at the mud obelisk, and bright purple light beamed through the small cracks.

Chips of mud began to fall away, and more purple light poured out. "Guys, I think we need to leave," Leise said as she backed up.

Detective Westin turned towards her. "What? I'm not——" He didn't get to say anything else before he hit the ground.

Bolts of lightning blasted outward, making everyone scatter. Leise hid behind a pine tree. Smoke rose from the detective's jacket, but the subtle movement up and down let Leise know he was still alive, just unconscious. Haviland's body lingered in the air with the amethyst clutched in one hand and the staff in the other.

The staff's tip glowed bright orange in his hand as he pointed it towards the puddle of water. A brilliant white light shot of the long stick, following the water back to its source. A bolt of lightning lifted Signet into the air and carried him a few yards away. Leise cringed as the older man's body hit a large tree and crumbled to the ground. He didn't move, and she couldn't tell if he was still breathing from where she hid.

"You." Haviland pointed his staff in Rum's direction.

"No!" Lucas screamed as he held his hands out. A tornado of pine needles, dirt, rocks, and leaves whipped up. The powerful winds created a whirlwind around Haviland. Flashes of light illuminated the inside of the tornado. Bolts of lightning struck some treetop branches, and Haviland controlled it from within. The lightning tore through the tornado, as the tree stump crashed with a thud. Lucas jumped out of the way.

Rum crawled to her brother.

Leise rushed behind Haviland to where Ari's body had fallen. She moved the mass of hair to reveal a blank stare on her friend's face.

Leise shook Ari's unresponsive body. "Ari? Can you hear me?" She waited. "Ari?"

Nothing.

She wanted desperately to hear her friend's voice, but she heard Ari's steady breaths, and knowing she was still alive would have to do for now. Leise looked around the clearing, and bodies were laid out. They were losing this battle.

Blossom limped behind her with the two girls. "How is she?"

"I can't wake her." Leise held Ari.

"We need to get out of here. I'll help you carry her. He's going to kill us all if we stay." Blossom held out her hand.

"He will kill you no matter what. He will track you down. You gotta know that." Leise yelled over the wind. Lucas wasn't out of the fight yet. "He wants something you have, and he's not going to stop until he gets it."

Blossom pushed the girls gently, but one fought out of her grip. "Momma, she's telling the truth. I've seen. He won't stop. Not until he has her." She looked down at Ari.

"He wants Ari? Is that what this is all about?" Leise asked. But she knew in her heart, she wouldn't give Ari to that monster.

The young girl shook her head. "He needs Ms. Ari," she said then closed her eyes.

"Don't do it, Oriana." Blossom touched the young girl's shoulder.

Oriana threw her hands up above her head and pointed. "He wants her!"

A virtual image of a smiling, dark-skinned, green-eyed woman filled the clearing. She was running and a young Haviland who looked a lot like Heath, chased her until he caught her. Then he took at the woman in his arms, leaned her back and kissed her.

"Stop it!" Haviland's strained voice cried out.

"Oriana, don't make him even madder. Stop it," Blossom said. Her eyes glued to the man across the clearing.

"No, wait," Leise said to the mother. Leise looked back at Haviland, then to the girl. "Oriana? Is it?" When the girl nodded, she continued. "Where is this woman now?"

"She's trapped. He carries her soul around his neck. That's why he needs Ari. That's why he wanted me and Drew. For her," Oriana whispered.

"For Nyah," Leise said at the same time.

Haviland stomped back towards them. "I said stop it! I will have her in this life."

"Could you take that down before I try this?" Leise said to Oriana.

Oriana slumped back into her sister's arms. "Are you okay?" Drew wiped sweat from Oriana's forehead.

"I will be," Oriana said slowly.

Leise had an idea that could possibly get her killed. Doing it might confirm her insanity. She didn't have any powers, but maybe she could give Haviland the one thing he wanted, without losing her friend. "You guys might want to leave now," she whispered to the group behind her.

"No. You're right. We'll stay," Blossom said from behind her. "Girls, get behind me."

Leise walked out into the clearing with her hands up. "Haviland, you don't have to do this," Leise pleaded.

"Human. You must want to die," Haviland said. He had made it midway to the clearing when he went down to one knee.

A strong gust of wind pressed him down. Leise could see Lucas's hands thrust downward. The moment Haviland stood on two feet, the force of the wind snapped her hair back and Haviland down. This went on two more times before the ground shook and Haviland dropped out of sight. Vines shot out over Leise's head and snatched the staff and necklace from Haviland's upthrown hands just as a large hole had opened up beneath him and swallowed him whole.

"Don't kill him!" Leise threw her hands out.

"I can't hold him for long. We need to kill him. Now," Rum said through grunts.

"He has to wake Ari."

Leise heard Rum grumbled something in Latin before she twisted her hands in the soil. The dirt where Haviland was buried alive began to swirl down revealing only his head. His eyes were closed as his head lulled to the side.

"Is he?" Leise moved in closer.

Signet limped over holding his side. "I hope he is."

Instead of finishing the job like Leise thought he would when he raised his wand, he pulled water from the various puddles, then flicked them into Haviland's face. The water formed something similar to a cat o'nine tails whip and cracked the air. Leise flinched with each lash. It only took two before Haviland gasped back to life.

Leise closed her eyes to give a little thanks.

"Can you get on with it." Rum's strained voice snapped Leise out of it.

Leise squatted down. "I understand why you did what you did, but there's another way without taking Ari from us...from me."

"You know nothing, human. When I get free. I'm going to destroy you. Every last one of you!" Haviland yelled, while only moving his eyes to look around.

"It doesn't have to be this way."

"She's my only hope." Haviland closed his eyes. Then they snapped open. "She's my last chance. I can't, no, I won't let her go."

"Last chance for what?" Leise was confident she knew the answer but wanted him to confirm it. He nodded with a smile. It looked genuine, and for a moment Leise could see the gorgeous man he used to be.

"To get my family back."

Leise frowned. "Who? Brennan?"

"Who?" He let out a hearty laugh. "My nephew is still alive. Amazing." His laugh died down, then softly he said, "No. My Nyah."

Leise stared at him. "Why have you wasted all these years, when you could have been inside with her?" She pointed towards the necklace.

"I only sensed its power a few months ago," Haviland said.

"Two months? Really?" After her mother died and when she received the necklace, and her insomnia began. In a way, this was her fault. She couldn't let that train of thought derail her. She had to get Ari back.

"I've been inside and so has Buster." She looked up at the Jamaican man, and he gave a half smile. "It's beautiful. You can be with her. All you have to do is release Ari."

Tears welled in his eyes but didn't fall. "You lie."

"I wouldn't lie. Not about this. Brennan is alive."

"But I need her." Haviland looked past Leise.

Leise's eyes followed his to Ari's body, then moved to block his view. "No, you don't, but I do. Like Nyah's your family. Ari is all I got. I promise you, when you wake her, she will put you inside with Nyah. The real Nyah. And maybe you could tell us how to get Brennan out. I'm sure you two would like some alone time." She waited with bated breath, not sure if her pitch got through to him.

They looked into each other's eyes for a long minute. Leise

didn't think she had persuaded him and stood up when he gave a sharp nod. Leise turned to the group with a huge smile and nodded.

Lucas held his ribs with one hand. "You sure about this?"

"Of course. Did you see Nyah? Ari would never forgive us if we let some woman take over her body who walked around barefooted," Leise said with a grimace and head shake.

Lucas smiled. "Absolutely unforgivable."

CHAPTER 31

*H*aviland rubbed his wrists and stretched his neck from side to side. He moved towards Ari, and a line of people blocked him. He lifted his hands and backed up. "I need her back over there." He pointed towards the circle of bright moonlight.

"I got her." Lucas lifted Ari with a wince and carried her to the center of the clearing.

Haviland stood over Ari's body. He lifted his hands and Ari's body rose. When her body reached his waist, it hovered. "I need it." He held his hand out.

Leise looked at the amethyst but didn't move. How could she trust him? For one, when Rum released him, he hadn't killed everyone where they stood.

"If you want her back, you are going to have to trust me."

Trust. No, she didn't trust him, but she would do anything to get Ari back.

"What exactly are you going to do?" Leise rubbed her fingers back and forth over the rough edges of the amethyst.

"The Gem of the Tortured Soul is a portal. It can move a person's spirit from one object to another, locking them in. Right now, Ari's halfway between this life and the aether."

"She's in purgatory?" Leise bit her bottom lip. She didn't even want to imagine what her friend was going through.

"Something like that. She will stay there until May Day is over and the moon has set," Haviland said.

"Bring her back." Leise gave him the amethyst...again and hoped she was doing the right thing. It wasn't just Ari's life she placed in his hands. It was Brennan's as well.

Leise missed the words Haviland chanted over Ari, but her body began to convulse, as she rose another six feet in the air. On the last convulsion, her body held in a long arc before falling.

Lucas threw his hand out. Dirt and puffs of dust kicked up under Ari, slowing her descent and giving her a soft landing. Haviland fell to his knees, almost like the life was drained out of him. Lucas, Rum, Buster, and Leise ran out and surrounded the two.

"Ari?" Leise caressed her face. "Can you hear me?"

When they were kids, Ari told her lots of things about magic that she hadn't believed at the time. She just thought Ari had a fun imagination. Ari had told her when they were children saying someone's entire name was a kind of magic. She never believed it, but today she had faith. Her best friend in the whole, wide world was going to come back to her.

"Aramais Delphine Mason. You are all I have, and I love you. You hear me? I love you. I don't know where he sent you but come back to me. Don't leave me."

Lucas rubbed Ari's hand on his cheek. His breathing changed like he was holding back sobs. Leise hadn't even noticed the first drops of moisture, but soon she couldn't breathe.

"Is she?" Rum asked softly. When no one responded, she turned into Buster's shoulder.

Leise's tears fell unbidden, and she let them.

"Did you just say my whole name?" Ari asked as she cracked open her eyes.

"Alive? Yes, she is." Leise held her friend's face with both hands. "For a minute, I thought you were..." She just stared Ari's huge hazel eyes, "never mind what I thought. You are here, and that's all that matters."

Ari squinted as she looked around. "Where? Hell, why are you all here?" She moved to get up. When she wobbled, many hands reached to help her.

"You!" Ari yelled and shook everyone off. She moved carefully, but purposefully, towards Haviland. "You tried to kill me!"

Ari thrust her hand outward, and Haviland grabbed his throat. Without touching Haviland, she moved her hand upward, and his body lifted to his tiptoes.

Haviland's body swayed limply. "Well, not really. Your body would have still…"

Leise could see the imprint of a hand around his throat as it constricted. She's much stronger than when she levitated the pocket-watch that released Remy.

"Just. Shut. It." Ari's eyes were golden brown as she squeezed her hand tighter, and Haviland's throated mimicked the same action. The gurgling noises went from wet sounds to a dry gag.

Leise looked around. No one was going to stop this. They were just letting this happen. Leise touched her friend's extended arm. "Ari. This isn't you."

Ari didn't move. "He kidnapped the girls. He killed so many. He doesn't deserve to live."

Leise touched both sides of her friend's face, turning it towards her own, but Ari's eyes didn't move from her target. "Please, Ari. Without him, we can't save Brennan. We can't save Telly."

Ari blinked, and tears fell, but still, her eyes were on Haviland. "You have no idea where he sent me."

"You're right. I don't know, and I have no right to ask you to let him live. I know he's not worth it. Let him suffer, but don't kill him."

Leise knew her friend had come back to her. "Look. The girls are okay."

Finally, when Ari looked at Leise, her eyes were the lovely hazel again. Then she turned her head to look at the girls. Blossom clutched them both tightly.

"Don't do it, Ms. Ari," Oriana yelled.

Ari exhaled, and tears ran down her cheeks.

Leise nodded. "See. You gotta let him down now."

Ari waved her hand, and he dropped. "Oh, my. I almost...in front of the girls." She shook her arm then hugged Leise. When Leise went to pull away, Ari held her tighter. "I thought I was going to—"

Leise rubbed Ari's back, cutting off any admission. "Shhh, I knew you wouldn't." She had hoped she wouldn't.

Haviland rubbed his neck.

"Tell her the spell," Leise demanded.

"What spell?" Ari asked.

Leise looked between Haviland and her friend. "A spell to send him in and get someone out."

"How can I trust her—" Haviland started but couldn't get the question out.

"Don't you dare!" Leise cut him off. "After everything you just put us through, you are going to have to just trust us." Not to kill you. She didn't say it, but was sure everyone was thinking it.

Leise walked back to the Blossom and the other witches. "You should take the girls home."

"Not until he's dead," Signet said with a growl.

"I know—" Leise started.

"No, you don't know. He killed my wife."

Leise cringed but didn't back down. "I can't begin to understand that kind of loss, but I've lost a mother and a close friend. They can't be replaced, but we are going to try to save some lives now."

"But, I want justice."

He wanted vengeance, but she let it go. "When this is over, you will never see him again. He will be in a prison of sorts. He won't hurt anyone again."

When did she become the voice of reason? This is hard work.

"Come on, Signet," Blossom said while still looking at Leise. "I think we should let them handle this."

Leise gave her a wan smile. Blossom pulled the girls closer to her as they walked away. The men followed, but not without grunts of complaint. Leise went back to the others.

"So we don't get to kill him then?" Lucas looked between Ari and Rum.

"Lucas, when did you get so bloodthirsty?" Ari asked.

Lucas walked closer. "I don't know. Maybe when a mofo abducts my favorite cousin and makes us drive to the backwoods of Texas to find her, that might cause some animosity."

"Favorite cousin, huh?"

"Shut up. What are we going to do with him?" Lucas asked as he watched Haviland.

"I think I know," Ari smiled at the druid.

"And what about him?" Leise said pointing to Detective Westin's body.

Ari threw her hands up. "What did y'all do, post an invite on Facebook?"

Leise looked around. "Yeah, well, he sort of invited himself."

$$\mathrm{D}\mathrm{O}\mathrm{C}$$

LUCAS USED mini whirlwinds to float Haviland's lifeless body and Detective Westin's comatose one back to their vehicles. The detective's body took a hit of magical electricity. He wasn't dead, but he hadn't woken up yet either. As a sign of good faith, Haviland agreed to go into the amethyst in exchange for the spell to save Telly and free Brennan.

"Why do I have to do all the heavy lifting? Why don't you use that swanky telekinesis to move the bodies?" Lucas asked.

Ari walked ahead of him. "Because you're here." But in reality, it made her feel too much like her mother.

When they made it back, Lucas flicked his wrist, the small tornados dissipated and the bodies dropped.

Ari looked around at the motley crew. Remy floated behind them. "If I didn't say it. Thank you for saving me. Buster, I don't know the story behind you being here, but thank you." Ari walked towards him with open arms.

"I'm sure Remy will fill you in," Buster said, then leaned back to look her over. "You okay, girl?"

Ari nodded. "I will be."

Buster squeezed her hands. "Well, I need a bath, something to eat and I'd really like to get that bottle of Chardonnay now. This outdoors life is not for me, and that ghost of yours wore me out. If I sense him ever again, it will be too soon."

"I think he knows." Ari looked up at Remy who held his hands together and yelled, "Sorry."

Buster waved his hand as got into the back seat of the car.

Ari hugged Lucas and Rum. "You sure you're going to be okay?"

"Yep. I'm sure, Haviland's locked away." Ari pointed, and Leise pulled the amethyst from her pocket and waved it. "He can't hurt any of us."

"And you're sure he can't get out?" Rum asked.

"As sure as I can be," Ari said. "Anyway, I gotta drop him off." She pointed to Detective Westin crammed in the backseat of her car.

"Here." Rum held out her bag to her. "I found it inside."

"Call us if you need help," Lucas said before driving away.

"So," Leise dragged out the word. "What are we going to do with the good detective?"

"Find his car, for one. Two, I'll work on while we drive."

CHAPTER 32

A nice hot bath, that's all Ari wanted, but it wasn't in the cards, at least not yet. Driving around with a comatose Houston police detective and another man that looked all but dead was disconcerting, to say the least. She'd decided to take the good officer back to the last place he'd seen her. Leise explained how he'd been following her and had seen the battle with Haviland.

Ari knew only one memory spell, and it hadn't come from her solitary good witch book. Her mother used it often, and she'd decided never to use it. There's a real possibility to erase more than just one day of a person's life. But she couldn't let him remember what he had seen.

It was hard to see Leise under Detective Westin's broad shoulders, but Ari could hear the heavy panting from her friend and knew she was struggling. Ari was a strong woman but she wasn't fairing any better. This man was solid.

"This isn't going to work." In for a penny, in for a pound. Ari summoned her power and lifted the man's weight off their shoulders.

"That's so much better. Thank you," Leise said as she rolled her shoulders.

The door to the White Cauldron opened, just as they walked up. When they got fully inside with the door shut, the detective's body hit the floor.

Hard. They both cringed.

"Ouch," Ari said. "I'm still working on controlling this power."

"You think he's okay?" Leise said.

Ari touched the big man's forehead. No blood and his chest moved up and down at a steady clip. "He's okay." She turned to the shop's owner. "Elizabeth, I didn't know where else to take him."

"No, please. We would have lost the girls without you and your friends. So, whatever you need, it's yours." Elizabeth waved around her.

"He saw some things tonight."

Elizabeth nodded. "A memory spell."

"Can you perform it? Do you know a way, so that I don't...."

"Have to use black magic? I'm sorry. I know someone who can persuade, but not all out forget."

"I figured as much. I guess if I could use your circle and some salt."

"Done. Come this way."

Elizabeth led the way as Ari used her power to lift Detective Westin up the stairs. Floating him up was infinitely easier physically lugging him, but mentally — this was exhausting work.

Leise collapsed into the wingback chair after they rolled away the rug and moved said chair out of the way. Detective Westin barely fit inside the carved circle. Ari removed his shirt, she didn't want to get blood on it. The man beneath surprised her. His torso was covered in old scars and burns. It looked like he'd been to hell and barely made it back. The perfectly round burn on his back marred his beautifully tanned skin. Since the lightning was magic, she wasn't absolutely sure a magically enhanced salve would remove the wound. But she had a small jar in her bag and applied it to his back.

After prepping him, Ari turned to ask for a knife, but the shop owner had the uncanny ability to know what you needed without asking. Elizabeth held out something better.

An athame.

These knives had been used in sacred magical rituals for thousands of years. Each person in her old coven carried a small knife in necklaces, keychains, even boots — to be prepared for blood magic at any moment. She'd stopped carrying a knife the day she left.

"I could see the turmoil and how much you didn't want to do this. This athame is much like you. It was my late husband's, but it has only been used for good for last few years. It will serve you well."

Elizabeth had a wan smile as Ari took the bone handled knife. The carvings in the ivory were intricate, but she didn't have time to study it.

"Thank you."

Ari looked at the ladies for a little longer than what felt comfortable. She kind of thought they would leave. They hadn't. "You guys staying?"

Leise leaned forward in the chair. "I've never seen you do this type of magic. You've only worked with herbs and your cards. Plus, I can't leave until you're done. You're my ride."

"I could totally call an Uber for you," Ari said dryly.

Leise blew a raspberry and waved her off. "Not a chance."

Ari noticed that her best friend had been a regular *Chatty Cathy* since she'd woken up in the clearing. What in the world happened to bring this on? "Fine," Ari said before turning back.

She hadn't really thought beyond performing the ritual, but it was weird having an audience. It made it all feel real now as she felt the weight of the sacred knife in her hand. Yes, she was born into a coven of black magic users, but it wasn't who she was. Not entirely. She loved helping people and growing things. She loved nature, but after tonight that was sort of debatable. White magic brought her solace and a balance.

"I'm ready," Ari said this aloud, but it was more for herself.

Elizabeth had already poured the salt circle to enclose her and the detective. Ari took the knife, began the ritual Latin words, and nicked her finger. A flood of dark but familiar power rolled over her. She used to hate the feeling it brought up in her, but today she greeted it like an old friend. Her entire body tingled. The power had never felt like this. She could smell every power that had been and what was in the room. Every distinct magic melted like candy on her tongue. She flexed her fingers, and knew fire dwelled there. But with her mind clear like this she could feel the other parts of her eager to be free. She probably could have lifted the chairs with Leise and Elizabeth in them with a thought.

She took a deep breath and exhaled. She didn't want the power to consume her. That's the other danger with dark magic, especially blood magic. It could seduce, entice, then consume your will. Much like a drug.

Blood pooled, and she used her finger to create a memory rune on the detective's forehead - A blinding rune for his eyes and forgiveness rune over his heart. This was the one thing she hated about using blood magic, so damned messy. By the time she finished the words, the blood had dried. She wiped away the particles and the spell that would erase a day of Detective Westin's life was complete.

With the power still thrumming through her, she tried to capitalize on it. Telekinesis is not as easy as TV made it out to be. True, Leise appreciated not carrying the large man down the stairs, but he was going to have some unexplained bumps and bruises along with a slight headache. It couldn't be helped though. They still had to get to the hospital, and Ari still had a rather dead looking body in her car.

They put Detective Westin back in his car and reclined the seat. Leise parked it on the other side of the street, down about a half a block. A good view of the front door of the White Cauldron. It looked like he'd been watching her, then just fell asleep.

Next stop, the hospital. Ari had some souls to save.

)〇(

THEY STEPPED into the hospital well after visiting hours. But they couldn't wait. Telly was scheduled to be disconnected from life support tomorrow. Ari was prepared to use her powers to cause a diversion. Even Remy offered up his rarely used poltergeisting skills. But in the end, they only needed tears.

Leise cried as she explained to the one nurse on duty that this would be his last night on earth. That was closer to the truth than what she knew. They were shocked to see Buster sitting next to the hospital bed.

"I thought you went home. Something about chardonnay," Leise said when they entered.

Buster hunched his shoulders. "I was having a drink for a reason." He looked over to Telly's still form. "What are you ladies doing here? After...well after, I didn't think you'd be here."

"We're going to try and help him," Leise said.

Buster looked at Leise then Ari. "That sounds like some strong magic. Can you do it?"

"I'm going to try, but there's something I need to tell you. About the spell," Ari said.

Haviland told her what he did to Telly couldn't be undone. She didn't have the heart to tell Leise, but she had intentions on saving both Telly and Brennan as best as she could. Brennan needed a body and Telly's body needed a soul.

"Will it save him?" Leise asked.

"Yes, but," Ari started.

"Ari, it doesn't matter. If you can save him. Save him." Leise wiped at the tears.

The actual Telly, or at least his spirit, stood behind a crying Leise.

Remy held Ari's hand. "Are you sure about this?" she asked Telly.

Telly nodded, then said, "This is what's best. I'm sure I've been here too long as is." His non-corporeal body flickered. The heart monitor flatlined for a moment, sending the alarms off, then quickly they returned to normal when a heartbeat blipped on the screen. He looked at Ari, "You might want to hurry. I don't know how long I can hold out."

"Telly, I'm sorry this happened to you. I won't ever forget you." Leise whispered to Telly's body before she kissed him on the cheek.

Ari nodded, then looked at Buster. "Now is the time if you want to say anything."

Leise moved away, and Buster wiped away tears as he sat on the edge of the bed. "Boy, I know you can hear me. You know I love you more than anything. I'm happy to have met you and even happier to call you my friend. Just know I'm here if you ever need to talk." Buster kissed Telly's cheek and moved the long blond hairs out of the boy's eyes.

Buster gave Ari a stiff nod.

Ari looked between the two Tellys. The spirit Telly moved to stand behind Leise, then nodded at Ari. She moved to the other side of the bed, kissed Telly's forehead, and placed the amethyst over his heart. She pulled the athame from her bag and cut her thumb and placed it on his chest. Her blood trickled over the amethyst, and his blood pooled below it. If a nurse were to walk in right now, they all would get tossed into jail. Blood wasn't pouring out of her, but it was trickling over the amethyst and sheets.

With her hand over Telly's cool cheek and her other hand over the amethyst, Ari closed her eyes, pressed her forehead to his, then began the chant.

Even through closed eyes, she could see the purple light. Ari lifted her head when the chant came to an end and saw the tears stream down her friend's face. Telly held Leise from behind, and her hands were on top of his.

He kissed Leise's cheek, and her entire body shivered. "Goodbye Annaleise."

"You okay?" Ari asked.

"Was that him?"

Ari nodded, and Leise closed her eyes, let out a long sigh, and rubbed the spot where Telly held her. Ari watched him fade away.

"I'm sorry you couldn't save him," Leise said through tears. "But he's at peace now." Leise touched Telly's arm.

She seemed to be saying it more for her own peace of mind, but Ari nodded anyway.

Leise jumped back with a squeak.

"What? What happened?" Buster was on his feet.

"He just moved. Ari, what did you do?" Leise looked between Telly and Ari.

Telly blinked a few times, then looked at Ari, then Leise.

"Is he a zombie?" Leise whispered.

In a scratchy, yet deep voice he spoke. "No." He reached out towards Leise, but she didn't move any closer. He then said a few more words, that no one understood.

"I believe that's Irish, Leise," Ari said with a smirk.

"Ari, what did you do?" Leise asked with a frown.

"Yes, girl. What did you do?" Buster chimed in.

"Haviland said, in order to save Brennan he'd need a body and what he'd done to Telly couldn't be reversed. He'd ripped Telly's soul from his body, and it had begun to dissipate the moment it was snatched out." His soul would have just disappeared. Even if there is a heaven or hell, he wasn't going to either.

"I kinda knew he needed a body. But honestly, I thought we would raid the morgue or something." Leise tightened her lips and looked back to Telly. "But I'm happy we didn't."

"So that's…" Buster's words trailed off.

"Brennan?" Leise said staring at Telly's body.

"Táim Brennan," Brennan said in a thick Irish brogue, as he nodded and touched his chest.

Leise reached out and touched his cheek. He curled into her palm like a kitten. He began to speak so fast.

Buster and Ari looked at each other. Buster hunched his shoulders. He had no clue what Brennan was saying either.

Ari felt weird witnessing this. She cleared her throat, "Um, I thought you said he spoke English."

"He did, in Otherworld," Leise said through tears and laughter, as her hands covered his. His eyes shimmered with unshed tears.

Pure love.

Now, they just had to work through that language thing. She felt a coolness just before Buster's eyes went white. Ari knew precisely what had happened.

"Could you come with me, please? Just for a moment," Buster said with a hand out towards Leise.

Leise wiped her tears. "I'll be right back." She followed him to the other side of the room. Ari wasn't trying to overhear, but she couldn't help it. Hospital rooms were small.

"What's wrong, Buster?" Leise asked.

Buster's blank eyes looked towards Leise. "No. It's Telly. I just wanted to say thank you. I know you couldn't save me, but I'm happy that I could help someone you loved. All I ever wanted to do was protect you. Because..." Buster's hand touched Leise's face, then his eyes blinked normal brown, then white, then brown again. He shook his head, "Whew. That boy packs a punch."

Tears were streaming down Leise's face, "Because what? What was it he was about to say?" Leise sounded near frantic.

Ari walked over and hugged Leise. "It's okay. Calm down," she whispered against Leise's head.

"Honey-Pie, I have no idea. I am just the phone spirits use to make the call," Buster said.

"He...loved you," Brennan struggled to get the words out.

Buster looked at Ari. "Ari, your aura has changed. It's simply," he paused, just looking all around her, "magnificent. There is some darkness trying to creep in, but stay gold, sister. You can fight whatever that is." He pointed over her head.

He walked over to Brennan. "You, sir, will take a bit to get used to. I'm Buster." He extended his hand. "Buster Calivares."

Brennan spoke excitedly in Irish as he took the offered hand.

Buster looked around. "Gaelic, huh?" He closed his eyes, then opened them with a smile. "I think he remembers me."

"Okay, I'll just..." Ari turned to leave, but for a man just out of a coma, he moved lightning fast.

"No." Brennan released Leise and grabbed Ari's wrist. "Go raibh maith agat."

Ari looked at the man in the bed. Telly's big blue eyes were now a bright lavender. Telly was truly gone.

Brennan kept saying something that sounded like 'go rav may a gut,' which she took to mean thank you. "If you are saying thank you, then you are welcome." She squeezed his hand, then reached for Leise's hand as well.

Ari gave their hands one last shake, and then winked at Leise. "I could get used to him speaking Irish, but you might wanna invest in Rosetta Stone."

Brennan kissed Ari's hand. "Thank. You." The English words came out tentatively. He tapped his fist over his heart.

Ari smiled as she squeezed his hand back; she understood every gesture and word. "And that's my cue." She left the lovebirds and walked as fast she could and used every power she owned not to cry.

She was happy for her friend, truly, but hearing that accent brought up so many feelings and memories about Heath. She needed to move on.

The sooner she got rid of Haviland's body, the sooner she could put this behind her. But before she left, she wanted to say goodbye to Nurse Francesca. She knew she couldn't save her, but she didn't want the woman to be alone in her last hours.

CHAPTER 33

*L*ater that week, Ari cleared her throat when she entered Brennan's room. Leise and Brennan pulled apart from a long kiss. Ari wasn't a shy person, but even she needed a glass of ice water after witnessing that lip lock. The language barrier didn't seem to be a problem.

"Hey, kids," Ari said smiling. She laid a few children's books and magazines on the end of his bed.

"What are those?" Leise asked as she grabbed the reading material.

"I thought that might help him,"Ari said, then leaned in to kiss Brennan on the cheek. "Hey."

"Hello," Brennan said slowly. "Good to see you."

Ari lifted an eyebrow. "That's good."

"I got him Rosetta Stone. He's learning so quickly," Leise said.

Brennan pointed. "Remy is…there…here."

Leise looked Brennan. "You can see him?" She looked to Ari, "Is Remy here?"

"Yes, he's right over there." Ari lifted her head to where Brennan pointed.

Remy smiled and came close to the bed. Brennan extended his

hand to shake. Remy did the same. When they couldn't actually shake they both laughed.

Leise asked, "What is Remy doing?"

"They were trying to shake, and his hand passed straight through."

"Brennan said he was a druid in his previous life. What does that mean?" Leise asked.

"It means he still has power," Ari said. "Magic comes from the soul. Speaking of which," she rummaged through her messenger bag and pulled out a black velvet bag, "I brought you this."

Leise shook her head. "I don't want it."

"Sorry, but it's your family's and a gift from your mom."

"You are my family. Remy and Brennan are my family. I don't need that to remind me. Plus, you can protect it better than me."

"Only if you're positive."

Leise nodded. "And if you have it, maybe Remy can visit Other-world whenever he likes. Even with *You-Know-Who* in there. The place is big. They may never see each other."

"Otherworld?" Brennan's eyebrows lifted up in question.

She pointed to the necklace. Ari pulled it out and waved it. "That's what I call it," Leise said with a smile. Brennan nodded with understanding.

"Ahh, yes. I would like to visit *Otherworld* again. Tell her thank you, Cher," Remy said. He floated to Leise and wrapped his arms around her.

Ari shook her head. "Remy likes that idea."

Leise shivered. "I can feel the love." Each word was followed by little puffs of cold air.

"Oh, has Brennan told you what happened when his uncle appeared?"

"Total chaos. They fought until we retrieved him. Three hundred years of anger unleashed. A fitting punishment I think." Leise walked towards Ari as she rubbed her arms, seemingly to warm up, but then bumped Ari with her elbow and tilted her head. A direct indicator she wanted to have a semi-private conversation.

"I know this is a sore subject, but did you find a place for Haviland?" Leise lowered her voice.

"Yeah. I, um, had to drive with him in the car an extra day because I needed his grimoire to perform an invisibility spell."

"What? Are you serious? You can make people disappear now? So, you're like a," she lifted both hands and mimicked air quotes, "fixer?"

Ari grimaced and shook her from head side to side. "Kinda. I wouldn't go around performing it at parties, but he's safe for now." She gave a small grimace, but didn't give voice to the niggling feeling that he wasn't secure. And then she definitely didn't go into how she hid his body inside a mausoleum with someone named, Landers O'Malley. That's a story for another day.

"When are you sending Nyah inside?"

"I'm not sure. That's the other reason Haviland gave me his grimoire. It has the spell to retrieve her essence, restore her soul, and then send her to Otherworld. It's a little bit complicated."

"No offense, but why do it at all. He killed a lot of people. He doesn't deserve a happy ending."

"I know, but in case you didn't realize we got our asses handed to us. We couldn't beat him. I certainly couldn't. And going by the spells in his book, he's more powerful than any witch around today. He's old and powerful. Who knows one day, we might need him, and I want him to remember that I did this one thing. That I reunited him with the one person he loved more than himself," Ari said.

"Okay, when you put it like that. I hope you figure it out." Leise looked back at Brennan, who seemed to be talking to himself.

"Alright, I have to prep for tonight," Ari put the amethyst back into the velvet bag and hid it away.

"What are you going to do tonight?" Leise asked as they walked back to Brennan's bed.

Ari smiled and thought about an old cartoon she used to watch and was half tempted to say, 'Same thing I do every night — try to take over the world.' But she didn't. When she thought about it, the real answer sounded just as crazy.

"I have a date with some ghosts at the cemetery."

)O(

A CLOAKED FIGURE with a small lantern walked through the head-stones in the dead of night.

Remy walked behind Ari. "Why are you dressed like that? What's in that bag, Cher?"

"I didn't know how long this would take and I might need to sit, have something to eat," Ari whispered.

"You brought a picnic? Sacre Dieu," Remy said, with a groan.

"Krista, are you here?" Ari called in a loud whisper.

An empty swing moved back and forth under the large oak tree in the middle of the cemetery. "Where else would I be?" The swing stopped and Krista, the young ghost, appeared. "I was beginning to wonder if you were ever coming back."

"Sorry, I've been a little busy."

Krista walked around Remy. "I guess this is him?"

"Remy, this is Krista. Krista, Remy."

"Enchanté, mademoiselle." Remy bowed with a flourish, then took the young ghost's hand and kissed it.

If ghosts could blush, Krista would have been a bright pink. But the giggle was proof enough that she was smitten.

"Now, Krista, did you have any luck?"

"I found a couple of women," Krista said, still smiling at Remy. "And a few ancients. They had to be at least thirty when they died."

"Girls for what?" Remy looked between Ari and Krista.

Ari knew their devious smiles didn't give anything away.

"Krista, could you bring them please?"

The young ghost clicked her Mary Janes as she gave a stiff salute, then disappeared.

"Cher, what have you done?"

"Nothing, but remember when we talked about you dating? I decided on, Ghost Bachelor." Ari sat down and pulled out a bag of popcorn. "One night in Otherworld."

"No."

"Too much?" She threw a popcorn up and it floated towards her mouth. "Match - Ghost edition, then."

Remy stood straight with arms folded, nose in the air. "No, I refuse."

"And here are the ladies now."

He twisted his head to peek. "Well, it wouldn't hurt to see."

EPILOGUE

The memorial service for Nurse Francesca was touching, but sad. The entire staff and all of the residents attended. Her grandchildren said their gran had one request for when she passed on.

That there be music and that people danced.

There was food, drinks, and music from Francesca's youth. Fifties music blared through the speakers, and she enjoyed an evening with Elvis, Chuck Berry, and the Everly Brothers. They laughed over stories of Francesca and Ari danced with the newest resident, Mr. Miller.

Mr. Pauppen Miller.

Ari introduced herself during one slow dance and she talked about a little girl who missed her Pop-Pop. Mr. Miller said he had a granddaughter named Krista who'd called him that. He laughed as he reminisced about the little girl who couldn't say his name correctly with her New York accent, but she could say Pop-Pop, and it stuck.

"This is the first time in a while it didn't hurt so much to remember her. Thank you," Mr. Miller said with a smile.

Ari hugged him tightly. "This is from Krista. She misses you."

They cried, but it was a good cry. A cathartic one. Ari looked at Mr. Miller's aura. Not all of the blackness had left, but it was whole. He was complete now. Something about the words or the hug was what he'd needed to start the healing process. She'd explained how she visited the cemetery for those who couldn't, and he was more than welcomed to come. He didn't say, yes, right off, but she left the invite open for him to visit with her one day. She had a good feeling he would go someday.

Ari went to the White Cauldron sometime later. Her hips still swayed to the music from the party. She felt good about life, and the choices she'd made. Before she reached the door, she heard a car door slam a few feet away. A man's voice she knew well called out. "Wait up."

His dark shadow blocked the sun and the front door. Just when things were looking up, Detective Westin shows up.

"Ms. Mason, how are you today?" the detective squinted his eyes and stared at her.

"I'm fine and you?" Ari smiled when she spoke.

"Odd. I seemed to have lost an entire day. Would you happen to know anything about that?" He scrutinized her every motion. Like he was waiting for her to confess all.

Ari frowned. "How could I? I haven't seen you in more than a week."

He nodded. "The murders have stopped."

His voice kept pausing like he wanted her to fill in the gaps. That wouldn't be happening in this lifetime.

"Good for you. You solved the case."

"That's just it. I didn't. The murders just stopped."

"Maybe the person knew you were hot on their trail and just moved on." Ari was surprised at how serious she sounded. Maybe she should have been an actress.

His stare looked like it would sear her soul. "I don't buy that for one minute."

Or not.

"I don't know what you and your friends here do," he waved

behind him. "But I'm sure you had something to do with those murders. I'll be watching you, Ms. Mason. You can count on it."

Ari didn't get a chance to make a witty retort, because he just stomped away. Even a memory wipe didn't clear his suspicion of her. She'd watched him stomp off when she heard the store bell jingle. She turned at the sound and Elizabeth appeared in the door. "Merry meet, Ari."

Ari blinked away the detective's comments, then smiled at the petite woman. "Merry meet."

Elizabeth waved her hand. "Are you ready to work on your blue firepower?" When Ari nodded, she said, "Come on in, everyone's waiting."

Ari stepped through the door. By a simple twist of fate, she had found friends, family, and a place to call home.

AFTERWORD

Thank you for reading, MAY DAY - A Gray Witch Novel. I really appreciate you taking the time to read my story.

If you enjoyed this book, please take a few minutes and place a review on Amazon and/ or Goodreads. It helps other readers who enjoy books about witches and magic, find this one.

Again, thank you.
R.R. Born

ACKNOWLEDGMENTS

I want to thank Karen Huang for always reading the roughest of the rough drafts, and still being my friend afterward.

Many thanks to Kavita Self. You held my hand through Grammar Hell, and led me out the other side a better writer.

Undying thanks to Lisa M. Knight. Your words of advice were priceless and helped set this book on the right path.

Thanks to Jennifer A., Kristina T., Peter W., & Arturo S. - You guys in your own way were my support system. Always helping, be it with time, art & crafts, or encouraging words. I want you to know it meant the world to me.

And to Ken Wallen. You saved me, and no amount of words can express my gratitude. I salute you. *Whiskey, no water.*

I'm happy all of you were with me on this writing journey.

ABOUT THE AUTHOR

R.R. Born lives in Texas with her husband, and an orange tabby terror named Pele. She graduated from Houston Community College where she studied Photography, then graduated with a degree in Film from Long Island University in Brookville, NY. She's worked as a Production Coordinator, and Second Assistant Director on local commercials, TV shows, and movies.

For more info on upcoming books
http://www.rrborn.com

CPSIA information can be obtained
at www.ICGtesting.com
Printed in the USA
LVHW090038291118
598419LV00005BA/999/P